Miss Dimple
Disappears

Miss Dimple Disappears

MIGNON F. BALLARD

Minotaur Books
NEW YORK

MISS DIMPLE DISAPPEARS. Copyright © 2010 by Mignon F. Ballard. All rights reserved. Printed in the United States of America. For information, address St. Martin's Press, 175 Fifth Avenue, New York, N.Y. 10010.

www.minotaurbooks.com

The Library of Congress has cataloged the hardcover edition as follows:

Ballard, Mignon Franklin.
    Miss Dimple disappears : a mystery / Mignon F. Ballard.—1st ed.
      p. cm.
    ISBN 978-0-312-61474-4
    1. Female friendship—Fiction. 2. Elementary school teachers—Fiction.
3. Women teachers—Crimes against—Fiction. 4. Missing persons—Fiction.
5. Georgia—History—20th century—Fiction. I. Title.
    PS3552.A466M57 2010
    813'.54—dc22

                                    2010035814

ISBN 978-0-312-62682-2 (trade paperback)

10 9 8 7 6 5 4 3 2

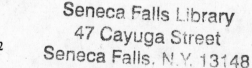

Dedicated with love to my dear sister and friend
Sue Marie Franklin Lewis

Acknowledgments

To my wonderful editors at St. Martin's, Hope Dellon and Laura Bourgeois, who, in their gracious manner, don't let me get away with a thing, and to Laura Langlie, my loyal agent and friend, THANK YOU! Special thanks to my nephew, John F. Lewis, for his expertise on World War II planes, and anything else that flies.

CHAPTER ONE

*H*e *froze as brittle magnolia leaves crackled underfoot. There she was, just like clockwork! Did she hear him? Maybe he should've found a better place to hide, but in the murky predawn light, cascading limbs of thick, glossy foliage concealed him from view. She couldn't see the car he'd parked, waiting, behind the thick hedge of holly that bordered the fountain, and if she followed her usual route, she would circle it and turn left toward town. Parting the boughs, he took a cautious step forward. He had what was needed in hand and would be on her before she knew it.*

Look at the silly old woman, spearing trash with her umbrella just like this was any other day. The man smiled. Wouldn't she be surprised? The colonel would be pleased, but God help him if he failed— and this was only the beginning. Well, this should prove he could be trusted.

Miss Dimple Kilpatrick spied the scrap of paper wedged between two loose stones on the far side of the narrow bridge during her early-morning walk through the park. It was probably swept there by the wind or left by someone who was too lazy to find a trash receptacle, she thought as she speared the offending litter with the point of her umbrella and deposited it with other debris she had collected in the paper bag she carried for that purpose. It had been almost a year since the Japanese bombed Pearl Harbor and brought them into the war, and one couldn't afford to be wasteful. As a first-grade teacher of long standing at Elderberry Grammar School, she encouraged her young charges to keep that in mind.

It was barely light as she crossed over the quaint stone bridge and took the curving path between two dark magnolias and around the circular pond where sluggish goldfish hid beneath lily pads in the dark, icy water. The park was one of her favorite places. She often visited there with her good friend Virginia, who served as librarian in the quaint log cabin building at one end of the park, and on summer days took much pleasure reading to children on its rustic porch. Usually she relished the deep serenity of the place in the gray hours just before dawn when peacefulness settled upon her like a comfortable cloak, and Miss Dimple, like most of the people of Elderberry, Georgia, treasured any moments of peace that came her way with the world at war and their young men— many of whom she had taught—shipping out to fight in foreign lands. Even her brother, Henry, although too old to serve in the military, was involved in something for the war effort, something he wouldn't discuss. She knew it involved planes because of his work at the Bell Bomber Plant in nearby Marietta and that it was important. Henry had been eight and she, fourteen, when she stepped in to help raise him when their mother died, and Dimple Kilpatrick was as proud of her younger brother as if he had been her own child.

This morning seemed unusually quiet, even for this early hour, and Miss Dimple began to feel uncomfortable in her aloneness. She paused briefly to glance behind her in time to see the jiggle of a limb in the dark magnolia. A bird, perhaps? Although it was the second week in November, many of the hardier varieties were still about, but usually not this early in the morning. Swinging her umbrella, Miss Dimple walked faster. It was probably just her imagination, but she'd had the same peculiar sensation the day before on her walk in the deserted north end of town until she'd met up with one of her former students. Angie Webber, on her way to serve up breakfast at Lewellyn's Drugstore, had walked the rest of the way with her, and Miss Dimple was glad of her company. Now, instead of following her usual Monday route through the deserted streets of town and the hills behind it, she decided to cross the railroad tracks and circle the cotton gin on Settlemyer Street before starting for home. The houses were closer together there and she could take a shorter way home. This morning, because Odessa had promised grapefruit and a poached egg on whole wheat toast at the rooming house where she lived, Miss Dimple was willing to forego her usual fiber-filled muffins.

Lifting the lid of the trash can in the corner of the park to dispose of her collected litter, Miss Dimple risked a second look behind her. Shrouded in shadow, the magnolia tree remained motionless. Relieved, she glanced at her watch in the growing light. Almost seven already. She would have to hurry if she were to have breakfast and get to school on time.

It was not until she had crossed the railroad tracks and neared the vacant lot that Miss Dimple again sensed the feeling. Her mother, long dead now, would've said a rabbit ran over her grave, but it was more threatening than that. Not one to become unduly alarmed over matters real or imagined, she attempted to suppress her anxiety by continuing at her usual steady pace and thinking of the egg and grapefruit soon to come, but like an annoying headache the sensation persisted. *She was being watched!*

Crossing the street, she sat on the low wall fronting the cotton gin and rubbed her ankle as if it were giving her pain. A car, partially hidden by ragged undergrowth and a few pine saplings, waited on the other side of the vacant lot across from her, and Dimple Kilpatrick had walked these streets long enough to know *there was no street or driveway there.*

Not a soul was in sight and Miss Dimple quickly got to her feet and turned in the other direction. There were several homes on that side of town, and not only did she know most of the people who lived in them, but had taught many of them. She walked faster now, chancing a brief look over her shoulder to see the car— which, in the dusk, seemed either black or dark gray—move slowly to the corner and turn toward her. *And the driver wasn't using his lights.* Dimple Kilpatrick picked up her feet and ran.

Ida Ellerby stood in the doorway wearing a pink tufted robe over her purple flannel gown. "Why, Miss Dimple! Are you all right? Here, come in the kitchen where it's warm and sit down. You're all out of breath. Is anything wrong?

"Ralph! Get another cup for Miss Dimple." Ida put a steadying arm across her shoulders. "My goodness, you look like you've done been rode hard and put up wet. What on earth has happened?"

Dimple Kilpatrick sank gratefully into the kitchen chair, glad for the warmth of the oven at her back, and held the coffee cup steady in her hands as strength returned with each sip of the bitter hot liquid. She had glanced behind her to see the dark car speed away as soon as she ran onto the Ellerbys' front porch. But would it return? And what if the driver was out for a perfectly innocent reason? Perhaps he forgot to turn on his headlights or was reluctant to shine them into the windows of sleeping neighbors. Then wouldn't she be like "The Boy Who Cried Wolf"?

"A dog," she said. "Must be a stray, but it seemed as large as a small pony, and I really thought it was going to attack." Miss Dimple set the cup firmly in the saucer. "It was quite threatening— gave me a bit of a fright." She smiled. "I'm sorry for bursting in on you like this, Ida. I hope you'll excuse me for making a spectacle of myself."

"Now, don't you think another thing about it. Ralph will be leaving for work in just a few minutes and he'll be glad to give you a ride home."

Miss Dimple blushed at the memory of her hasty glimpse of Ralph's long white underwear as he'd fled the kitchen at her entrance, and said she'd be most grateful for the favor.

Ida sighed as she shook her head. "If there's a dangerous animal on the prowl around here, we'll have to do something about it. It just won't do to have things like that on the loose."

Miss Dimple agreed wholeheartedly.

CHAPTER TWO

*G*eneva Odom ladled a spoonful of pancake batter into the skillet and tugged her robe tighter around her. Was that the first bell already? Surely not! She glanced at the clock over the stove and sighed in relief. She had almost an hour to finish breakfast and open her classroom on time. Must've been the wind.

❧

Charlie Carr unlocked the door of her third-grade classroom and made a face. Christmas had bypassed her again—Christmas being the school's janitor, Wilson "Christmas" Malone, so named because he was as slow as. Shavings from the pencil sharpener littered the floor and the trash can was filled to overflowing with wads of paper, an apple core from somebody's lunch, and a couple of day-old banana peels that reeked to high heaven. Charlie set the trash can out in the hall and turned on the overhead lights. The whole world seemed washed in gray and the lights did little to dispel the gloom. Outside she could hear the voices of children playing on bare red earth and slate rock where no grass ever grew. It hadn't been many years since Charlie had been one of them chanting,

"Mother, may I?" and "Red rover"; building moss and stick houses under the sheltering oaks, and declaring war on the boys who tore them down.

But that was before she knew what war was.

Charlie pulled her faded green cardigan around her. She had sewn patches where the elbows had worn thin in an effort to make it last. Wool was hard to come by since the war began, and who knew how long it might last. *Use it up, wear it out, make it do, or do without,* the government was fond of saying, and Charlie couldn't see that they had much choice.

She looked at the rows of empty desks, all fastened to the floor, and each with its little inkwell in the right-hand corner, although nobody used inkwells anymore. What on earth was she doing here? This wasn't the place she had meant to be. She had dreamed of becoming an archaeologist discovering ancient treasures in some mysterious land or an explorer hacking her way through the jungles of Africa, but of course she knew that would never be. Professional choices for women were limited, and Charlie Carr had no desire to become a secretary or a nurse.

Well, here she was, and that was that! And how could she not care for these children who had become like her own? Charlie agonized over the boy who came to school barefoot on a frosty October morning, the girl in shabby clothing often absent because she had to help at home.

"Well?" Annie Gardner spoke from the doorway.

"Well, what?" Charlie smiled as she erased from the blackboard all twenty-five sentences of *I will not make faces in class,* which Willie Elrod had laboriously written the day before, and pretended to rearrange pencils in the jar on her desk.

Annie's sigh sounded bigger than she was and she did a couple of steps of her own choreography in place. A zealous would-be dancer and thespian, this was her first year at Elderberry Grammar School since the two received their teaching certificates from

Brenau College and—unlike Charlie, who towered over her at five feet ten—she wasn't a whole lot taller than some of her fourth-grade students. Now she tapped an impatient foot. "You know very well *what*. I know you went out with Hugh last night, so don't pretend with me."

Charlie turned away from her friend's sly, expectant smile and held a hand to the radiator. "Is it cold in here to you?"

Annie crossed her arms and shivered. "Looks like Christmas is late again. Does the man *ever* get here on time? I haven't heard a peep out of the furnace, and it'll probably take half the morning for that old monstrosity to heat up."

"Trash hasn't been emptied, either," Charlie said, nodding toward the wastebasket in the hallway. "I heard our principal reading him the riot act after school yesterday, and was hoping he'd improve. Maybe we should all chip in and get Christmas a new alarm clock. Do you think he'd get the hint?"

"I think you still haven't answered my question," Annie persisted. "What happened with Hugh last night?"

Charlie busied herself wiping chalk dust from her fingers and sneezed. "Are you sure you can handle the excitement?"

"Try me," Annie said.

"We went to see that *Thin Man* movie at the picture show—the new one with Myrna Loy and William Powell—and then he brought me home and ate up what was left of the lemon meringue pie in the Frigidaire."

"And that's *it*?" Annie asked.

"'Fraid so. Anything else you want to know?"

Annie shook her head and paused, and Charlie knew she was thinking up an appropriate quote from the great bard. "'Lord, what fools these mortals be!' Surely he said *something*."

Charlie frowned as if in serious thought. "Right. 'You be sure and tell Miss Jo that's the best pie I ever put in my mouth,'" she mimicked, stretching to her full height. She hadn't told him that the pie had been made by Evie McDaniel, who cooked for them occasionally. Her mother, Josephine Carr, could do little more than scramble an egg, which was why Charlie took her noon meal with several of the other teachers at Phoebe Chadwick's boardinghouse.

Charlie had been seeing Hugh Brumlow almost exclusively for over a year now and he would soon be called up for service, so naturally just about everyone—especially Annie—expected him to propose. But Charlie, caught up in the tide of war and romance, found herself in a tug-of-war with her emotions. His kisses stirred desires in her that terrified and thrilled her, and the thought of him soon going off to war was like an icicle piercing her heart, but she was distressed as well about her brother, Fain, and others who had left to fight.

Looking over her shoulder she saw that Annie was still there. "Don't you have some place to go—like your own classroom maybe?"

Annie looked at her watch. "Guess I had better skedaddle. It's almost time for the bell and they'll be lining up outside . . . but, Charlie . . ." She hesitated in the doorway.

Charlie cocked an eyebrow and grinned. "Annie . . . ?"

"Hugh cares about you. Really. I know he does. Just wait and see."

Charlie shook her head as Annie rumbaed into her classroom next door, and hurriedly began writing the reading assignment on the board. She wasn't going to think about Hugh Brumlow. She wasn't going to think about his eyes so blue they could burn a hole in your heart, or the funny, stubborn tuft of hair no amount of brushing or hair tonic could conquer.

And she certainly wasn't going to think about his mouth . . . mmm . . . oh, no—and how his lips felt against her own. Charlie Carr had enough on her mind without worrying about Hugh Brumlow.

Everyone knew Hugh would've already enlisted if his mother hadn't had to have her appendix out, then suffered what she claimed were "setbacks," taking what seemed forever to recuperate. Doc

Morrison, who performed the surgery, had told his wife, who told Charlie's mother, that when he made the incision her appendix looked perfectly healthy to him.

The early-morning sun hadn't worked its way to their side of the building and the classroom seemed drab in the gray November chill in spite of the colorful drawings of Indians and Pilgrims marching along the walls, the American flag above the portrait of George Washington, and the purple felt banner the class had won for having the most mothers attend the last PTA meeting.

In an hour or so, when Christmas Malone finally got around to stoking the furnace, the room would become so close and warm Charlie would have to open windows to let in cooling air. Already the place smelled of dust, mildewed galoshes, and forgotten bananas, and she decided a room cleaning would have to be a priority since it was apparent the school's janitor had skipped them once again.

Charlie glanced at the bulletin board to be reminded that Mary Ann Breedlove was scheduled to lead her classmates in a selection of patriotic songs that morning. Classes always began with a ten-minute period during which students recited the Pledge to the Flag, listened to a brief verse of scriptures from the Bible, and were led in a morning prayer. From time to time the ritual centered on a theme, and freedom, loyalty, and courage had been popular subjects since the war began the year before.

Throwing a jacket around her shoulders, Charlie stepped into the hallway and was on her way to greet her third-grade students at the back steps when the first bell rang.

For blocks around, school-age children in the small Georgia town kissed their mothers, grabbed their books, and started out on a run when they heard the lusty clanging. The bell hung in the belfry over the red brick building that housed grades one through four as it had when Charlie's parents went to school there. If a child wasn't present to line up when the principal rang the second bell five minutes later, he or she was marked tardy and required to "stay in" during recess—or worse, after school.

"Did you hear the bell ring earlier?" Geneva Odom, who taught second grade, stood in the hallway outside her classroom, brimming wastebasket in hand. "I could've sworn it rang while I was cooking breakfast this morning, but it was much too early, so I guess it was my imagination."

"Or a bad dream," Charlie answered, "except I thought I heard it, too."

Annie gave a little shiver. "I must've been in the shower, but it was probably mice gnawing on the bell rope. I know they're around. One chewed clear through a box of cough drops I left out on my desk, and Christmas doesn't halfway clean around here. I know he has trouble with his back, but you'd think he could do better than this."

"If it's not his back, it's his blood pressure," Geneva said. "All our able-bodied men are in the service, and I guess the poor man does the best he can, but he's late more often than not and it seems he's always complaining about something." She set the wastebasket in the hallway. "I hoped that little talk he had with Mr. Faulkenberry would give him some incentive, but apparently not. Since he missed my room again yesterday, I'm going to leave this right here in the hall as a reminder."

"I found my door unlocked, so it seems he's at least been in my room, but I can't see that he's done any cleaning." Miss Dimple Kilpatrick appeared from the first-grade classroom next to Geneva's wearing her customary purple. Today it was a long-sleeved cotton dress in a paisley print with a plain gold bar pin at her throat and a lace-trimmed hankie peeping from a pocket of the bodice. Her graying hair was swept up and held in place by tortoiseshell combs, and bifocals hung from her neck on a chain. Now she spoke softly as she shrugged into what once had been a lavender sweater. "The flu has been going around, you know, and

Wilson complained of a sore throat yesterday. I do hope he hasn't come down with something." She never referred to the janitor as Christmas.

If he had caught the flu, Charlie wished he'd stoked the furnace first, but she kept her thoughts to herself. Miss Dimple might think she was being selfish.

Miss Dimple Kilpatrick had taught first grade in Elderberry Grammar School for almost forty years, and for most of those forty years she had made it a point to arrive at the school before anyone else, including the principal and the janitor. It gave her time to think and plan in peace and quiet, she said. Charlie herself had sat in one of the little green chairs in the first classroom on the right and read about the adventures of Tom and Nancy from a bright pink primer, and when she first began teaching there, she had been shocked to discover that Miss Dimple actually went to the bathroom like ordinary humans do.

"Did you hear the bell ring earlier this morning?" she asked the older woman as they parted at the second bell.

"Why, no, but then I doubt if I would've. Do you know I walked almost as far as the peach orchard this morning before I realized how far I'd gone." And Miss Dimple hurried after Geneva to stand at the top of the front steps as "commander in chief" of the first grade class. She had deliberately taken a different route on her walk that morning after her peculiar experience the day before, although she was probably letting her imagination run away with her, she supposed. Miss Dimple knew she read entirely too many mysteries but had no intention of giving them up. Whenever a new Agatha Christie arrived at the local library, her friend Virginia always saw that she read it first.

A champion of healthy living, Dimple Kilpatrick seldom missed her brisk early morning walks and was the only person Charlie knew who didn't seem to mind cutting back on sugar, even going so far as to decline desserts and Phoebe Chadwick's occasional breakfasts of crisp hot waffles with syrup. There was a secret contest among the other faculty members to guess the ingredients of Miss Dimple's Victory Muffins, which were supposed to make one healthy and patriotic as well as regular. Even Miss Phoebe, who gave her permission to use the boardinghouse kitchen, claimed she didn't know what was in them.

When Christmas still hadn't shown up by mid-morning, the school's principal, Oscar Faulkenberry, also known as "Froggie" because of his likeness to that amphibian, had begrudgingly rolled up his sleeves and stoked the ancient furnace, and during recess Charlie tricked her third graders into believing it was a special treat to be allowed to sweep the classroom floor.

"You don't suppose something's really happened to Christmas, do you?" Annie asked as the two of them watched the usual game of tag during the noon lunch break. "He might actually be sick. It could be his heart or something."

Charlie smiled as one of her students hid behind the oak tree to avoid being caught. "I hope not," she said. "I heard Froggie say he tried to call his house but nobody answered. I think his wife works at the cotton mill."

"As far as I know, he's never done this before," Geneva said, joining them. "It's one thing to be late, but we should've heard something by now."

"If he was that sick, he's probably waiting to see a doctor," Annie said. "There's just the two of them now since Doctor Stewart left for the navy, and Phoebe said she had to wait over an hour the other day just to have her blood pressure taken."

Charlie realized Miss Dimple was standing silently behind them and wondered what she was thinking. Unless a student was misbehaving, the older teacher usually kept her opinions to herself, but Charlie had known her long enough to realize there was more to Dimple Kilpatrick than any of them could ever guess.

It wasn't until the children filed in for the afternoon session that one of Alice Brady's expression students went to the upstairs storage closet for a box of Thanksgiving props for their upcoming theatrical production and discovered the janitor's body.

The child's scream was so loud and shrill that Ruthie Phillips, who happened to be giving a book report on *Nancy Drew and the Message in the Hollow Oak* for Charlie's English class, dropped the book she was holding and ran to crouch under her desk. She thought they were having an air raid, she said afterward.

❧

"A heart attack, I'll bet," Annie said. "You know how he was always complaining about being out of breath."

"Well, I hope it isn't anything contagious! I sent the Cooper girl home with a fever just the other day, and frankly, I haven't been feeling so well myself." Lily Moss, the pencil-thin sixth-grade teacher, spoke as if she had marbles stuck up her nose.

"I heard Doc Morrison say it looked like a stroke to him but he injured his head when he fell," Geneva cut in, giving the woman a long-suffering look. "Of course he'll have to do a more thorough examination before they know for sure. I expect there'll be an—"

"Oh, don't say that awful word!" Lily clasped a hand to her ironing-board chest. "I just can't bear the thought of anyone cutting into the poor man, even though he *was* too lazy to hit a lick at a snake."

"Why, Lily Moss!" Geneva gasped.

"Well, he was . . . bless his heart," Lily mumbled, as if the expression would make everything all right.

Charlie stood at the window watching empty swings zigzagging in the wind. The children had been dismissed early for the day and she wished the faculty had been allowed to do the same. Instead, the teachers were instructed to gather in Lily's classroom until the principal could address them.

The structure that housed the fifth, sixth, and seventh grades

14

was smaller than the belfry building and sat on the other side of the school grounds with a play area in between. Built in more recent times, the upper-grade classrooms were spacious, but without the heat-sucking high ceilings of the older building, and the desks were large enough to accommodate most adults although Charlie found it difficult to fold her long legs underneath.

While some of the teachers chatted or roamed restlessly about the room, Miss Dimple Kilpatrick, Charlie noticed, sat primly in one of the front desks with an open book in front of her, although she didn't appear to be reading. With fragile hands she clutched the worn leather handbag in her lap, and for a minute Charlie wondered if the woman might be praying.

Maybe it wouldn't be a bad idea if we all did, she thought. Charlie caught Annie's eye and took a seat across from her. It made her think of their years together in college. The two had been roommates all four years at Brenau and after graduation it was only by chance they found teaching positions together. With the recommendation of a college professor, Charlie had been offered a teaching job in her instructor's California hometown and was excited about the opportunity for travel and adventure, but then the war came along. With her brother enlisting in the army and her younger sister marrying and leaving home, Charlie's widowed mother would be left alone, and although she knew Josephine Carr would never stand in the way of her leaving, Charlie just couldn't bring herself to desert her. She was thankful that Annie had not yet signed a contract to teach and was willing to fill one of the openings in Charlie's hometown of Elderberry.

It was now half after three and her mother would be rolling bandages for the Red Cross, after which she would probably stop for a visit with her sister Louise. The two worked three days a week at the ordnance plant in Milledgeville, and still spoke to one another most days. Charlie's father, who had died a few years earlier, had claimed the two sisters could talk the ears off a mule.

Annie marked the last of the papers she'd been grading and returned them to the folder. "Poor Christmas! I feel awful for having doubted him," she said aside to Charlie. "Just think, all this time he's been trying to tell us he wasn't well . . . 'but what's gone and what's past help should be past grief,' I suppose," she added mournfully.

Geneva, who had been wandering the aisles, plopped on the desk in front of hers. "That must be why we heard the bell," she said, speaking so that everyone could hear.

"What bell?" Lily asked.

"Didn't you hear it? The school bell rang early this morning before we even had breakfast, but I knew it wasn't time for school to begin." With one finger Geneva traced a carved initial in the desktop and lowered her voice. "I'll bet it was Christmas Malone. They found him in that upstairs storage room, you know. That's right above the principal's office and the bell rope comes down through the ceiling in there."

"Dear God!" Annie propped her head in her hands. "The poor man must've been making one last effort to summon help."

"Or to warn us." Miss Dimple spoke softly. She didn't look up.

Now, what does she mean by that? Charlie wondered, but she didn't have a chance to ask because "Froggie" Faulkenberry came in just then to announce in solemn tones that the janitor's body had been taken by ambulance to the hospital in Milledgeville where they would determine the cause of death, and that he was on his way to notify Wilson's family.

Charlie didn't envy him that unhappy job. She stayed in her seat as one by one the other teachers left silently. Only a few minutes ago she would have been eager to join them, but now she would rather sit and let numbness overcome her. If she moved she would have to think of the questions that plagued her. If Christmas needed to summon help, why didn't he use the phone, or even ring the bell, in the principal's office on the main floor? And earlier she'd overheard the speech teacher confiding to Kate Ashcroft, who taught music, that she'd found Ebenezer with a broken wing. The school's mascot, a heavy, carved wooden eagle, sat on a stand directly across the hall from the storage room where the janitor died. "I know it wasn't broken yesterday," she said, "because it was facing in full view. It looks like whoever broke it turned it sideways, probably hoping no one would notice the missing wing."

And then she would have to think about Christmas Malone's two teenaged children and his wife, Madge, who always brought pinwheel cookies to the faculty during the holidays. And she would have to think about Christmas himself, a round, red-cheeked man who could sing all the lyrics to "Froggie Went A-Courtin,'" and at barely over forty, was much too young to die.

CHAPTER THREE

*Y*ou hush up, now, Rags! You ain't supposed to be in here
and if Mama finds out, we'll both be in trouble." Willie
Elrod dragged the reluctant terrier from underneath his
snug quilt and tiptoed down the dark stairs. "Go on, now, and get in
your box," he said, letting the small dog onto the side screen porch, "and
she won't never know the difference." But why was that car stopping
out there with no lights? What if it was a spy? You never knew where
one might be lurking, and Willie was always on the lookout. He held
his breath and prayed the puppy wouldn't bark. For a minute it looked
like Miss Dimple from next door standing there in the pre-dawn gloom.
But then she was gone. And so was the car.

~

It was colder than she thought, and Miss Dimple had almost
reached the corner before she decided to turn back for a heavier
wrap. Except for a light in the Sullivans' house across the street,
the sleeping neighborhood stared at her with dark windows, but
the Sullivans had just welcomed a lively baby boy. Miss Dimple

smiled and hoped she would still be around to teach him when he started first grade. Surely this dreadful war would be over by then. With sadness she remembered the Hopkins child, her student fourteen years before, who had been killed somewhere in the Marshall Islands. Peyton. He could read faster than anybody in his class and insisted on writing with his left hand.

The Sullivans' light went out and it comforted her to think about this small new life and all its possibilities. This business with Wilson Malone had upset her more than she liked to admit. First the frightening experience with the car two mornings ago, and then Wilson dying in that upstairs storeroom. What had he been doing up there? And several people said they'd heard the school bell ring earlier. No, something wasn't right.

A truck rumbled past in the street below, and maybe it was because her mind was on other things, or perhaps the noise of the truck distracted her, but Dimple Kilpatrick didn't hear the car pull up quietly behind her.

A rough hand covered her mouth before she could scream and something unpleasant was crammed over her face. Miss Dimple swung her purse, heavy with a worn copy of *Winnie-the-Pooh*, a storybook about the Indian chief Tomochichi, who had been a friend to the early settlers of Georgia, a Thermos of tea, and two vitamin-enriched Victory Muffins. The purse grazed the bare branches of the crape myrtle next to the street and landed with a muffled thump on a solid surface she hoped was her abductor. But Dimple Kilpatrick remembered the sweetish sickening smell from having her tonsils removed several years before, and although she kicked and struggled, she knew it wasn't going to do any good.

***

"Any news about Christmas yet?" Annie popped her head in Charlie's doorway as they waited for the bell to ring.

"Haven't heard a word since yesterday, but I just can't get his family off my mind. I thought I might stir up some of those applesauce muffins this afternoon—if we have enough sugar, that is. I can take them over there tonight."

"I'll go with you," Annie said. "I'm sure I can talk Phoebe out of a jar of her bread and butter pickles.

"Froggie must've found somebody to wrestle with the furnace or else he took care of it himself," she added. "It's practically toasty in here."

Charlie took the spelling sentences she had graded the day before from her desk drawer in preparation of returning them, smiling again at Marshall Dodd's use of the word *behind.*

My mama seys if I don't do beter in school shes gone whip my be-hind.

"How are we going to explain to the children about what happened to Christmas Malone?" Annie asked.

Charlie hadn't thought of that. "I don't know, but we'd better think fast. It's almost time for the second bell. Miss Dimple will know how to handle it. She must be in her room."

She followed Annie down the wide hall to the classroom on the right, but the door was closed and the room, dark.

"Where could she be?" Annie asked. "She's always here before everybody else. You don't suppose she's sick, do you?"

Charlie thought immediately of Christmas Malone. Was some sort of deadly disease going around? Soon the bell would summon the children to file into their classrooms. The two older classes lined up in back, while grades one and two marched in the front way with teachers maintaining order at the head of the lines. She glanced outside to see if the older teacher was taking care of a problem on the playground as they were often called upon to administer first aid or put an end to occasional fights, but Miss Dimple was nowhere in sight.

"Maybe she's in the teachers' lounge." Charlie hurried to the small narrow room at the end of the hallway and opened the door. If Miss Dimple were inside, it would be impossible to miss her.

The toilet flushed and Geneva Odom darted from the cubicle, tugging at her undergarments as she scurried. "Blasted girdle! I must've put on ten pounds since I bought it, but try and get another one!"

Charlie resisted the impulse to laugh. She hadn't worn a girdle since she bought that slinky gown for a college dance, but knew they were next to impossible to find since rubber was being used in the war effort.

"Have you seen Miss Dimple?" Annie asked. "She's not in her room and the children are getting ready to line up outside."

"*What?*" Geneva couldn't have looked more startled if she'd been told the war was over and they had lost. For the venerable teacher not to be at her post when expected was unheard of.

"I can't imagine where she'd be, but if she doesn't show up soon, we'll have to ask Froggie to call in a sub," Charlie said.

The three huddled in the hallway as the bell tolled above them. "Did you see her this morning at Phoebe's?" Geneva asked Annie, who lived in the same rooming house with Miss Dimple and several other teachers.

Annie frowned. "She wasn't at breakfast, but you know how she goes for those early-morning walks. And it's not unusual for her to skip breakfast and come straight here—makes do with some of her muffins, I guess."

Charlie made a face. "I hope she hasn't had an accident," she said, thinking of Miss Dimple walking alone in the early-morning gloom. But in a town as small as Elderberry, surely they would know by now if anything like that had happened.

The voices of the children grew to a swell as they clamored around the entrances without supervision, and the remaining teachers quickly agreed to take time about watching Miss Dimple's classroom for a while until it became apparent she wasn't going to show up. Fortunately, Geneva had exchanged classroom keys with the missing teacher and was able to unlock her door and see the children to their seats. When Charlie looked in a few minutes later, one of Annie's fourth graders was reading a fairy story to the class while the smaller children, apparently enjoying the break from their usual routine, happily colored stenciled drawings of Thanksgiving turkeys with their fat, broken crayons in anticipation of the holiday ahead.

During her usual morning ritual Charlie listened for Miss Dimple's rapid footsteps in the hallway and checked frequently to see if she had finally arrived. From her doorway across the hall, Geneva shook her head and frowned. It was becoming obvious that something had happened to Miss Dimple Kilpatrick.

Wouldn't the demure Miss Dimple be mortified to know she was the central subject during the noon meal that day at the boardinghouse? Charlie thought.

"She couldn't just disappear into thin air," Geneva said as she helped herself to the cornbread. "There has to be a logical explanation." She paused as if considering whether or not to continue. "And that's not all that piques my curiosity. One of my second graders found Ebenezer's broken wing in that drainage ditch behind the toolshed during recess this morning."

"What on earth was it doing there?" Charlie asked.

"What I want to know is *who put* it there," Geneva answered. "It has to have something to do with what happened to Chri— uh, Mr. Malone. Froggie locked it away in that cabinet in his office and I saw Bobby Tinsley from the police in there a little while ago. I'll bet anything he took it with him."

"But why?" Lily Moss looked about. "I assumed Mr. Malone knocked the eagle from its stand when his poor heart gave out on him, just before he rang the bell."

Geneva eyed her silently. "Then what was the wing doing in the ditch?" she asked with a barely audible sigh.

"But surely that has nothing to do with Miss Dimple's curious absence." Noticeably flustered, Lily seemed near to tears.

"Perhaps she has a reason." Elwin Vickery pounded the salt shaker on the table before shaking some into his hand.

"Then I wish somebody would explain it to me," Annie said. "None of us saw her leave the house this morning, and as far as I know, nobody's reported an accident. Frog—I mean, Mr. Faulkenberry telephoned the hospital *and* the police when she didn't show up today. He even checked with her friend Virginia Balliew at the library to see if she'd heard anything. Poor man! He's had his hands full with this on top of what happened to Christmas Malone. Anyway, they don't seem to know any more than we do." She sighed. "'Something's rotten in the state of Denmark!'"

"What a shame about Mr. Malone!" Lily Moss spoke in a quaking voice. "His heart must've just given out on him, and I understand he probably hit his head on that old metal filing cabinet when he fell. And now Miss Dimple's disappeared! It's most upsetting with all this happening right before the holidays.

"I just hope they find her soon," she added. "Why, the poor soul might be lying in a ditch somewhere. Or worse, some fiendish person has carried her off and—" Lily covered her mouth with a napkin as if the notion were just too indelicate to mention.

As, of course, it was, Charlie thought. It seemed unlikely, though, that the prim spinsterish Miss Dimple would be the victim of such an attack. After all, there were few men left in Elderberry who were young enough to be that lustful.

Elwin Vickery cleared his throat. "I should think Miss Phoebe would've been informed if Miss Dimple intended to leave," he said, referring to the owner of the rooming house. A fastidious bachelor and relative newcomer to Elderberry, he was Phoebe Chadwick's one male roomer and the only person who had accommodations downstairs. Annie sometimes referred to him as "Aunt Mildred," claiming he was every bit as stuffy as her maiden aunt.

"Well, if she was, you couldn't prove it by me!" Odessa Kirby, the Chadwick's cook, bumped through the swinging door into the dining room fanny-first with a steaming tureen of vegetable soup.

Charlie's stomach growled in anticipation. Using home-canned vegetables from the Victory garden and only a few bones for stock, Odessa could make soup fit for President Roosevelt himself.

Now Odessa set the tureen at the end of the table where Phoebe Chadwick usually sat. "She say for Miss Velma to serve today," she announced, nodding to Velma Anderson, the senior member at the table and, with the exception of Miss Dimple, the one who had been there the longest. Miss Velma taught secretarial science at the high school and, besides Elwin and his sleek new Nash, was the only roomer who owned her own vehicle, a 1932 Ford V-8 that looked every bit as good as the day she bought it.

Geneva dropped saccharine into her glass of iced tea and stirred vigorously. Now that sugar was in short supply, they had to make do, although few cared for the peculiar taste. "Where is Phoebe?" she asked, frowning. "Don't tell me she's sick, too."

"She be too busy helping the po-lice hunt for Miss Dimple." Odessa snatched up the near-empty bread basket and started to the kitchen for more. "Been like a crazy house here all morning. Don't know what that woman be thinkin' goin' off like that without so much as a by-your-leave!"

The cook's angry muttering didn't fool Charlie for a minute as she knew Miss Dimple was Odessa's favorite among all the teachers and she was as worried as the rest of them.

Geneva tasted her tea and made a face. "It's not like her to do a thing like this."

"Not like her at all," Elwin echoed as he began scooping all the

24

green peas from his soup and transferring them to a small bowl provided for that purpose.

"Surely she has relatives," Annie suggested. "Hasn't anyone tried to contact them?"

"She seems to be close to her brother," Lily said. "Remember, Velma? He sent that huge crate of fruit last Christmas."

Velma made little catlike dabs with her napkin. "Such delicious oranges! And those tiny little sour things—kumcubers, I think they're called."

"Kumquats," Elwin whispered under his breath, and Charlie smiled behind her napkin and tried not to meet Annie's eyes.

"Does anyone know how to get in touch with him?" Annie looked about as she spoke, but no one had an answer.

Charlie had seen Miss Dimple walking to the post office with letters to mail but she had no idea who they were for. The older teacher was not in the custom of engaging in personal chitchat. "I don't guess any of you have noticed who she writes," she said, but this was met with only blank stares.

"I suppose we could look in her address book," Geneva suggested.

"*If* we can find it," Annie said, "but wouldn't you think the police have already thought to look there?"

Charlie bit her lip. Knowing the police in Elderberry, she wasn't so sure about that.

Charlie didn't know how Odessa accomplished it, but she usually managed to come up with delectable desserts in spite of rationing and shortages. Today it was gingerbread made with molasses, orange peel, and spices, and she was relishing the last bite when Phoebe Chadwick appeared looking like she'd been plowing the north forty with a blind mule.

"I know you're all wanting news of Miss Dimple," she told them, pouring herself coffee from the sideboard, "so I'll tell you what I know: She had made her bed this morning as usual, and I couldn't find a thing missing from her closet, but Bobby Tinsley noticed a small piece of paper under the console table in the front hall. I suppose it must've blown there when somebody opened the door because we didn't see it earlier."

Bobby Tinsley was Elderberry's chief of police, and his daughter, Bobbie Ann, was in Annie's fourth-grade class. As well as Charlie could remember, the most recent "crime" the chief had to deal with was when several members of the local football team got carried away with some bootleg liquor one night and turned a pig loose in the sacred halls of Elderberry High.

Phoebe paused while she stirred cream into her coffee and everybody leaned forward to hear what she had to say. The spoon clinked as she set it on her saucer and turned to face the diners at the table. "It seems," she told them, "that there's been a family emergency and Miss Dimple has gone to look after an older sister who has fallen ill."

Charlie couldn't imagine the longtime teacher having a sister—especially one who was older than Miss Dimple herself. In fact, she had always thought of the woman as arriving in this world fully grown, handbag in hand. "Is that all she said?" she asked.

"Surely she gave an address where she could be reached," Velma reasoned, but Phoebe shook her head.

Noticing the time, Annie pushed back her chair. "She might not have slept in her bed last night at all," she said. "And why would she leave in the middle of the night without saying anything? Are you sure that note's in Miss Dimple's handwriting?"

Odessa, lingering in the kitchen doorway, put down her tray with a rattle. "Ain't no way Miss Dimple could'a wrote that note," she said, looking stormier by the second.

"What do you mean, Odessa?" Phoebe grasped the back of a ladder-back chair until it seemed it might break in two.

"'Cause she done told me back when I first come here the only sister she had died when she was just a little old thing, so I don't see how she could've gone to see 'bout her . . .'lesson, of course, dead folks be coming back to life."

And with that, Odessa Kirby made her exit.

CHAPTER FOUR

Something was terribly wrong! She knew Dimple Kilpatrick as well as . . . well . . . as well as anyone did, and better than most, and Virginia Balliew was absolutely certain that something had happened to her friend. Something horrible. She was so upset with worry she almost dropped an armful of books she was shelving when Emma Elrod came into the library to return Willie's books, two of the orange-backed series based on the semifictional childhood of historical figures. "And which of these did Willie like better? Benjamin Franklin or Thomas Edison?" Virginia asked, hiding a smile because she knew the child had read neither.

Willie's mother, however, was a determined woman and immediately selected two more. "He didn't say, but probably the one about Edison. Our Willie has an inventive mind, you know. Such an imagination! Says he saw poor Miss Dimple being kidnapped by spies! Spies, now! Can you believe it?"

Virginia frowned. "And where was this, Emma?"

"Why, right out there in front of our house. Says she got into a car."

"What kind of car?"

Emma shrugged. "Willie claimed it was too dark to tell, but of course it wasn't true. Just like all those other wild stories he tells. Worries me nearly to death—the child doesn't seem to know fact from fiction." She patted the selections on the desk in front of her. "That's why I want him to read about real people."

Virginia stamped the date on a Hardy Boys Mystery that had just come in and slipped it in with the rest. "When he's finished those others, he might enjoy this one," she said. After all, reading was reading.

Josephine Carr tossed her blue felt hat on the needlepoint footstool and kicked off her shoes. "What's all this about Miss Dimple?" she asked, hovering as close to the fireplace as possible. They had been gone all day and the house was cold, although Charlie had lit a small coal fire in the sitting room when she got home from school.

Wednesday was one of the three days during the week her mother worked at the ordnance plant over in Milledgeville, along with Charlie's aunt Louise and several others from Elderberry, including their neighbor, Bessie Jenkins, and Odessa's husband, Bob Robert. At eight every morning, a bus picked up workers in front of Clyde Jefferies Feed and Seed for the forty-five-minute drive, returning them several hours later. Jo and her sister worked in offices in one of the main buildings, and Bessie's job had something to do with fuses, but Bob Robert, being colored, was assigned to another facility.

"It's like she dropped off the face of the earth," Charlie said. "Didn't show up for school, or even bother to get a substitute, and you know that's not like Miss Dimple. Poor old Froggie had a terrible time finding somebody to fill in. Finally, one of the mothers felt sorry for him and volunteered to help—and all this on top of what happened to Christmas yesterday!"

The principal had done his best to assure the bewildered children that everything would be all right, but his grating voice and authoritative manner overwhelmed some of the smaller ones and little Margaret Bailey had cried until her mama had to come and take her home.

Charlie's mother frowned. "I don't suppose they've learned any more about that?"

Charlie shook her head. "Nothing definite. Everybody seems to think it was a stroke, but I heard he had head injuries as well."

"Injuries? You mean he had more than one? How can that be?"

Charlie shrugged. That had bothered her as well. "I'm just repeating what I've heard. I guess he could've hit his head on the filing cabinet when he fell, and then again on the floor."

"Hmmm . . ." Jo Carr contemplated that, and having warmed her front, turned her back to the flames. "Poor Madge! Don't you think we should take something over?"

Charlie nodded. "Applesauce muffins are in the oven. Annie and I plan to drop by for a few minutes tonight."

"And now Dimple Kilpatrick. Do they have *any* idea where she might be?"

"She did leave a note, or at least they *found* one, and Miss Phoebe says it looked a little shaky to her, but she's fairly sure it's in her handwriting. She left instructions on where to find her lesson plans for the rest of the week. Bobby Tinsley saw it underneath the hall table, but all her clothes are here, and Miss Phoebe said her luggage is still in the basement with everyone else's."

"That doesn't make any sense at all," Jo said, ramming a hairpin into a cascading lock of brown hair. At fifty, she was just beginning to get a few strands of gray. "Is that all she said?"

"She *said* there'd been a family emergency and she was leaving to take care of an older sister," Charlie said, "but Odessa swears up and down Miss Dimple told her once that her only sister died as a child."

Jo gave the fire a poke, sending red embers spiraling. "Where does she usually keep her lesson plans?"

"In her desk at school, but, knowing her, Miss Dimple probably has all her lessons planned through the end of the year, so that wouldn't necessarily mean she knew she would be away."

"Are the police even trying to find her?" Jo shook her head. "I reckon Bobby Tinsley does the best he can, but his daddy was a couple of years ahead of me in school, and he didn't have the sense God promised a billy goat!"

"They're trying to locate her brother to see if he knows anything, but Miss Phoebe can't find her address book and nobody remembers his name. You know how private Miss Dimple was—*is*."

"Well, it all sounds mighty peculiar to me," Jo said, "but Miss Dimple always had her own way of doing things, getting up at the crack of dawn to walk all over town! Lord, her poor feet must be worn out by now, not to mention her shoes—and they don't grow on trees these days. And you know she won't wear any color but purple."

Charlie nodded. It was rumored that Miss Dimple wore that color for a long-ago beau who was killed in the Spanish American War, but she thought it was probably because she just liked purple.

The fragrance of cinnamon and nutmeg wafted from the kitchen and Charlie was heading there to check her muffins when the phone rang. Her mother, who was nearer to the telephone, gave her a questioning look, but Charlie shook her head. If Hugh was calling, it wouldn't hurt him to wait. In fact, the way Charlie felt about Hugh . . . well . . . she wasn't exactly sure just how she felt about Hugh Brumlow. There were times when she was *almost* certain he was the one, but she couldn't be sure what his feelings were.

But it was her aunt Louise on the phone, and she could tell by the one-sided conversation Louise had heard about Miss Dimple's disappearance.

"No, she didn't show up for school . . . as far as I know, they don't have any idea where . . . left a note, right, but her clothes are still there . . . no, she doesn't know, either. . . ." Jo smiled and rolled her eyes at Charlie. "Yes, you'll know when we know, Lou. I promise."

"Faster than a speeding bullet," she said, following Charlie down the long cold hall and into the warm kitchen. "Your aunt should be the one working for a newspaper the way she noses out the news—and speaking of, I have to write up Linda Harkins's wedding if I want to get it in on time for next week's *Eagle*. Do you mind stirring up something for supper?"

Charlie, who was usually the one who "stirred up something for supper," said she didn't mind at all. She would much rather throw sweet potatoes in the oven to bake and warm up leftover chicken and green beans from the day before than write the lengthy, saccharine descriptions of social events her mother turned out weekly in her position as society editor of the local paper.

Although Jo Carr still owned a small share of the drugstore her husband, Charles, had left her when he died several years before, she had been forced to sell most of the family-owned farmland in order to send Charlie and her brother to college, and the money she earned at the ordnance plant and the newspaper supplemented Charlie's small salary to help with expenses.

Jo was quiet as she helped with the dishes after supper and Charlie knew her mother was thinking of Fain. Charlie's older brother, a brand-new second lieutenant in the infantry, was somewhere in Algeria with General Eisenhower as part of the Allied forces that had landed earlier in the month, and except for what they read in the newspapers or heard over the radio, they knew little else. Charlie came to dread seeing the Western Union boy delivering messages on his bicycle because it usually meant someone's son, brother, or husband was either killed or wounded..

If only she could be a part of it—do something to help further the war effort! Once, Charlie had even considered joining the Women's Army Auxiliary Corps, or WAAC, or its navy counterpart, the WAVES, and would have if it hadn't been for Delia. She and her sister had been drying dishes together two years ago when Delia announced she intended to marry Ned Varnadore. Charlie, home for Christmas break during her junior year in college, pointed out that Ned was only in his sophomore year at the University of Georgia; that she, Delia, was to begin at Shorter College in September after she graduated from high school, and what could she possibly be thinking?

Delia dumped the dried silverware in the drawer with a clatter and, arms folded, turned to face her older sister. "I love him," she said, "and he loves me."

There was a finality in her statement as shocking as a dash of cold water, and Charlie knew that in the long run her sister would have her way.

When the country went to war a few months after they married, Ned enlisted with most of his fraternity brothers. Now, far away in Texas where she lived in cramped quarters on her husband's army base, Delia was lonely, homesick, and pregnant. Well, it served her right! If her sister had stayed at home where she belonged, Charlie thought, she herself could be contributing more than used cooking fat and scrap metal while also seeing a whole new part of the world.

"You can't do it, Charlie. You can't leave Mama alone," Fain had told her. Her brother had been accepted into officers training school at the time, and Charlie knew he was right. Besides, Fain didn't need anything else to worry him.

Although Delia's letters home were upbeat and newsy, Charlie recognized a "brave front" when she saw one. She knew her mother worried over what her sister had obviously omitted, and once in a while she even felt guilty for resenting her.

Now Jo hung her damp dish towel on the back of the pantry door. "I think I'll go ahead and take my bath before I get back to that wedding write-up. Want me to leave on the heater in the bathroom?"

Charlie felt suddenly tired, and a warm bath seemed tempting, but she had promised to meet Annie at Miss Phoebe's, where they would then walk together to pay their respects to the Malones.

"I want to take those muffins over to Madge Malone before it gets too late. Maybe there'll be a little warm water left when I get home."

In order to have a hot bath in a warm room, first one had to light the iron gas monstrosity that would heat water in the tank, then the smaller heater in the bathroom, but it would be worth waiting for, Charlie thought as she grabbed her coat and stepped into the cold night air.

Phoebe Chadwick sent a loaf of Odessa's homemade bread and a jar of peach preserves with Annie, and the two of them left their offerings on the Malones' kitchen table along with numerous cakes and casseroles before paying their respects to the family. Charlie noticed that their neighbor, Bessie Jenkins, who was leaving as they arrived, had brought her customary contribution of orange nut bread, wrapped in wax paper and tied with a lavender ribbon.

Madge Malone, red-eyed and quiet, thanked them for coming and even smiled when Charlie told her she would always remember her husband's joyful rendition of "Froggie Went A-Courtin'." After speaking to several other members of the family, she was glad to work her way toward the door where Annie stood talking with a short, dumpy woman with obviously hennaed hair.

"I've been telling Wilson he works too hard," she said, introducing herself as the Malones' next-door neighbor. "Why, he was out here the other day cuttin' stove wood, face as red as that chair cushion over there. I told him—'Wilson,' I said, 'you'd better ease off on all that choppin' or you're liable to end up just like your daddy!'

"Wilson's daddy had the high blood, too, you know. Keeled over playing softball at the church picnic. Didn't even make it to second base."

"Are they sure it was Chri— Wilson's heart?" Charlie asked. "Someone mentioned earlier they thought it might've been a stroke."

34

But the neighbor waved that idea aside. "Stroke, heart, what does it matter? If you're not careful, that high blood will get you in the end." She shook her head. "If only he'd listened to me—"

Her attention was distracted by a new arrival whom she snared by the arm. "Pearl, I was tellin' these folks here I wasn't a bit surprised—"

"Lord, I thought we'd never get away!" Annie said as they finally made their escape. "It's peculiar that nobody seems to know exactly what it was that killed Christmas. Wouldn't you think they'd have learned something definite by now?"

Charlie tucked her muffler closer under her chin. "I hated to ask Madge, and they might not ever know. I've heard he had more than one head wound, but nobody has explained that, either. Besides, we can't bring him back, can we? Dead is dead."

"I guess you're right, but it does seem a shame. I wonder if the bell you heard was Christmas calling for help." Annie pulled her tam about her ears and walked a little faster.

Charlie didn't even want to think about that. Eager to reach home and relax in a hot bath, she hurried to catch up with Annie who waltzed along ahead of her to some unheard tune. It amazed her that somebody with such short legs could outpace her. There was no moon tonight and few streetlights in this part of town. The dull yellow glow from neighboring windows gave sporadic illumination to the dark streets where an occasional wind sent leaves rattling into gutters.

After parting with Annie at Miss Phoebe's, Charlie walked even faster, periodically glancing over her shoulder. Had someone shadowed Miss Dimple on her last early-morning walk?

Threatening characters from every frightening movie she'd ever seen seemed to hover just out of sight: Lon Chaney, Peter Lorrie, Boris Karloff, and Bela Lugosi in his dark, sweeping cape, who, to Charlie was the scariest of all.

For heaven's sake! This is ridiculous! What would your third grad-ers think of you now? Charlie deliberately slowed her steps and sang all she could remember of "Chattanooga Choo Choo" until she finally reached the safety of her own front porch, where she hur-ried inside and locked the door behind her.

A light shone from beneath the sitting room door and Charlie peeked in to find her mother dozing by the dying fireside with what looked like the completed wedding write-up still in the note-book on her lap. Charlie tiptoed past to quietly add a couple of coals to the grate, but Jo Carr sat up with a start.

"My goodness! I must've dozed off. What time is it?"

Charlie kissed her mother's warm cheek. "Time for you to go to bed, and I'll be doing the same after I've thawed out in the tub. I think it's getting colder out there."

"I can't help thinking of poor Miss Dimple. Wherever she is, I hope she's safe and warm." Jo covered a yawn. "And how did you find Madge Malone? Any word on what happened to Wilson?"

"I didn't ask, but their neighbor thinks it must've been his heart. Said he had high blood pressure, and I suppose that could've con-tributed to it." Charlie sat to pull off her shoes and held her cold feet to the flickering blaze. "Frankly, I think Madge is still numb, but they have two teenaged daughters. What will happen to them now?"

⟡

What must it be like to lose your life's mate? she thought later as she relaxed in lilac-scented water using crystals someone had given her the Christmas before. Her own parents had been especially close and she knew her mother still had difficulty with her husband's death, although most of the time she tried not to show it.

Her sister Delia had loved Ned from their first date when she was fifteen and had never given anyone else a second look. Boyish and handsome in his uniform with his cap set at a jaunty angle, Ned smiled from the photograph they kept on the sitting-room mantel across from her brother's more serious pose.

Would she be willing to live on some remote army base to be with Hugh? Charlie sank lower in the tub until water covered her shoulders. What did it matter? On their last date, he had seemed unusually quiet, almost impersonal, as if his thoughts were somewhere far away. She would probably never have a chance to find out. Closing her eyes, she pictured Hugh in uniform; pictured how her head came almost to his shoulder so that she could smell the spicy scent of his aftershave as she had when they had kissed good night. The delicious memory of it sent an electric tingle through the secret places of her body and Charlie's face grew warm at the thought of what it might be like to make love with Hugh Brumlow.

But she wasn't going to think of him. Charlie pulled the bathtub plug with her toe and wrapped a towel around her as the water gurgled down the drain. And that was when the telephone rang.

Shivering, she clutched the towel around her and hurried down the cold hall to answer the demanding summons.

"About the other night . . ." Hugh began. The pause was so heavy Charlie could hear him breathing. "I feel—well, I feel I should apologize."

Charlie didn't reply.

"I had a few things on my mind," he continued, "and some major decisions to make."

"Uh-huh," Charlie said. She wasn't going to make this easy.

"How about dinner tomorrow night? There's a rumor Rusty's might have steak."

Rusty's was a cozy little restaurant on the outskirts of town where people went for special occasions. Soft music played in the background while guests dined by candlelight on tablecloths wedding-cake white. And *steak!* Charlie couldn't remember the last time she had eaten steak since rationing began.

"What time?" she said.

CHAPTER FIVE

How long was she going to sleep? The woman was as still as . . . he wasn't even going to think that. And small. Smaller than he'd expected. What if she died? What good was she then? He hadn't planned to kill that janitor. How was he to know the man would be at the school that early in the morning? From all he'd heard, Miss Dimple was always the first one there and everybody complained that janitor fellow was never on time. It would've been so easy to knock her out with chloroform and lower her out the window to the waiting car below. It was still dark that early. Who would see?

So what was he to do? He remembered the panic on the janitor's face when he unlocked Miss Dimple's classroom door and found him waiting there. Didn't waste a minute before he bolted to the school office across the hall to call for help. He had to stop him, didn't he? Malone, the man's name was. Wilson Malone. It was too bad, really. He hadn't counted on that. When Malone didn't have time to unlock the office door, he ran upstairs—grabbing the bell rope in that storage room up there before he could stop him.

But he had stopped him, stopped him with the first thing that came to hand. Came down on him hard with that big wooden bird. There was no question he was dead. Too bad.

And now this. From across the room he stared at the figure on the bed. If only she had stuck to her usual route, all that could've been avoided, but he reckoned the woman got spooked that day in the park. Well, he'd done what was expected of him, hadn't he? But that was only the first step. He sighed, rubbing his neck to ease the tension. Maybe this wasn't such a good idea after all. Maybe he'd made a mistake. And then he thought of his papa and how hard he'd worked to make ends meet. What did the government ever do for him? Drove him into an early grave, that's what! He clenched his teeth to keep from crying out with anger and resentment.

❧

Dimple Kilpatrick slowly pulled herself erect and carefully placed her feet on the floor. The room was dark and smelled of mothballs and mildew. Why did her head hurt so? She felt faintly nauseated and her mouth was dry. Had she eaten something that didn't agree with her?

And then she remembered.

As she sat on the side of the bed, her eyes became gradually accustomed to the darkness and she could distinguish the pattern of a quilt that had been thrown over her. It was of an intricate log-cabin pattern, and old. Very old. Her feet rested on a rag rug, the kind made of scraps of cloth, like her mother used to make. A glass of water sat on the table beside her along with a lamp and her glasses. Miss Dimple reached for the glasses first, then drank the water. It hurt at first to swallow.

She was reaching for the lamp when the man spoke.

"Don't be afraid. I'm not going to hurt you."

He sat in a chair on the other side of the room. He must have been there all along, and on closer look, she saw that he wore a Halloween mask like the kind you could buy for a nickel at Murphys' Five-and-Ten. A Harlequin, she thought. "What do you want from me?" she demanded, and her voice, usually calm and authoritative, surprised her with its rusty pitch.

He stood and placed pen and paper on the table beside her. "First, I'll have to ask you to write a brief note. We don't want your friends worrying now, do we?"

Dimple Kilpatrick wanted everyone to worry. She wanted them to worry day and night. She wanted the whole town of Elderberry, the entire state of Georgia turned upside down until they found her. "Why have you done this? What do you want?" she asked again.

His silence was as terrifying as the shocking answer she suspected, and although Miss Dimple wasn't much of a one for bothering her Maker on a regular basis, she prayed it wasn't so.

"I know what happened to Miss Dimple!" Willie Elrod said the next morning at school as he offered his dime for a savings stamp.

"Is that right, Willie? And what would that be?" Charlie gave him the stamp and made sure he pasted it in the book for that purpose. She noticed that Willie's mother had made an attempt that morning to smooth down his wild, haystack hair.

Junior Henderson plonked down three dimes for his purchase. "I'll bet it was Martians that took her! She's probably in a spaceship right now." And he glanced out the window as if he expected to see the missing teacher waving from afar.

"Naw! I reckon the Japs got her . . . or maybe it was the Germans," Willie insisted. "I saw—"

"We'll probably never see her again." Lee Anne Stephens looked as if she might break into tears, and Willie, noticing that, continued. "And they'll question her until they make her talk. No tellin' what they might—"

"That's quite enough of that, Willie," Charlie said, sending him to his seat. "I can't imagine what information Miss Dimple might have that would be useful to the enemy. Now, let's all get out our *Adventures in Arithmetic*. I'm sure we'll hear from Miss Dimple soon, perhaps even today."

But they didn't.

The mood was somber during the noon meal at Miss Phoebe's. Lily Moss declared she just couldn't bear to think of what had happened to Poor Miss Dimple, and it was all she could do to keep from crying. "But of course I have to put on a brave front for my students," she added, sniffing. "Sixth graders can be so emotional, you know."

"Crying isn't going to get her back," Elwin said, buttering a biscuit. Because Phoebe Chadwick purchased milk and butter from a local farmer, her boarders continued to enjoy at least some of the dairy products that had become in short supply.

"Haven't they heard *anything* more?" Annie asked their hostess, but Phoebe concentrated on passing the black-eyed peas and didn't answer.

"What about her address book?" Annie persisted. "Hasn't that turned up yet?"

Phoebe's voice was as bleak as her face. "We can't find it anywhere. She must've taken it with her."

Phoebe Chadwick was a small woman, but she seemed to have shrunk even more in the last two days, Charlie thought. Usually immaculate in her appearance, she looked as if she had slept in her clothes.

"And her purse," Phoebe continued, "you know, the one she always carries? Well, that's gone, too."

"The one with the yarn flowers on it?" Velma asked. "She probably had it with her. Dimple carries that bag everywhere."

It would've been hard not to remember Miss Dimple's handbag. Made of purple leather with a drawstring, it was adorned with yarn flowers of every hue, and Charlie was certain it dated back to the War Between the States.

"We've looked everywhere to try to find any kind of correspondence with her brother," their hostess said, ladling chow-chow onto her turnip greens. "She spends most holidays and part of her summers with him and his wife. If only we knew how to get in touch with him!"

Lily Moss spoke up. "I've tried my best to think of his name and it seems his first name is Henry, but I haven't the faintest idea where he lives."

"That's at least a start," Charlie said. "What made you remember that?"

Lily shrugged. "Henry's my father's name and I remembered Miss Dimple mentioning her brother's name when he sent us that big box of fruit last Christmas."

"Of course!" Velma laid down her napkin and abruptly pushed back her chair. "How could I forget? I got his address from Miss Dimple to send him a thank-you note. I'm sure I still have it somewhere." She rushed from the room.

"Here it is!" Velma Anderson was more excited than Charlie had ever seen her when she reentered the room, flushed and breathless, a few minutes later. "He lives in that little town near Atlanta. There's a mountain there where they fought a big battle . . . Kennesaw—that's it! I have the address right here." She presented the small slip of paper to Phoebe Chadwick as if it had been a guarded treasure.

"I don't suppose you have a phone number," Elwin said.

"No, but we can call the operator and find out," Phoebe said, frowning as she studied Velma's spidery handwriting. "Now, where did I put my glasses?"

Annie laughed. "They're around your neck."

"Where's everybody going? We got that prune cake you all like for dessert." Odessa bustled in from the kitchen as the group filed out of the dining room and gathered around the telephone in the hallway while Phoebe again studied the address.

"We're going to call Miss Dimple's brother," Charlie explained above the hubbub.

"Will everybody please be quiet? I'm trying to get the operator and I can't even hear myself think!" Phoebe exclaimed. "Hello, Florence? I need to get long distance, please . . . that's right, long distance. I need the number for Henry Kilpatrick in Kennesaw, Georgia. Kennesaw, that's right . . . no, Florence, Miss Dimple's not in Kennesaw—at least not that I know of. We don't know where she is. That's why I'm . . . thank you!" She repeated her request and hastily scribbled a number on the back of the paper Velma had given her.

"It's ringing," she announced to the others after what seemed like hours dragged by.

But apparently no one at that number was at home although the operator rang several times. Charlie looked about her at the downcast group. She almost felt like crying herself.

"I suppose we ought to pass this number along to Bobby Tinsley," Annie suggested. "The police should follow up on this.

"Don't worry," she added, apparently noticing Phoebe's disappointed expression. "We can try again later."

❧

"Okay, out with it," Annie said as she and Charlie walked back to school after lunch. "What's going on?"

"What do you mean?" Charlie walked a little faster.

Annie stepped in front to block her way. "What do you think? Have you heard from Hugh? You know you're going to tell me sooner or later."

She was right, of course. It was hard to keep anything from

Annie. Even though they had only met in college, she felt the two of them might as well have grown up together.

"That sounds serious," Annie said when Charlie told her about her telephone conversation with Hugh the night before.

"Oh it is. We hardly ever smile." Charlie managed with great difficulty to maintain a straight face, but Annie let the comment pass without so much as a blink.

"I'll bet that *something on his mind* is you." She stopped suddenly in the middle of the sidewalk. "Do you think he might be planning to propose?"

"I think it's more likely he's going to enlist." Charlie glanced at her watch and walked faster. The first bell would ring in about five minutes.

Annie nodded. "Maybe both."

"His mother would have a fit."

"Why?" Annie asked. "Because he proposes to you or plans to join the service?"

"Both," Charlie said, wondering what she would say if he did. "Anyway, he hasn't done either one."

"Yet," Annie reminded her.

The closer they came to the school, the more Charlie found herself dreading going back into the building. Alma Owens had been delegated to take Miss Dimple's class until she returned or a permanent replacement could be found, and the children across the hall had been boisterous all morning.

"I wonder what Alma plans to do with them this afternoon," Annie whispered as they waited at the top of the steps for the second bell. "For a while this morning I thought a train was coming right through the building."

Plump, jolly, and fortyish, Alma considered herself to be a friend to the children and played with them accordingly. That morning she had kept them entertained with games of fruit basket turnover and musical chairs, with Alma playing the xylophone. During recess she led them around the playground in a parade of rhythm band instruments she had apparently pilfered from the supply closet.

"They should be worn out by now. Maybe they'll nap this afternoon," Charlie said, knowing it was too good to be true.

And of course it was. After several rounds of "Row, Row, Row Your Boat" and "Are You Sleeping, Brother John?" Alma had the class competing in some kind of quiz in which the answers were shouted, and by the end of the day, Charlie felt as if someone were pounding an anvil inside her head.

"Take an aspirin and rest for a while," Annie suggested as they left school that afternoon.

"I can't. I told Mama I'd pick up a few groceries from Mr. Cooper. We're completely out of butter, and I planned to make macaroni and cheese tomorrow." Charlie fumbled in her purse as she spoke. "Thank goodness I remembered to bring my ration book. Maybe they'll have some real butter today instead of that disgusting imitation stuff with the blob of food coloring in the middle."

"Let me drop off some of these papers at Phoebe's and I'll go with you," Annie said. "I need to get some writing paper from the dime store and I'm almost out of hand lotion, too."

"Heard anything from Will?" Charlie asked. She knew Annie was waiting to hear from a friend of her brother's she'd dated in college. Both men were training as pilots in the Army Air Corps.

But Annie frowned and shook her head. "They're just beginning their training and it sounds like they have a long way to go. The last time he wrote, though, he said he might try to get down here to see me."

Charlie laughed. "Maybe you're the one who'll get the proposal."

But Annie only grinned. "And maybe the war will be over tomorrow."

"Find out if they've heard any more from Miss Dimple," Charlie said as Annie hurried inside. But one look at her friend's face when she emerged a few minutes later told her nothing had changed.

"Phoebe said she passed the phone number along to Bobby at the police department but he hasn't been able to get an answer yet," Annie reported. "Bobby said he'd ask the police there to try and locate Miss Dimple's brother. He's hoping he'll hear something by tonight."

As far as Charlie could remember, nothing especially unusual had ever happened in Elderberry, but she had a horrible feeling that the events around the teacher's disappearance were going to involve them in something they weren't prepared for.

A brisk wind had picked up earlier in the afternoon and she buttoned her coat a little higher as dry leaves swirled in its wake. "Why would Miss Dimple leave a note saying she was going to be with her sister if she doesn't have one?" Charlie said as they hurried the few blocks to town. "And why didn't she tell anybody she was leaving?"

"Beats me. Maybe she was referring to a sister-in-law or a stepsister. Wherever she is, I wish she'd hurry back! I don't think I can stand another day of Alma's racket." Annie groaned. "Poor Froggie's tried just about everybody in town to find somebody to replace her. I heard he even plans to advertise in the newspapers."

She paused as they neared Lewellyn's Drugstore. "Don't look now, but I think we're being followed." Annie lowered her voice. "Willie Elrod's been behind us since we left Phoebe's. I think he has a crush on you."

Charlie looked behind her in time to see the boy dart into a store front. "Hello, Willie!" she called. "Is that you?"

The child emerged just long enough to hold a hand to his lips and wave her away.

"Probably some kind of game," Annie said, laughing. "Okay if we run in here for a minute? I want to see if they have that new lipstick in." But Charlie continued walking as if she didn't hear her.

Annie, noticing she didn't follow, hurried to catch up with her. "Charlie! Wait up! Didn't you hear me?" She grinned. "Or are you in just too much of a hurry to see Jesse Dean?"

Jesse Dean Greeson helped stock shelves and deliver groceries for Cooper's Grocery and it was obvious that he had a crush on Charlie. He had a prominent Adam's apple, wore gold-rimmed glasses with lenses thick enough to distinguish planets, and was so pale it was hard to tell where his face stopped and his fair hair began. Charlie felt sorry for Jesse Dean and made an effort to be kind to him because he was 4-F on account of his eyes, which made him ineligible for the service and he was sometimes taunted by others.

"Sorry. I was thinking about something Miss Dimple said. Guess I wasn't listening."

"About what? Do you think it might be important?" Annie asked.

"It was the day they found Christmas Malone and we were all waiting in Lily's classroom. Remember? You said something about Christmas ringing the bell to summon help, and Miss Dimple said maybe he was trying to warn us."

Annie frowned. "Warn us? Warn us about what?"

"I don't know," Charlie said. "But thinking about it makes me wonder about something else. What was Christmas doing up there in the storage closet that early in the morning? It's used mainly to store props and things for school assemblies and Alice Brady's expression recitals. I don't think he ever goes—went—in there."

"You're right. He usually started by stoking the furnace and worked his way up. If he wanted to summon help, he could've used the phone in the office or even rung the bell from in there." Annie shrugged. "Well, we'll never know now. Come on, let's go get a Co-Cola and think about something else."

CHAPTER SIX

*V*irginia Balliew locked the door of the library behind her and wondered what she would have for supper. There was the last of the meat loaf, of course, but she was tired of meat loaf, and it was monotonous having to cook for one. Albert had been gone almost four years now, and although he had been a bit prosaic, he was a kind man and good. She missed him. And Dimple! What on earth had happened to Dimple? Surely someone must know something by now. Really, it was quite frustrating! If her friend were here, she could invite her to share her meal, as she often did.

And even though it was two blocks out of her way, Virginia turned up the street by Phoebe Chadwick's rooming house where, according to his mother, the child Willie claimed he had seen Dimple Kilpatrick abducted. The evening shadows were deepening as she crossed the road, her eyes on the spot where Willie said he had last seen her friend.

An ardent reader of mysteries, Dimple might have had time to leave a clue, Virginia thought, and with one foot, probed a soggy mound of leaves by the curb. Nothing. The ground next to the street was brown and bare . . . but what was this on one of the lower limbs of the crape myrtle? A tiny tuft of color. Purple.

Virginia plucked the bit of frayed yarn from the branch and tucked it inside her purse.

❧

Although her father had been gone almost seven years, Charlie still looked for him behind the partition where pharmacists fill prescriptions at the back of the store and felt the familiar stab of emptiness it brought. The room was long and narrow with a black-and-white tile floor and pressed tin ceiling. In warmer weather a ceiling fan stirred the air above a scattering of tables in front of the soda fountain, but today the place felt stuffy and close. She smiled as Phil Lewellyn, Charles Carr's former partner, looked at her over his glasses and raised a hand in salute.

The two women found an empty booth in the back and treated themselves to fountain Cokes in crushed ice. Sipping the drink slowly, Charlie could almost feel her headache melting away.

Annie swirled her drinking straw in the bell-shaped glass. "Have you decided what you're wearing tonight?"

"That green suit, I guess. Remember? The one with the velvet collar." Charlie had worn the suit in college but it was still good except for the length, and her mother had promised she would ask their neighbor, Bessie Jenkins, to take up the hem that afternoon. In addition to her part-time job at the ordnance plant, Miss Bessie sewed for many of the women in town and sold tickets to the picture show on Saturdays.

Charlie wished she would have time to do something different with her hair. She wore her straight blond hair in a long bob that turned under just below her chin line, and to achieve this effect, it was necessary to roll it in kid curlers, rags, or socks, and sometimes even the hated metal rollers.

Annie waved at a couple of her students who were browsing through the rack of comic books in the corner of the store. "If you want, you can borrow my brown—" She broke off in mid-sentence.

50

"Uh-oh! 'Double, double, toil and trouble' . . . Don't look now, but there's her royal snideness."

"Who—" Charlie glanced behind her to see Hugh's mother, Emmaline Brumlow, thumbing through the greeting cards at the front of the store.

"I said, *don't look!*"

Too late. Emmaline had noticed them. "Charlie. Annie." She nodded in their direction, and Charlie thought she smiled, but it was hard to be sure.

Hugh's family owned Brumlows' Dry Goods, a small store that sold everything from shoes to hats, and his mother ruled the business and the family with a tight fist and a shrewd eye, and had, even before his father died when Hugh was twelve. At her mother's insistence, Hugh's sister Arden, who had graduated from high school with Charlie, left college early to help her mother manage the store.

"I wonder if she knows you're going out with Hugh tonight," Annie said, responding to the woman's greeting with a wave of her fingers.

Charlie didn't answer. She was trying hard to like Emmaline Brumlow even a little bit, but it was a difficult challenge. She couldn't help feeling sorry for Arden. Her mother had put her foot down when Arden wanted to marry Barrett Gordon before he left for the navy. She wanted to spare her daughter the heartbreak if anything happened to Barrett, she said, but everyone knew she was just too cheap to hire somebody to run the register if Arden left to be near her husband.

The music of Glenn Miller's "String of Pearls" bounced from a radio somewhere in the back and Annie's fingers danced in rhythm along the tabletop. "Have you thought about what it would be like to have *her* for a mother-in-law?"

"Huh!" Charlie said and concentrated on fishing the ice from the bottom of her glass. She'd first noticed Hugh Brumlow when he sold her a pair of fire-engine-red sandals when she was sixteen. He was working in the store during a summer break from college and Charlie had saved her money for the shoes from a part-time job helping out at the library.

Now that all seemed very long ago. Hugh still took care of orders and shipping and kept the shelves stocked with fabric and clothing—at least when he could get them—but with the current shortages and rationing, none of the stores had anything like their prewar inventories. And the red sandals had rubbed painful blisters on her feet. Now, even if Hugh did propose tonight, Charlie wasn't sure what her answer would be.

The two parted a few minutes later as Annie wanted to get a letter off to her brother, Joel. Annie corresponded with him faithfully as she did with Will and several others who were serving with the armed forces. Charlie wrote every week to Fain and kept up a steady correspondence with some of her high school classmates as well, plus a few of the men she had dated in college. She was particularly concerned about a friend of her brother's, who, in August, had landed with the marines on Guadalcanal. Just about all the young men she knew had either enlisted, been drafted, or were waiting to be.

A short way down the block she spied Willie Elrod dodging behind a poster in front of the picture show and tried hard not to laugh when he peeked slyly over the top and quickly withdrew his head.

"Come out, come out wherever you are!" Charlie called, pausing until the boy showed himself. "What are you doing down here, Willie? Does your mother know where you are?"

"Yes'm, I guess so. She sent me to get her a spool of thread at the dime store."

"And did you?" Charlie asked.

Willie shrugged. "No'me. Not yet."

"Well, don't you think you'd better hurry? It's getting kind of late and you have homework for tomorrow. She might be worried about you."

"She don't care," Willie said, shuffling along beside her.

"*Doesn't* care." Charlie smiled. "Except I happen to know she does."

She stopped when they came to Murphy's Five and Ten on the corner. "Well, this is where we part company. I'm on my way to Coopers.'"

Willie did an about-face. "I reckon I'll go along with you."

"William Elrod! If I didn't know better, I'd think you were following me!" Charlie frowned. "Now, what's all this about?"

The child's face flushed. "There's spies around, you know, and I ain't takin' no chances."

Charlie made a face at the bad grammar. "But, Willie, why do you think they'd be interested in me?"

"They got Miss Dimple, didn't they? I saw 'em. And you know what happened to Mr. Malone."

Charlie sighed. "Mr. Malone probably had a stroke or a heart attack, Willie, and fell and hit his head . . . at least they're almost sure that's what happened. And what do you mean you *saw* someone taking Miss Dimple?"

"I saw her. That is, I did, and then I didn't." Willie turned in the direction of Murphys' but Charlie put out a hand to stop him.

"Whoa! Wait just a minute. "Just when do you think you *might've* seen Miss Dimple, Willie?"

"It was just the other night—well . . . more like morning, but still dark, and I went out to put Rags back in his box—Rags is my dog—when I seen—saw this car pull up out front, and that was when they got Miss Dimple."

"Are you sure it was Miss Dimple? You said yourself it was dark." Charlie glanced up at the courthouse clock. She would have to hurry if she was going to stop by the grocery store and get home in time to try on her skirt.

"Sure looked like her to me." Willie searched in his pocket for a lint-covered jawbreaker, which he popped into his mouth.

Charlie stooped to face him. "Now, Willie, did you actually see anyone snatch her? Did she cry out?"

The child switched the jawbreaker to the other side of his mouth. "No'me, but I'm as good as sure it was her. It ain't my fault nobody will believe me!"

Charlie shook her head as she watched him walk away. She knew exactly why nobody would believe Willie Elrod. Back in September he had terrified half the girls in the class by telling them a dragon lurked in the drainage ditch that ran behind the school, and only a few weeks ago Froggie had whaled the daylights out of him for reporting there was a *big fight* out on the playground. Turned out it was pudgy fifth-grader Amelia *Fite*, who had to wear her mother's altered dresses because she couldn't find children's clothing to fit.

Jesse Dean, who was straightening shelves of canned goods, hurried to the front counter when Charlie entered the store.

"And what can I get for you today?" he asked, resting scrawny arms on the glass-topped showcase.

The bell jangled as she closed the door behind her and Charlie smiled. "Let's see . . . I need a couple of pounds of White Lily flour, and I hope you can sell me a little butter if you have any. My mother was supposed to call and ask Mr. Cooper to set some aside." The store smelled of stale peppermints and pickles, and faintly of the live chickens that were kept in crates in the back. Even if she were blindfolded, Charlie thought, she would know exactly where she was.

"I believe he did," Jesse said. "Just let me go and check."

Charlie took out her precious ration book, noticing again his peculiar gait, as he hurried to the refrigerated section in the back of the store. He took short galloping steps, pumping his arms up and down like a child riding a stick horse. Although Jesse Dean had been a few years ahead of her in school, Charlie knew he had suffered from a lot of cruel teasing, especially from other boys, and she had hoped he might overcome his awkwardness as he got older. Instead, it seemed to be getting worse.

"Miss Phoebe called earlier and said if you or Miss Gardner happened to come by, would you please bring her some baking powder and a bunch of bananas? That is, if you don't mind. She said to just put it on her bill." The young man flushed as he spoke and his hand trembled slightly as he put Charlie's purchases in a bag.

"Well, sure, Jesse Dean. Annie—Miss Gardner—is just down the street at the post office. I'll be glad to take them to her." She watched him tear the stamps from her book and was paying for the groceries when her aunt Louise practically blew in with a gust of wind.

"Jesse Dean," she began, "tell Mr. Cooper I want a small, plump hen, not like that tough old sister he sold me last time." She parked her worn black handbag on the counter and gave Charlie's arm a squeeze.

"Tell me, sugar, what's the latest on the evasive Miss Dimple?" Louise Willingham was as large as her sister Jo was small and her sizable bosom now rested on the counter alongside her purse. "First that poor Malone fellow, and now this! I'm just waiting for the next shoe to drop. Don't suppose there's any news?"

Charlie didn't even try to figure out the analogy of somebody with three feet. "Not much," she said, shaking her head. "They're trying to locate her brother." If she told her aunt about the newly discovered phone number, she was sure an entirely different version would be all over town by morning.

"From what I heard at choir practice last night, the woman was

55

afraid for her life." Aunt Lou waited until Jesse Dean went to see about the hen and dropped her voice. "Ida Ellerby—you know Ida—lives in that little yellow house on Melrose Street out past the cotton gin . . ."

Charlie nodded. She was almost certain, though, that Mrs. Ellerby's red brick was one block over on Settlemyer.

"She told us that Dimple Kilpatrick pounded on her door one morning so early the sun was barely up. Why, Ida wasn't even dressed, and here was poor old Ralph still in his long johns . . ." Lou paused to get her breath. "Anyway, she was hollering to wake the dead out there on the porch. Ida thought the poor soul must be dying."

"So what *was* the matter? What happened?"

"A dog, she *said*. Ida snatched her inside, gave her a cup of coffee to kind of settle her down some, and Miss Dimple told her a big old dog had frightened her . . . chased her all the way up on the porch, she said." Her aunt paused to thumb through her ration book. "Of course you have to wonder about somebody crazy enough to walk all over town before even the chickens are up. You'd think she'd be old enough to know better."

Charlie frowned. "But, Aunt Lou, I don't see how a dog could've had anything to do with Miss Dimple's leaving."

"That's just it, you see. Ida said nobody on her street even has a dog like that, but just the same, it could've been a stray, so Ralph got out in his truck and looked for it after he dropped Miss Dimple off at school. They have small grandchildren, you know, and you can't have a dangerous animal like that running loose."

"Did she say when this happened?" Charlie asked.

"I believe it was a day or so before she pulled that disappearing act. Of course Ida didn't know anything about Miss Dimple's vanishing the way she did until we told her about it last night." Aunt Lou pulled a grocery list from her purse and smoothed it out on the counter. "Jesse Dean," she hollered, "give me about a half a pound of streak-o-lean, too, if you have it. I'm going to cook me up a good mess of greens tomorrow."

"I hope she told Bobby Tinsley about this," Charlie said, making a face. She hated turnip greens.

"Said she was going to. Ralph never did find that dog, either. Now you know that doesn't mean I don't believe there *was* one."

"Uh-huh." Charlie knew that was exactly what her aunt did believe. She gathered her groceries along with Miss Phoebe's order and gave her aunt a kiss on the cheek. "Gotta run!" It was already getting dark and she still hadn't done a thing about her hair.

"Tell your mama if she'll bring me the sugar, I'll bake some of my teacakes for her circle meeting next week," her aunt called after her. Charlie hoped she would bake enough to have some left over. That was another thing the sisters didn't have in common. Aunt Louise was a fantastic cook.

"Stand still and let me see if this hem is even," Miss Bessie said. Charlie stood in front of the fireplace in her underwear while her neighbor slipped the skirt over her head. Charlie's daddy had claimed Bessie Jenkins was so buck-toothed she could eat an apple through a picket fence, and she had a slight lisp to her speech, but that didn't seem to bother Bessie's longtime boyfriend, Ollie Thigpen. Ollie helped out on Paschall Kiker's farm just outside of town and looked after the old man now that he wasn't able to get around much anymore. He didn't own a car and rode a bicycle just about everywhere he went, so most of their neighbor's "outings" took place at her house unless the couple walked to church or to the movies, although once in a while Ollie treated her to supper downtown at Ray's Cafe.

Turning slowly as she was directed, Charlie couldn't help but notice the woman's thinning reddish hair as she knelt below her.

Now, humming a slightly off-key version of "Don't Sit Under the Apple Tree," she painstakingly measured the length of the skirt.

"You were gone so long I just had to guess at this." Miss Bessie sputtered pins as she spoke. "So don't blame me if the hem dips."

Charlie didn't care if it dipped or not. She had hurried home from town to take a quick "splash" bath and to roll her hair under in those hateful metal curlers that pinched and pulled, and she was not in a patient mood. "I saw Aunt Lou in Cooper's Store," she said to her mother. "Said to tell you if you supply the sugar, she'll bake teacakes for your circle meeting."

Charlie also told the two women what her aunt had said about Miss Dimple's frightening experience with the dog.

"You know you have to take some of the things your aunt tells you with a grain . . . no, make that a big spoonful of salt," Jo told her. "She's always had a wild imagination. Still, if there's anything to it, I'm sure Ida Ellerby mentioned it to the police."

Bessie removed the pins from Charlie's skirt and stuck them into the pincushion she wore on her arm, groaning as she stood. "Huh! Sounds to me like your aunt Lou's been listening to too many ghost tales."

CHAPTER SEVEN

*I*t wouldn't be long now. He had done what he was supposed to do. Now, it was up to the others. If only that old woman would cooperate! Why couldn't she eat like everybody else? He had no idea she would be so hard to please. And now she claimed she was going to die if he didn't bring her some sort of pills she kept in her desk at school. For her heart, she said. You'd think she'd keep something as important as that in that big old bag she hauled around with her, but they weren't there. He'd searched every purple crevice, so he reckoned they had to be in her classroom at school, like she said. And hadn't he made a big snafu the last time he went there?

Ninety-eight . . . ninety-nine . . . one hundred. Dimple Kilpatrick fanned herself with a page from a 1938 calendar that had hung on the wall and sank gratefully into a chair. At least twice a day she walked the confines of her basement room a hundred times. It wouldn't do to let herself get out of shape. Her prison was long and rectangular, with brick walls that had at one time been painted yellow. Two small windows higher than her head were covered with grillwork that appeared to be sturdy, but she meant to look into that later. Partially screened on the outside by scraggly evergreens—cedars, she thought—they allowed in little light, and it was difficult to regulate the gas heater at the end of the room to keep the temperature in a comfortable range. She was either too hot or too cold. Most of the time she opted for cold and wore one of the sweaters her captor had brought her. This one was a man's gray cardigan missing most of its buttons. In addition to the clothing she wore when she was taken, Miss Dimple had been supplied with seven pairs of women's underpants made of some cheap fabric. Each was a different color that had been embroidered with the name of a day of the week. She found Thursday's white ones less offensive than the others but rinsed out her own modest teddies in the bathroom sink as often as possible. The rest of her wardrobe consisted of three cotton housedresses that were too large and smelled of mothballs but at least seemed clean, a couple of pairs of inexpensive stockings, and a long flannel gown with robe to match. Except for the undergarments, most of the clothing, she assumed, had at one time belonged to a former tenant of the room—possibly a grandmother or maiden aunt, or perhaps even a maid—and she was grateful for the privacy of the small bathroom at one end with its toilet, lavatory, and an ancient tub that sat on legs.

The calendar page was for a long-ago month of September and featured an illustration of a little boy in overalls giving an apple to his teacher. How appropriate, she thought wryly. But the picture made her smile and think of her classroom at school, and the boy reminded her of that rascal William Elrod. She knew he kept his puppy in his room most nights before returning it to its box on the porch and it evoked happy memories of her own dog, Bear, who had been her childhood companion. Had William been on the porch on the morning she was taken? And if so, had it been light enough for him to see? She could only hope.

Miss Dimple stiffened as she heard someone unlock the door at the top of the stairs and the slow heavy tread of footsteps descending. The man always wore a long raincoat that had seen better days along with that crazy Halloween mask, and left her tray of food on a table at the other end of the room. He never came close enough for her to get a better look. Today he wore a clown mask that made him appear even more ridiculous.

"You've hardly eaten," he said, examining the breakfast he'd left earlier and which she had barely touched. "What's the matter? My cooking not good enough for you?"

It most certainly is not! Miss Dimple's stomach turned just thinking of the huge glutinous biscuits soaked in greasy gravy, but she dared not express her feelings aloud. Who knew what this person was capable of doing? And she wouldn't be surprised if he had something to do with Wilson Malone's death. She'd eaten a little of the scrambled egg, however, and drunk all of her coffee, which was surprisingly good, but oh, she did long for a cup of hot tea!

"If you'll bring me the ingredients, I'll make some of my muffins. I believe you'll find them both nourishing and satisfying," she said. "I can make a list of what you'll need."

"Oh, I know what you're up to. Do you really think I'd let you near a stove?"

"There's no reason you couldn't make them yourself if you follow my recipe. It's quite simple, really, and extremely beneficial to the digestive system." Miss Dimple managed a faint but audible sigh. "My physician strongly recommends them for someone in my, ah, delicate state of health." She coughed daintily into her handkerchief. Ben Morrison, who was her doctor as well as just about everybody else's, had probably never seen the muffin recipe she'd discovered years ago in a copy of *The Farmer's Almanac*, and at her last checkup, he'd told her she'd probably outlive him.

"What's wrong with your health? You're not sick or anything, are you?" There was alarm in his voice and he moved a few steps closer to see, she supposed, if she was showing any outward signs of illness.

"I'm afraid I've always been rather delicate, and I haven't felt myself for the last several days." *At least that was the truth!* "It would ease my mind if you could bring me those pills from my desk drawer . . . for my heart, you know." It was true the pills were filled from a prescription, but they were intended for a slight touch of rheumatism she'd suffered earlier in the year.

"And just how am I supposed to do that?" he wanted to know.

"Oh, I'm sure you'll find a way. I'm afraid you'll have to jimmy open the desk drawer, though, as I seem to have misplaced the key."

She knew the man's concern was not that he cared about her well-being but it was obvious he needed her to remain in good health. Dimple Kilpatrick was certain now that she was being held for ransom.

"And if it's at all possible," she added, "a cup of strong hot tea would boost my immune system. Ginger mint usually works for me."

Miss Dimple reminded herself to rise slowly and walk with tottering steps to sit on the side of the bed. "It's sometimes a bit difficult to find now with the war on, but Mr. Cooper manages to get some in now and then." And Harris Cooper knew she was one of a few people in town who favored that kind of tea.

Arms folded, he stood in the center of the room until his silence became threatening. "I'll see about getting the pills after you've done a little favor for me," he said finally. The tone of his voice made her go rigid.

"And just what kind of favor might that be?" Miss Dimple took deep, measured breaths and folded her hands demurely. It wouldn't do to let him know she was afraid.

"Nothing to be concerned about. It will only involve your writing a brief note."

"A note to whom? What kind of note?" She didn't bother to keep her intense dislike of this person from her reply.

"You'll know that when the time comes, and if you know what's good for you, you'll do as you're asked!" He really seemed most annoyed, and his voice had a peculiar squeak, as if it needed lubricating.

Miss Dimple frowned. "I believe you might be coming down with a cold, Mister . . ."

"Smith. Just call me Smith. And I'm *not* coming down with a cold!"

"Well, if you are, you might want to rub your chest with warm camphorated oil, then cover it well with a flannel cloth. And a cup of hot ginger mint tea would do wonders for your throat. I can tell by your voice you're not in the best of health."

Miss Dimple shivered and drew the quilt about her. She was going to ask Mr. Smith if he would kindly provide her with some mysteries from the library but he had already stormed back upstairs.

Well, here we are, Charlie thought, but for the life of her, she could think of absolutely nothing to say. The restaurant was appropriately lighted for a romantic dinner. Starched white tablecloths made ghostly circles in the candlelit room, and on a phonograph somewhere in the background Frank Sinatra crooned, "Night and Day." The only thing missing was the wine, but because they lived in a dry county, there was no chance of that. It would've been comforting, she thought, to have something to sip, or just to hold as they waited for the waitress to take their order. And wouldn't the good people of Elderberry be shocked? Wine with dinner was fine for people in the movies, but it wasn't an accepted practice in their little town—especially if you were employed by the Board of Education.

Suddenly, she didn't know what to do with her hands. What was wrong with her? She had been going out with Hugh for over a year now, even before she finished college and came home to teach, and usually felt comfortable in his presence. Tonight, however, she searched for something to say.

In order to read the menu, Charlie held it to the light of the candle until she noticed the flame had begun to singe the edge of the paper, and in snatching it away, she almost tipped over the vase of yellow chrysanthemums in the center of the table. Good heavens, she almost set the restaurant on fire! Maybe she should've just stayed at home. Hugh, too, was unusually restless. He unfolded his napkin and folded it again until she was tempted to lean over the table and snatch it from him. Charlie wished the waitress would hurry and fill their water glasses. She was beginning to get a headache. Should she mention that she saw his mother in the drugstore that afternoon? Possibly not the best subject to discuss over dinner.

Charlie cleared her throat. "What does Arden hear from Barrett?" she asked. Hugh's sister's fiancé was in San Diego with the navy and she wrote to him almost every day.

Hugh, who had apparently been experiencing a similar dilemma, spoke at the same time. "So, any news from the elusive Miss Dimple?"

Charlie laughed and so did he. "You first," she said, relieved that they could make light of the situation.

"I think Barrett expects to be shipped out soon. He just doesn't know when." Hugh frowned. "It's hard for Arden . . . being here, you know."

Charlie told him they were still trying to speak with Miss Dimple's brother in Kennesaw. "We're hoping he might know where she is. Phoebe says the two of them have always been close.

"Aunt Lou says she heard Miss Dimple ran to Ida Ellerby's for help early one morning not long before she disappeared," she added. "Said she was being chased by a dog."

Hugh smiled and shook his head. "I'm crazy about your aunt Lou, Charlie. Nobody makes a better sweet potato pie, but you'll have to admit she does exaggerate just the tiniest bit." He shifted in his seat and suddenly reached across the table for Charlie's hand. And that was when the waitress chose to come and take their order.

They ordered steak, which cost valuable ration stamps, and now she had lost her appetite. Charlie wished Hugh would just go on and tell her whatever it was he planned to say—good or bad. She was about to tell him that when again he took her hand, and gently stroked her fingers. The warmth of his touch steadied her and Charlie found herself immersed in his blue-eyed gaze.

Hugh's voice was calm. "Charlie, I signed up last week."

"What?" Had she heard him right? From the tone of his voice, he might have said, "I think it might rain tomorrow."

"I've been accepted . . . as a navy corpsman." He smiled and gave her fingers a squeeze.

"What?" *Why did she keep saying that? She sounded like a honking goose!*

"This way I'm able to choose. If I waited for the draft, I'd have to go where the Selective Service sends me."

"But why that? I thought you had to have some kind of medical background."

"That's what I'll get in Virginia. I'll go on from there to get further instructions as a corpsman." Hugh smiled. "It's what I want to do, Charlie."

"Are you sure about this?" *Now, that's a brilliant question, Charlie! A little late to back out now.*

"As sure as I'll ever be." He released her hand as the waitress brought their salad course. "You will write to me, won't you?"

"You know I will." Suddenly she wanted to cry. "When . . . ?"

"I leave next week for Portsmouth, Virginia. That's where I'll begin my medical training." Hugh concentrated on buttering his bread.

Now, of all times, Harry James, in the mellow tones of his

trumpet, began to serenade them with "I Don't Want to Walk Without You," and it was all she could do to hold back the tears.

"I'll miss you, you know I will. I don't even like to think about your leaving, but I *am* proud." Charlie hoped he wouldn't notice the break in her voice. And she *was* proud. Of course she wanted him to serve. Already she had heard whispered gossip about draft dodgers, able-bodied men who managed to evade the draft. And like so many others, Hugh would probably be in danger. Eddie Thornton, who had been in the class behind hers, was taken prisoner by the Japanese in the Philippines and his parents didn't even know if he was dead or alive, and one of Delia's friends had been wounded in the Battle of Midway back in June. And medical corpsmen—why, they had to dodge fire during battle just like everyone else, yet with very little chance to defend themselves. But she wouldn't think of that right now.

When their steaks came, Charlie could hardly choke hers down and felt guilty for leaving half of it on her plate. She asked the waitress to wrap it in brown paper so she could take it home. "Don't you dare laugh!" she said to Hugh, who laughed anyway. "I'll make tomorrow's hash from this.

"Have you told your mother yet?" she asked over coffee—or what passed for coffee. Charlie wondered how many times the cook had used the same grounds.

"Not yet." Hugh made a face and shook his head. "I think I'd rather face the enemy."

Charlie laughed. Wouldn't bossy old Emmaline have a fit? She'd met her match with Uncle Sam. Still, she couldn't blame a woman for not wanting to send her son to war. What kind of mother raised her sons to be killed? But would she really want him to remain at home and become a subject of derision like poor Jesse Dean?

"I wanted to tell you earlier," Hugh said on the drive home. With one arm, he drew her closer. "But I thought the news deserved a more intimate setting."

Charlie nestled against his shoulder, inhaling the spicy scent of his aftershave. "I shouldn't be surprised," she said. "I suspected it was coming after what you said on the phone last night."

Hugh was silent as he turned into her driveway and shut off the motor. "That wasn't exactly all I had in mind," he said, drawing her into his arms.

Whoa, Nellie! Here it comes, Charlie thought. Was this a preamble to a proposal? Was she absolutely sure she was ready for this? No matter. Charlie Carr closed her eyes and abandoned herself to the moment.

Brushing her hair from her face, Hugh kissed her forehead, her cheek, her lips, and buried his face in the nape of her neck. Charlie surprised herself by crying as she returned his kisses, and Hugh gently wiped them away with his fingers. "I'm not going to ask you to wait for me, but I want you to know, well, how I feel. . . ."

"And how *do* you feel?" Charlie had trouble speaking because of the elephant in her throat.

His hands were firm on her shoulders and she could barely see the outline of his face in the dark. "I think you know how much I care—"

She found his hand and raised it to her lips. "And how much is that?"

"Look, Charlie, nobody knows how long this war is going to last." Even in the darkness she could see his resolute expression. "I can't and don't expect you to hang around waiting for me for what might turn out to be years . . . or maybe even—"

Charlie stopped him with a kiss before he could continue. She knew what he was going to say and she didn't want to hear it. She didn't even want to think about it.

☙

"But you told me yourself you weren't sure you'd accept even if he did propose," Annie reminded her the following day as they stood in the shelter of the doorway watching the children at their morning recess. Several in Charlie's class were choosing someone to be "it" for a game of hide-and-seek, chanting:

Eeny, meeny, miney mo,
Catch a Nazi by the toe!
If he hollers, make him say,
"I surrender to the U.S.A!"
O-U-T spells out you go,
You old dirty dishrag, you!

Ruthie Phillips, who had the misfortune to be chosen, hid her face against a tree and began to count as the rest of the children scattered.

"No peeking, Ruthie!" Charlie warned her, seeing the child peer slyly over one concealing arm.

"Thirty-seven, thirty-eight, thirty-nine . . ." Ruthie buried her face and continued.

❦

"Well, would you?" Annie reminded her. "Would you have said yes to Hugh?"

"Maybe. I don't know." Charlie dug in her coat pocket for her gloves as a gust of frigid air sliced through her. She *was* in love with Hugh, wasn't she? Or maybe she was just in love with love as were some of the women who married hastily before their men left for the front.

Annie must have been thinking the same thing. "You'd rather be left single and wondering than married and miserable like poor Janet Delaney, wouldn't you?" And Charlie had to admit she didn't envy Janet, who was six months pregnant and living with her new husband's grim-faced mother and ailing old-maid aunt.

"Janet used to be such fun back in high school," she said, "and now she goes around looking like the end of the world is just around the corner. I know I should go and visit her, but she makes me feel so sad, and I never know what to say."

"From what I've heard about her mother-in-law, she'd probably rather you ask her to visit you," Annie suggested. "At least she's not running around on her husband with anything in pants." She scowled as she drew her coat more closely about her. "You know that woman who works at the five-and-ten? The skinny one with the blue pop eyes?"

Charlie nodded. "Ruby somebody. Works in the housewares section?"

"Yeah. Well, she got engaged to a soldier right before he left for overseas. Showed me her ring and all, and he hadn't been gone more than a month before she was cozying up to that Lem who works at the hardware store—and him old enough to be her father and married to boot!"

Charlie, whose sister had been a classmate of Ruby's, didn't doubt it for a minute. "I hear she's always been the friendly type," she said.

"*Friendly?* I'll say she was friendly! I went in the hardware store to pick up batteries for my flashlight and that woman was sitting on the back counter in there with her skirt hiked up to kingdom come, and she was all over that Lem like honey on a hot biscuit." Annie snorted. "So, you will see Hugh before he leaves for Virginia, won't you?"

Charlie nodded. "Sunday. And guess what he wants to do?"

Annie giggled. "I can guess. Oh, 'get thee to a nunnery!'"

"Oh, hush! Wants to take a picnic to Turtle Rock—roast marshmallows—that sort of thing. It's kind of a special spot. We all went there a lot growing up—mostly in the summer, though. We'll probably freeze."

"Ahh!" Annie said, and smiled. "Somehow I doubt that."

"Ahh, yourself," Charlie said, as the bell summoned them inside.

It was a relief to be back in a warm building again after Froggie hired someone to replace Christmas Malone. She had caught a glimpse of the custodian at a distance earlier that morning when she arrived at school as the principal was showing him around the building. It wasn't until later when Froggie introduced the new janitor to the school assembly that Charlie recognized her neighbor's "beau," Ollie Thigpen, who made the children laugh when he took a "sweeping" bow with his broom.

Geneva Odom, seated behind Charlie, leaned over to whisper, "Let's hope he can manage to get to work on time. The man rides a bicycle everywhere he goes. I don't think he even owns a car."

Charlie told her she didn't care if he came on roller skates if only he would keep that monster of a furnace going.

The old auditorium smelled of the oily cleaning compound Christmas Malone had used on the hardwood floors whenever the mood struck him, and chairs were arranged in rigid rows, evidence that the newly hired custodian had already been at work. Both sides of the stage were decorated with dried cornstalks, pumpkins, and squash, and even the upright piano, where the music teacher sat in anticipation, looked as if it had been polished. The children had been assembled for a special program to commemorate the upcoming Thanksgiving holiday, and the students in Miss Brady's expression classes, dressed as Pilgrims, Indians, turkeys, and a variety of vegetables, waited expectantly behind the canvas backdrop as the floor reverberated with the shuffling of restless feet.

Annie, Charlie noticed, had left two of her mothers in charge of her class while she waited backstage with a small group of sixth graders dressed in patriotic colors. After weeks of rehearsal, the young dancers would end the program with a loosely choreographed jitterbug to "American Patrol," a song Glenn Miller had made popular.

The large white oak tree just outside the building clawed the wind with bare branches, sending its remaining brown leaves twirling past the window. The sky was heavy with clouds and it looked as if rain might be coming soon. Charlie thought of the missing Miss Dimple and hoped she would be warm and dry—and safe—wherever she was. Annie reported earlier that the police had not yet been able to locate her brother and Charlie was beginning to wonder if he had disappeared as well.

The blue velvet stage curtains, now worn bare in spots, began to part with a tantalizing rattle. A loud harrumph and a warning glare from Froggie finally subdued Alma's squirming first graders into quiet attentiveness. The pianist raised her hands as a signal, and crashed down with a chord. As one, the entire student body stood amid scraping of chairs to begin singing "America the Beautiful." The program had begun.

It wasn't until everyone returned to their homerooms that Alma discovered someone had broken into Miss Dimple's locked desk drawer.

CHAPTER EIGHT

*E*lderberry? *What kind of place was that? She was going to have her work cut out for her here, but that was what happened when you dropped your guard—even for a minute. You couldn't trust a soul. Well, no one would be the wiser for it, and she'd soon straighten things out in short order. They didn't call her "The Eagle" for nothing, and she didn't have time . . . no . . . not even a minute to waste. She wasn't looking forward to this, but she didn't have a choice, did she? After all, her country was depending on her.*

❧

"Are you sure the desk was locked?" Charlie asked Alma as they stood in the hallway after the children were dismissed for the day. They were joined there by Annie and Geneva Odom. The rain had started in earnest and because the school had no lunchroom facilities, their principal had declared a one-session day, which enabled the students to go home at one o'clock.

"The wood's been splintered around it," Alma explained, absently fingering the pin at her throat. "Must've happened while we were all at assembly, and it looks like whoever did it used a screwdriver to force it open because they left it right there on my desk." She frowned. "I'm afraid Miss Dimple's going to be most upset."

Charlie thought that was the least of their worries. "That screwdriver might have prints on it. Where is it now?"

"Mr. Faulkenberry has everything locked away in his office until Bobby Tinsley can get here," Alma said, fumbling inside the bodice of her dress for a handkerchief, which she used to blow her nose. "All this has been most upsetting! I just don't know how much more I can take."

Make that two of us, Charlie thought as she put an arm around her. "Try to get some rest over the weekend. You might feel differently by Monday," she said, although she doubted if the fidgety woman would last another week.

"I can't imagine why anybody would be interested in the contents of Miss Dimple's desk," Annie said. "It just doesn't make sense . . . but then neither has anything else that's been happening around here lately."

"I'll have to admit, I'm dying of curiosity," Charlie said. "What *was* in that drawer, anyway?" Miss Dimple had kept the mysterious drawer locked even when six-year-old Charlie was reading about *The Three Billy Goats Gruff* and singing the alphabet song.

"I've always wondered about that, too," Geneva added. "She seemed to have sort of a hush-hush air about it like she was guarding some great secret."

Alma shrugged. "I can't see anything secret about a can of Ovaltine, a couple of Hershey bars, and some vanilla wafers."

"Ah-ha!" Charlie laughed. "I guess one can't live by muffins alone."

"Is that all you found?" Annie asked.

"The only thing of value was a couple of sheets of savings stamps and a coin purse with a few bills and some change in it,"

Alma told them, "so it doesn't look like whoever did it was after money or it seems they would've taken all of it."

"Then what were they after?" Geneva said.

CR

That was what everybody at Phoebe Chadwick's boardinghouse wanted to know as they sat around the table a short while later. Elwin Vickery gnawed the last shred of meat from his chicken drumstick and placed the bone carefully in his plate. "How did this person get into the room if the door was locked?"

"That's just it," Annie explained. "Alma *thinks* she locked it behind her when they went to assembly but she said she couldn't be absolutely sure."

"Alma Owens couldn't be absolutely sure she put on her drawers in the morning," Geneva, sitting beside Charlie, mumbled under her breath.

"Aren't her windows fairly low to the ground?" Phoebe asked. "I'd think anyone who was fairly agile might climb in. The shrubbery around the concessions area would screen them from view."

"Do you think it might've been that Ollie fellow who took Chr— uh, Wilson's place?" Lily Moss pressed praying hands to her lips. "He's always seemed kind of peculiar to me. A grown man like that riding a bicycle!"

"Ollie Thigpen's been courting our neighbor for years," Charlie said. "And I can't imagine why he'd want to get into Miss Dimple's drawers."

Her face grew warm at the resulting undercurrent of laughter when she realized what she'd said.

"Why would anybody?" Annie whispered, barely suppressing a giggle.

"Well, it felt great to walk into a warm building this morning," Geneva added, obviously feeling sorry for Charlie's embarrassment.

"Ollie's been working for Paschall Kiker for as long as I can remember, and he's a pretty fair carpenter, too. He built a sweet little gazebo for my cousin Eunice, and put a new porch floor in the Methodist parsonage." Phoebe said. "I'm sure Mr. Faulkenberry is familiar with his background."

"Poor Alma was really shaken about all this," Annie said. "And I don't blame her. "It would make me nervous, too, to think a stranger might enter my classroom when I wasn't there—or even worse, when I was. What if she had returned with the children and surprised him?"

"Who, besides the principal, has a key to Miss Dimple's classroom?" Velma asked.

Geneva, who was reaching for a second yeast roll, paused with her hand in midair. "Ollie would, of course . . . and, well, I guess I'm the only other one."

"Do you still have it?" Charlie asked. "Where would it be?"

All eyes were on Geneva as she spoke in a flat, measured voice. "On a nail inside my supply cabinet, where I also keep a screwdriver. That blasted roller that holds the maps is always coming loose and I finally bought one of my own so I wouldn't have to keep bothering Christmas."

"Was your room locked during assembly?" Phoebe asked her.

"Of course—but not during recess. One of us is always close by, so I didn't see the need. There's nothing in there of any value, and of course I keep my desk drawer locked."

Lily's face paled. "So, it could've been anyone."

Geneva shoved back her chair. "Well, don't look at me. I'm not *that* desperate for stale Hershey bars and a few vanilla wafers. Still, Miss Phoebe, if I might use your phone, I'll try to catch Froggie before he leaves school and ask him if those things are still in my cabinet."

But it had to have happened while everyone was at assembly, Charlie thought, as Annie explained to the others about the edible contents of Miss Dimple's desk drawer. And as far as she knew, everyone, including Ollie Thigpen, had been in the auditorium for the Thanksgiving program.

Phoebe Chadwick ladled cream gravy over her rice and passed the gravy boat to Velma. "Speaking of telephones, I'm afraid we've hit a bit of a dead end with Miss Dimple's brother."

Elwin frowned. "Don't tell me they were still unable to find him!"

"Oh, they found him all right," Phoebe explained, "but Henry said he hasn't heard from her and wasn't even aware she was missing. He seemed concerned, of course, but gave me the impression there was probably a rational explanation." She shook her head as if trying to rid herself of a bad dream. "Naturally, I didn't believe that for a minute, and, frankly, I don't think he does, either. He phoned me here after speaking with Bobby to say there was a possibility she might be visiting some distant relatives and that he planned to do some investigating on his own." She sighed. "Poor man! I could tell he was worried to death, although he was making an effort to hide it."

Velma spoke up. "I should think he would be worried. Did you ask him about an older sister?"

"It's just as Odessa remembered," Phoebe said. "Dimple's sister died of scarlet fever, and Henry's wife is the only sister-in-law she has."

"And just what *is* he planning to do about it?" Elwin asked, and he set down his cup so suddenly coffee splashed into the saucer. "Miss Dimple's been missing for three days now. I'm terribly afraid something dreadful may have happened."

"Oh, dear! Where in the world could she be? I just can't bear to think of it! Dimple Kilpatrick is the kindest, dearest soul you'd ever hope to meet, and who knows who might be next?" Lily Moss clutched her napkin to her mouth and began to cry silently, her shoulders shaking.

"My God, woman, get a hold of yourself!" Elwin turned almost as red as Odessa's pickled beets and looked as if he'd like to vault over the table and throttle the cringing Lily.

"Will everyone please calm down?" Phoebe said, and Charlie

was startled that anyone so tiny could speak in a drill sergeant's commanding voice. "They're doing their best to find Dimple. Bobby Tinsley has had several men out searching this town from top to bottom. He even checked the depot and the bus station and there's no record of her buying a ticket."

"She didn't have a car and couldn't drive one if she did," Annie said. "Good heavens, you don't suppose she *hitchhiked*, do you?"

Charlie laughed at the image of the decorous Miss Dimple holding up her skirt to reveal her knees, like Claudette Colbert did in the movie, *It Happened One Night*.

"I don't find that one bit amusing," Elwin informed her, including in his look the several who laughed. "It shocks me to hear you make light of a friend's possible misfortune, and I'm sure Miss Dimple would never—"

"They're not there." Geneva stood in the door silhouetted in the gray light from the hallway and she spoke so softly it was hard to hear her above the steady drumming of the rain. Slowly she made her way back to her seat and took a sip of water. "Froggie said the key and the screwdriver are both missing from my cabinet. It looks like my screwdriver is the one Alma found on her desk, but my key to Miss Dimple's room is gone."

"Won't Alma have a fit when she hears that?" Annie said. "After today, she's already scared of her own shadow. I'm afraid Froggie's going to have an awful time finding somebody to take that class."

Phoebe rang a bell to let Odessa know they were ready for dessert. "Fortunately that won't be necessary," she announced. "I'm told a replacement for Miss Dimple will be arriving soon. In fact, I'm expecting her sometime this weekend."

❧

"Cornelia Emerson," Annie muttered as they hurried back to school after lunch. "Sounds like a heroine from a Victorian novel. I wonder where Froggie found that one—and so soon, too."

Earlier, their principal had told Geneva that Bobby Tinsley would be at the school to speak with as many of the faculty as possible that afternoon, and even though the rain had slacked, the two struggled to keep their umbrellas from sailing away in the wind.

"She has to be an improvement on Alma," Charlie said. "Of course when the poor woman hears what's been going on here, she might turn tail and run. I wonder if she knows why she's taking Miss Dimple's place."

Head down, Annie frowned as she walked. "Does it bother you about Miss Dimple leaving that note?"

"You mean the handwriting?"

Annie shook her head. "I mean the fact that nobody saw it at first until Bobby Tinsley happened to notice it on the floor under the hall table."

"A little too convenient, you mean?" Charlie had questioned that as well. "Do you think it was put there later by somebody else? I can't imagine who it would be . . . unless . . . maybe . . . Elwin Vickery."

"*Aunt Mildred?* I think Elwin's sweet on Miss Dimple," Annie said. "I've never seen him get so hot under the collar. I thought he was going to bean us with the gravy ladle."

"I've seen the two of them walking to the library together a couple of times, but I don't think she considers him anything more than a friend. Maybe he became outraged because she rebuffed his attentions." Charlie sidestepped a puddle as they crossed the street. "I can't imagine Miss Dimple having a beau, but who knows what she might have on her mind?"

"Only *The Shadow* knows, I guess," Annie said, referring to a popular radio program. "And speaking of being shadowed, I believe there's one behind us."

Charlie did an abrupt about-face. "Willie Elrod, what *are* you doing out here in the rain. You go on home right now!"

The little boy slowed but didn't stop. "I'm not gonna bother nobody, honest, but I gotta keep an eye on things."

Charlie stood her ground. "What things?"

Willie jammed his hands into the pockets of his slicker and rolled his eyes heavenward. "I heard about what happened to Miss Dimple's desk drawer and I'm pretty sure I know who did it."

The raincoat, passed down from an older brother, was much too large for him, Charlie noticed, and almost touched the ground. "And who might that be?" she asked.

"Don't you trust us, Willie?" Annie's voice was soft. "We might be able to help, you know."

The child sighed in impatience, or maybe it was relief, and hesitated. Knowing he had their full attention, he apparently planned to make the best of it.

"*Willie!*" Charlie shook her umbrella at him.

"Well, you know that old man who lives in that little green house over on Fox Grape Hill?"

"Mr. Scarborough?" With impatience, Charlie shifted from foot to foot. Not only was she chilled to the bone, but she had to go to the bathroom. "What about him?"

Willie shrugged. "German spy," he whispered. "Carries secrets in his cane, don't you know. I've been following him, only he don't know it, and he sits on that wall next to the playground just about every day waitin' for his accomplice to meet him, but he can't fool me!"

"And have you seen this accomplice?" Annie struggled to keep a straight face.

"Not yet, but he'll show up, just you wait. And I'll be hot on his trail. I reckon President Roosevelt himself will give me a medal!"

"What you'll *get*, Willie Elrod, is a cold from being out in this awful weather," Charlie told him. "And poor Mr. Scarborough rests on that wall because he's *tired*! Why, that old fellow's probably never been out of the county, so you can forget about following him."

The little boy looked so crestfallen Charlie felt sorry for him. "You go on home and get on some dry clothes," she said, speaking softly now. "There are a lot of other ways you can help with the war effort, you know."

"That's right," Annie said. "I know there's a drive to collect metal, like aluminum cooking pots and things like that. Tomorrow's Saturday, and you have a wagon, don't you? I bet they'd be glad if you'd help them collect some.

"Some spy, that Willie!" she added aside to Charlie as they watched the child race home, apparently inspired with patriotic zeal. "I could hear his galoshes flopping almost a block away."

CHAPTER NINE

Jesse Dean adjusted his helmet and admired himself in the mirror. Too bad about old Hiram Hopkins breaking his hip! Fell down the back steps, they said. Well, somebody had to take his place, and it might as well be him. And if he kept his eyes open, he might just learn a thing or two. Let them laugh now!

Dishes clanged when he thumped the tray on the table, but Miss Dimple didn't look up. Something had upset him and she knew she would hear about it sooner or later. She would prefer later, or not at all. He wasn't the only one who was upset.

Earlier, she had discovered in an old chest of drawers in the bathroom a small sewing kit and a bag of quilting squares, intended no doubt for a long-ago project never completed. Miss Dimple had never enjoyed sewing and certainly didn't plan to undertake anything as involved as a quilt, but what was she to do with her time? Other than an age-spotted copy of *Oliver Twist* and someone's old geography text, the only books on hand were syrupy-sweet and featured such spineless, milque-toast characters she wanted to be sick.

Now she adjusted her glasses and concentrated on threading her needle.

"Have you written that note I asked you about?" Mr. Smith's voice was muffled behind the mask but not enough to drown out his impatience.

"I beg your pardon?" She doubled the thread and knotted it at the end just as her grandmother had taught her when she was six.

"I'm sure you remember—the one to your brother." He held up a small glass bottle she recognized as the one containing her pills for arthritis pain and rattled them about before putting the bottle in his pocket. "I managed to get this medicine you seem to find so important. It's yours as soon as you write that note."

She looked up as he approached, stopping only a few feet away. His shoes, she noticed, were scuffed and his tan socks had a run in them. And tonight he wore a Halloween witch mask. Murphy's Five and Dime must've had a sale, she thought.

"I'll manage to get by without them," she told him, returning to her stitching.

He sighed. Heavily. "Now, there's no need for that. I'm only asking for a short note in your handwriting so your brother will know you're all right. I'm sure you wouldn't want him to worry, now, would you?"

Tossing the quilting scraps aside, Miss Dimple stood suddenly, completely forgetting her ruse of fragile health. "You leave my brother out of this! He has no money to speak of. What could you possibly want of him?"

"Oh, come now, Miss Dimple. You're an intelligent woman. You must realize it isn't money we're after."

Dimple Kilpatrick had never been a violent person. In all her forty years of teaching she had never spanked one of her small charges, but at that moment she understood how someone could be driven to murder. Lifting her chin and straightening her shoulders, she spoke in a calm but chilling voice.

"How can you live with yourself? Do you realize what you're doing? Whatever it is you want from my brother, you're never going to get it, and I refuse to be a part of it!"

His silence seemed to go on forever as he looked at her from behind his mask. "How easy it would be," he said, in a voice as soft as quicksand, "to collect one of the children from your class as they walk home after school—"

Her responding gasp was audible and she knew it would be impossible to disguise her reaction. "Surely you can't be serious! How can you even think of such a thing?"

"You can imagine how frightening it would be," he continued, "but then that's entirely up to you. I'll expect that note by morning, if you please."

Dimple Kilpatrick closed her eyes and held her breath until she heard him ascend the stairs and lock the door behind him.

"Did you know that just one pound of waste fat makes enough glycerin to fire four thirty-seven-millimeter aircraft shells?" Charlie's aunt Lou rattled the pages of the *Elderberry Eagle* and peered over the top.

"Kinda makes me wish I hadn't eaten all that sausage back when we could get it," her sister said, looking a little bilious.

"I try to save as much as I can. Turned some in to Shorty Skinner at the butcher shop just last week," Lou said, "although I do like to keep a little bacon grease to cook with."

"Better lock up your aluminum pots tomorrow if you don't want Willie Elrod to get them," Charlie warned them, and she told them about the little boy's obsession with imaginary spies.

Her mother shook her head. "I'm afraid he's wasting his time trailing old Luther Scarborough, but there is something peculiar going on over at that school. They don't seem to have the slightest notion what happened to poor Miss Dimple, and nobody's yet been able to give us a satisfactory explanation about the way Wilson Malone died. Makes me uneasy about your being there, Charlie."

"They seem to think Wilson had a heart attack, Mama, and hit his head when he fell," Charlie said. "Or maybe a stroke. You know how he—"

"They? They *think*? They who?" Jo's voice rose. "I'll tell you this: if I were Madge Malone, I'd demand a better answer than that!"

Charlie didn't want to worry the older women, but she was beginning to think along the same lines. The local police, and even the doctor who had examined him, seemed strangely vague about explaining the reason for the janitor's death. She was almost sure Ebenezer, the school's carved wooden eagle, along with his broken wing, was being held as evidence at the local police headquarters, and their principal seemed curiously uncertain about its whereabouts. Also, no one had been able to explain exactly how Wilson Malone came by his mysterious head wounds.

Aunt Lou laid the paper aside. "I've been giving this some thought, and it appears to me that whoever took Dimple—if indeed that was what happened—it must have been someone who was familiar with her early-morning routine."

Charlie shrugged. "That would be pretty much everybody, wouldn't it?"

"Not necessarily," her mother said. "Most of us are asleep at that ungodly hour. It's more likely to be somebody who's usually out and about at the time Dimple takes her walks."

Her sister slapped the table with the palm of her hand causing teacups to clatter in saucers. "Exactly! Someone who has to be out early because of his job." She looked knowingly from Jo to Charlie. "Like Amos Schuler."

Jo laughed. "The *milkman*? I think his face would break if the man ever smiled, but I can't see him carting away Dimple Kilpatrick. Why would he want to do that?"

Why would anybody? Charlie wondered, yet someone obviously had. According to Phoebe, Henry Kilpatrick didn't seem to know what had happened to his sister and seemed to be making an effort to hide his concern. Perhaps he didn't want her friends in Elderberry to become unduly worried, but they were *already* worried! His suggestion about his sister visiting distant relatives certainly didn't sound like the Miss Dimple she knew, but maybe he knew something they didn't.

"Uncle Ed drilling with the Home Guard tonight?" Charlie asked her aunt in an effort to divert her mother from the warpath. God help them if the two sisters became involved.

"Lord, yes, if his feet don't give out on him first." Lou picked up the brown earthenware pot and added steaming tea to her cup.

Charlie had been happy to find her aunt in the kitchen drinking tea with her mother when she got home that afternoon. Lou's husband, like many other men who were either too young or too old to serve in the military, belonged to the Georgia Home Guard, so he wouldn't eat until after their drill that night, and Aunt Lou would be joining them for supper—which meant she probably would be cooking it as well. Now her aunt relaxed, with her stocking feet propped in a chair by the open oven door. The two women had walked the short distance from town after their bus ride from Milledgeville and both appeared tired after their shift at the ordnance plant.

"Remember it was just last Monday we had that air-raid drill," her aunt added, "and Ed had to run all over creation to see if anybody showed a sliver of light. Ridiculous for a man his age! But let that man put on a helmet and an armband and he thinks he's God Almighty!"

"Louise!" Jo protested. "For heaven's sake, he's just doing his job."

"Well, he could start by fixing that porch railing that's been loose since last spring," her sister said. "Thank goodness he's been assigned a shorter route now that Hiram Hopkins had that fall and can't get around. I understand the Greeson boy—that pale little fellow who works for Harris Cooper—will cover Ed's territory."

"Jesse Dean?" Charlie took eggs and cheese from the Frigidaire. "I'm glad they're giving him something that will let him contribute to the war effort. He's had to put up with a lot of harassment."

Jo snorted. "That crazy woman who raised him is responsible for a lot of that. His mother died giving birth to him, you know, and his father took off for who knows where. The grandmother brought him up. Put him in dresses until he was three years old!" She turned to her sister. "You remember old Addie Montgomery, don't you? Died when the boy was about twelve or thirteen and a cousin took him in." She shook her head. "Of course by that time it was too late."

"Maybe not," Charlie said, and hoped it was so.

Aunt Lou set eggs aside and began to grate the cheese onto a plate. "I don't know what Ed will use for an excuse once this war's over. Sure doesn't look like that railing's going to be fixed anytime soon. Looks like I'm gonna have to ask Ollie Thigpen to take care of it."

In spite of her caustic remarks, Charlie knew her aunt adored her husband and worried about his health. The couple had no children, only each other, and as one of the town's two dentists, he stood on his feet most of the day.

❦

Silence lay like a pall as the three went about preparing their simple meal, and Charlie sensed her aunt was dying to ask if they had heard from Fain. Of course, Aunt Lou knew good and well they would've shared any news if they had any. War made everyone antsy and brought out emotions as sensitive as a toothache. She had seen her mother caress her brother's photograph, running her fingers along the outline of his face; seen her stand in the door of his room with a look in her eyes that would wring out your heart like a dishrag.

She lined up slices of bread on a pan and shoved it under the broiler for toast. "We heard from Delia today," she said. "She says the baby's a real kicker. Ned thinks it's going to be a boy."

Her aunt made a mock sad face. "Then I guess they won't be naming it Louise."

Jo Carr set the table with the daisy spattered dishes she had collected from boxes of laundry detergent and a sudden smile transformed her face. "I don't care if it's Louie or Louise," she said, scattering silverware at each place. "I just want to hold it and sing to it, rock it the way I did my own. I do wish she could come home for the delivery."

Charlie knew from the impish look on her aunt's face that she was going to start down a path she'd rather not go. And she was right.

"From what I hear, things are heating up between you and Hugh Brumlow," she said, addressing Charlie, "so it looks like Delia might soon have some competition in the marriage department." She paused, smiling. "A candlelight dinner at Rusty's sounds mighty romantic to me, and I suppose he'll be leaving for the service soon. Has he proposed yet?"

Charlie made a face. She dearly loved her aunt, but if they gave awards for being nosy, Aunt Lou would have to add a room to hold them all. "If he does, you'll be the first to know," she told her.

"Make that the second," her mother said. "And it could happen yet. They're going on a picnic Sunday."

"Would you two *please* drop it? For heaven's sake, let's talk about something else!" Charlie took the toast from under the broiler and spread the browned slices with margarine. She wasn't ready to face that subject, and the thought of Hugh leaving for Virginia made her suddenly want to cry.

⟨⟨

"Didn't you tell me Miss Dimple has a brother?" Lou asked Charlie after they finished a hasty supper of rarebit on toast and applesauce. "I don't know his financial circumstances, but if he's wealthy it might be possible somebody's holding his sister for ransom."

"I haven't heard if her brother has money or not, but they finally located him somewhere near Marietta, and he hasn't heard from her, either," Charlie told her. "And I'm not sure if this has anything to do with it, but today while we were all in assembly, somebody pried open Miss Dimple's desk drawer."

"Ye gods and little fishes!" her mother exclaimed. "What could they be looking for in there?"

"You mean somebody just walked right into the building?" her aunt Lou asked. "Did they take anything?"

"Nothing that anyone could tell." Charlie told them about Geneva's screwdriver and the missing key. "Bobby Tinsley was there all afternoon asking questions but none of us could imagine what anybody would be looking for. Now Froggie's having the lock changed on Miss Dimple's door."

Jo groaned in irritation. "And I don't suppose they have the least idea who might be responsible."

Charlie cleared the dishes away and stacked them in the sink. "They've already hired a new teacher to take Miss Dimple's place," she said. "Woman named Cornelia Emerson. She's supposed to start Monday."

Her mother shook her head. "This quickly? Where in the world did they find her?" She sighed. "I can't imagine anybody taking Dimple Kilpatrick's place."

"Nobody can," Charlie added sadly. "And guess who started working as our new custodian today? Bessie's boyfriend, Ollie! If you want him to fix your porch railing, Aunt Lou, you might have to wait a while."

Her aunt's eyes widened. "*Ollie Thigpen?* You don't suppose he—"

Charlie shook her head. "Ollie has his own key to all the rooms, so why would he take Geneva's? Besides, he was in the auditorium with the rest of us during assembly."

"I guess there's not a whole lot to do out on the Kiker farm now with winter coming on, so this should give him a chance to earn some extra money," her aunt said.

Jo laughed. "Maybe he'll buy a car and learn to drive. Take Bessie out somewhere nice for dinner. Lord knows she's earned it with all the meals she's fed that man!"

"I don't know. I think he might have the right idea about that bicycle," Lou said. "I've thought of getting one myself since gas is so hard to come by."

Charlie tried not to visualize that.

Jo filled the kettle to heat water for the dishes. "I don't think old Paschall will be doing much farming anyway. Looked awfully frail the last time I saw him. Jesse Dean's been delivering their groceries from Cooper's."

"Well, Ollie didn't come a minute too soon for me!" Charlie said. "This morning the building was warm as toast, and he was mopping the front hall when we left this afternoon." She tied an apron around her middle and added soap to the dishpan. "Everybody was crazy about Christmas Malone but spit and polish wasn't his strong suit."

"Still, it seems obvious to me that *something's* going on over there." Her mother frowned. "What do you all know about this man who rooms at Phoebe's? He hasn't been there very long, has he? Wouldn't hurt to keep an eye on that one."

"*Elwin Vickery?*" Charlie laughed. "I believe he moved into Phoebe's just before school started, and he's always seemed fond of Miss Dimple. The man wouldn't hurt a fly."

Lou, who had been swirling a soapy dishrag over the blue-and-white oilcloth table cover, looked up and frowned. "That's exactly what they want us to think," she said.

Charlie grinned. "They? They who?"

"The enemy," her aunt said.

CHAPTER TEN

It was here. He was really leaving. Thanksgiving would come, and then Christmas, and Hugh wouldn't be here to sit by the fire after dinner and eat sweet potato pie with a thin slice of watermelon rind preserves on top like only Aunt Lou could make it. Who would go caroling with her and kiss her under the mistletoe? Who would help her find the perfect cedar tree on what was left of the family farm? Charlie swallowed hard and was certain he could hear her. Her mouth felt so dry her lips stuck together.

They drove down familiar streets past the yellow Victorian house on the corner, where years ago she and Delia had picked daisies from the neighbor's yard and sold them back to her for a nickel a bunch. There was the stone arch at the edge of town, the bright blue water tower. Things she loved. Things Hugh loved, and soon he would be leaving all this behind and facing a dangerous and unfamiliar world.

Charlie clutched the cold quart jar of potato salad her aunt had made as if it were a cherished treasure. It's a normal day, she told herself. Act as if it's just a day like any other with many picnics to follow.

It was the Sunday afternoon before Hugh was to leave and they were on their way to picnic at Turtle Rock a few miles outside of town. Charlie struggled to speak in a light voice. "I'm going to have to keep a close eye on Mama and Aunt Lou," she said finally. "They're suspecting practically half the town of snatching away Miss Dimple. It wouldn't surprise me if the two of them didn't take matters into their own hands and go sleuthing."

Hugh laughed and reached for her hand, covering it with his own. "What makes you think that?"

"Because I know them, and they don't have enough patience between them to fill a thimble. Nobody, it seems, can do anything fast enough to suit them. If Aunt Lou weren't too old and too . . . well . . . out of shape, she probably would've joined the WAACS the day after Pearl Harbor."

A cat streaked across the road in front of them and Hugh braked to avoid it. Charlie was glad it wasn't black. "And who do they suspect?" he asked.

"Elwin Vickery, for one. Poor man! I don't know when they think he'd have time to do it . . . and where would he take her?"

To Charlie's surprise, Hugh didn't laugh, but kept his eyes on the road in front of them. "He does own some land, you know. It used to have a house on it but I haven't been there for a while, so it might not be there anymore."

"Where? And what would Elwin Vickery want with land?"

"Off the Covington Highway, not too far from here. He bought it for an investment, I guess. Rents out the pasture to somebody else."

Charlie studied his face. "Are you making that up? How do you know all this?"

Hugh laughed. "Because my uncle Martin sold it to him back in the spring. We used to go out there every fall to pick cotton . . . and wade in the creek. Mostly wade in the creek, but he always gave us fifty cents anyway."

"Still, I can't see him kidnapping Miss Dimple. Besides, I think he has a crush on her," Charlie said.

"You see! You have your motive already." Hugh smiled when he said it, but the image of Miss Dimple being held prisoner in an abandoned farmhouse did occur to her, however fleetingly. Elwin Vickery worked alone, selling insurance in a small office above the jewelry store in the middle of town, and he had a perfect reason to make sales calls that took him all over the county and beyond.

Charlie was beginning to wish she'd never mentioned it to Hugh when he brought up the subject again. "Who else?" he wanted to know.

"Who else what?"

"Who else do they think might have made off with Miss Dimple?"

"The milkman, of course. Amos Schuler. Really, Hugh, you need to bone up on your detective skills. He's always out at an early hour like Miss Dimple, and he has a grouchy expression on his face."

"I'd be grouchy, too, if I had to get up before dawn and milk all those cows." Hugh made a face. "Of course, it won't be long before I'll be rising with the sun as well."

Charlie didn't want to talk about that.

"And then there was that problem with his son," Hugh added. "Boyd. A year ahead of me in school. Bad news, that one—got into some kind of trouble in Atlanta. Woman said he sexually assaulted her, and he was convicted and sent to prison. Claimed he didn't do it, of course."

Charlie frowned. How terrible it would be if he really didn't! No wonder the milkman never smiled.

"Looks like I'll be missing all the excitement," Hugh said. "With any luck, your mother and Aunt Lou will have all those problems solved by the time I finish my training in Virginia."

"Well, if they don't, Willie Elrod will." Charlie told him about her student's recent preoccupation with trailing 'spies.' "I ran into his mother at church this morning and she said he'd taken every one of her aluminum pots to the salvage drive. She had to go down there and reclaim a few so she could cook supper!"

The sun had come out after several days of rain, and now in the afternoon, the temperature had climbed into the sixties, unusual for mid-November. It was almost as if Mother Nature were blessing them with a farewell gift before Hugh left for his training. The fried chicken Hugh's sister Arden prepared for their picnic filled the car with its tantalizing smell, and, when she learned of their plans, Aunt Louise had insisted on contributing potato salad.

"If you think that tightwad Emmalene Brumlow's going to put herself out cooking, you've got another think coming," her aunt had said when Charlie told her Hugh insisted on bringing the picnic. And as it turned out, she was right, but, Charlie learned, Hugh had managed to help himself to a bottle of homemade blackberry wine from the family cellar.

Turtle Rock was a large granite formation remotely resembling a turtle on the banks of a creek by the same name and had been a popular picnic spot for as long as Charlie could remember. As a child she had come there often on Sunday school picnics and, later during her teen years, on wiener roasts and hayrides. The family who owned the property and farmed the adjoining land had always been glad to share it with others as long as they first asked permission, as Hugh had done, and cleaned up after their outings.

Hugh pulled off the road and parked the car in a grassy area where, not too many years before, they had hunted four-leaf clovers, made daisy chains, and played innumerable games of ball. Charlie helped him carry the picnic items to a rustic table, which they spread with a cloth Arden had tucked into the basket. Although most of the trees were bare; star-shaped remnants of red fluttered here and there in the sweet gum trees, and the occasional scattering of hickory leaves mottled the ground in gold. Other than the scampering of a squirrel in the underbrush nearby and the soothing lap of tea-colored water over mossy stones, the woods were quiet, and Charlie let the silence envelop her in an effort to sense its peace. This was a familiar place, a favorite place for both of them. Why did everything feel so strange?

"Let's go for a walk before it gets too dark." Taking her hand, Hugh led her under an archway of hardwoods onto a narrow path that meandered around the hill above the creek. "I helped to blaze this trail with my Scout troop about a million years ago," he said. "Look, you can still see the mark we left on that big sycamore." His words sounded proud, yet sad in a way for a time that was lost. Charlie watched his face as he looked about. He was storing up mind pictures of this place he loved, and she felt privileged that he chose to share it with her.

"Here's where we camped out overnight," Hugh said as they moved farther up the trail, "and Dennis Chastain got homesick and cried." He laughed. "To tell you the truth, I was homesick, too, but I was too embarrassed to admit it."

Charlie thought of lanky Dennis, who was such a smooth dancer all the girls wanted to be his partner. Years ago in high school, she had been lucky enough to dance the Lindy with him and it spoiled her for anybody else. One of the first to be called for the draft, Dennis was now with the marines somewhere in the South Pacific where he surely must long for home. His aunt Sarah taught at Charlie's school and a few months ago, she and some of the other teachers had mailed him a box that they hoped would reach him by Christmas. Sarah had later confided that she'd even tucked in a sprig of red cedar so Dennis could at least have the smell of Christmas. Charlie considered telling Hugh about it, but thought better of it. She didn't trust herself to speak.

It had grown colder by the time they tramped by a circuitous route to the top of the hill where they drank in the view over the outskirts of the town stretching before them in the dying sunlight:

a gray and brown quilt stitched with roads and streams and dotted with splashes of green.

Hugh drew her close as they stood, not speaking until a chill wind made her shudder. He tightened his arms about her. "This place is special to me, Charlie," he said, taking in the scene below. "And so are you."

And for a time Charlie Carr forgot about being cold, forgot about the war that was taking him from her, and thought only of the warmth of his lips and the brisk clean smell of his face next to hers.

She also forgot momentarily about the school custodian's mysterious death and the puzzle of Miss Dimple's disappearance. And she almost—but not quite—forgot she was hungry. On the hike back to the campsite they collected dry tinder from fallen pine boughs, and with a lot of patience and an armload of dry kindling he had brought from home, Hugh built a respectable campfire on a flat part of the rock that had been blackened by past fires over the years.

Charlie pointed out the spot where she and her brother and sister had attempted to dam up the creek for a swimming hole and disturbed a water moccasin under a rock. "It was at least two years before I'd go wading here again," she admitted, laughing.

It was comfortable sharing stories of growing-up days as they warmed themselves by the fire surrounded by the pleasant smell of wood smoke and the nose-tickling scent of leaves, and the two managed to put away their share of the picnic with surprising ease. The wine, rich and pungent, tasted of summer, warming her as she watched the fire send an eddy of bright sparks into the darkness. Charlie could feel the throbbing of Hugh's heart as she leaned against him, encircled by his arms.

"I wish we could stay this way forever," Hugh said, nuzzling her cheek, and she sighed in response. Neither spoke for a while as the fire popped sporadically, burning lower, a flickering orange nucleus of their small world. They watched it diminish to a mound of ruddy embers when Hugh spoke again, his voice little more than a whisper. "When I think of coming home after the war, I think of you. Will you still be here, Charlie?"

Would she? Of course! She was sure she would. Well . . . almost sure. "Hugh—"

"I know. I said I wouldn't ask you to wait, and I'm not. I'm not asking you to make any kind of commitment right now. I just want to know . . . well, I guess I just want to know if I have a chance."

Charlie turned and took his face in her hands and kissed him. "You've always had a chance, Hugh Brumlow. Let's just leave things as they are for now. Just come back. Come back safe and sound."

He rose to add a few more pieces of wood to the fire and draped one arm loosely about her shoulders when he sat beside her again. "You'd think I was going off to battle next week when I'll be coming home on leave after I finish my medical training—that is, if they don't throw me out first."

Charlie ignored his last comment, realizing he was making an attempt to be amusing. "And after the medical training, then what?" she asked.

"If I survive that, they'll move me to one of the marine bases to complete my instruction as a corpsman."

"Christmas is going to be strange with Fain clear on the other side of nowhere, Delia in Texas, and now you'll be away." Charlie stopped herself before she said more. What right did she have to complain when she wasn't the one who was having to put her life on the line? She thought of happier Christmases before Fain enlisted and her sister married and moved away. Christmases when war was an intruder that disrupted *other* people's lives.

"You'll have to write and keep me informed about the whereabouts of our Miss Dimple," Hugh said, jarring her back to the present. "I've had a soft spot in my heart for her since she let me help with the scenery instead of giving me a speaking role in our first-grade play. I was scared to death I'd forget my lines, so Jimmy Lay got my part as the Big Bad Wolf. I guess she felt sorry for me."

Charlie smiled and snuggled closer. "I hope I'll have something positive to tell you," she said, sobering. "I still don't understand why she would leave a note saying she had gone to care for her sister if her only sister's been dead for years."

Hugh was quiet for a minute. "Are you sure she was the one who wrote that note?" he asked.

"Phoebe Chadwick said it was in her handwriting but it does seem strange that nobody saw it until Bobby Tinsley found it underneath the hall table. I guess it could've fallen there." She shrugged. "Who else would've left it?"

"Could've been one of the other roomers." Hugh chuckled. "Most likely the suspicious Elwin Vickery! Or, I suppose anybody might've walked in there unobserved while everyone was either asleep or busy. I don't think Phoebe ever locks her doors."

"But why would anybody do that?" Charlie asked. "Unless—"

"Unless they don't want anyone looking for her," Hugh said grimly.

❦

Charlie arrived at school the next day to find Annie waiting by her door. Pulling off her glove, she held out her left hand for her friend's inspection. "Go ahead and take a look. I know that's what you're waiting for," she said. "Notice anything different?"

Puzzled, Annie shook her head. "Not that I can see. What do you mean?"

"*Nothing's* different. That's what I mean." Charlie unlocked her door and deposited a sheaf of papers on her desk. "I'm not saying that can't change, but we've decided to leave things as they are for now."

Annie followed her inside and perched on a front row desk. "And are you satisfied with that?"

Charlie draped her jacket over the back of her chair. "I think

Hugh was ready to propose, and actually, he did in a way, but something held me back . . . held us both back. Remember when we had to go off the high dive back in college? That water was a long way down and it seemed like I stood there forever before I had the confidence to jump."

Annie laughed. "You never did, you chicken! I had to push you, remember?"

"Oh. Well, I never would've passed phys ed if you hadn't, so I guess I should thank you," Charlie admitted. "But I don't want to be pushed into matrimony. The world's too unstable right now."

Annie stood and faced her. "Do you love him, Charlie?"

"I don't know. I think I do . . . maybe." *But shouldn't she know? Other people did. Delia, her mother, even Aunt Lou admitted she fell for her husband Ed the first time she set eyes on him.* "I feel comfortable with Hugh. We share so much in common . . . and he's good looking, too . . ."

Annie looked up at her. "What about his kisses?"

Charlie smiled. "His *kisses*? Hmm . . . nice! Maybe I'm just holding out for something that isn't going to happen."

"Then I suppose you'll know for sure when the time *is* right," Annie said, her statement lingering like a question in the air.

"I think Hugh was trying to say good-bye to his past yesterday. We've both had a lot of happy times at the rock so it was good to share them, and sad, too, but I believe it brought us closer—as friends if not for something more." Charlie took reading workbooks from her cabinet and stacked them on her desk. "He leaves for Virginia in the morning."

"What about tonight?" Annie asked, but Charlie made a face.

"This is Emmalene's night—just family—and that's fine. We've said our good-byes for now."

"Will he be home for Christmas?"

Charlie shook her head. "He won't get leave until after he's finished his medical training," she said. "Like forever and a day."

Annie paused on her way out. "I talked with my brother last night and Joel wants to come here for Thanksgiving. It's too far for him to go home, and he and his friend Will have a chance to hitch a ride on a plane to Fort Benning. Do you think you might put them up in Fain's room? There's just no space at Phoebe's."

"Well, of course! We'd love to have them," Charlie said. "And I think it would do Mama a world of good. Our house is much too quiet with Fain and Delia gone. Besides, it will give me a chance to get even with him for that rotten telegram he sent." She knew Annie's brother from the times she had visited with her roommate during their college years and was aware that her friend hoped the two would develop a romantic relationship, but it hadn't worked out that way. Joel, who had more girlfriends than he could count, looked on Charlie as another little sister and teased her unmercifully. Earlier in the school year, Joel had sent her a telegram proclaiming his undying love and promising to keep their recent "elopement" a secret, so naturally Ben Whitfield at the local Western Union circulated the news of her sudden "marriage" all over town. And the coward hadn't even signed his real name!

Charlie smiled as she distributed workbooks on the children's desks. Annie had gone out with her brother's friend a couple of times, wrote to him regularly, and kept a snapshot of Will Sinclair in the frame of her mirror. It was going to be an interesting Thanksgiving after all.

She had been so preoccupied with Annie's news that Charlie didn't even think to ask her about the new first-grade teacher. The first bell hadn't rung yet when the principal tapped at her door and called her into the hallway with Geneva and Annie to meet Miss Dimple's replacement.

CHAPTER ELEVEN

*M*iss Dimple stood at the foot of the stairs and listened. As instructed, she had written the required note to Henry. Of course she had no choice, but Henry had a choice, and she was certain he wouldn't do anything foolish because of her. Her brother knew or had something these evil people wanted (she was sure Mr. Smith wasn't working alone), and Dimple Kilpatrick knew Henry well enough to realize he would never let them have it.

Everything was quiet upstairs so he must have gone out. She had detected enough of his routine to know he came and went during the day and sometimes even at night. At least he had begun to include fruits and vegetables in her diet: a few carrots and some cabbage— overcooked, of course—a banana or two, and wrinkled apples that looked as if they had been stored in a cellar. The night before he had even brought down a stack of magazines, which he had dumped unceremoniously on the floor. All were outdated issues of The Country Gentleman, The Woman's Home Companion, and The Saturday Evening Post. Miss Dimple devoured the Post from cover to cover, and had especially enjoyed the stories about Tugboat Annie. The name of the subscriber, she noticed, had been torn from the front of the periodicals.

Now, with great effort, she pushed the table intended for dining next to the wall under the small window. Then, taking one of the drawers from the chest in the bathroom, she used it as a step to climb onto the table. At five-feet-five, Dimple Kilpatrick had never considered herself short, but even standing on the table, she couldn't see out of the window.

Determined, she climbed down from her perch, emptied the second drawer from the chest and turned it upside down on top of the table. This time she was able to see just over the edge of the window, but the filthy glass had obviously not been washed in years, if ever, and a small cedar and several berry-laden nandina bushes blocked most of her view. There was a small crack in the corner of the window pane and she saw that the cement that held the outside grille in place had begun to crumble. If she could push out the glass and pry it loose enough . . . Miss Dimple looked about. Mr. Smith had not yet collected her tray from the midday meal, which had included a bowl of canned tomato soup and a metal spoon with which to eat it. If she could manage to dislodge a large enough piece of glass, maybe—just maybe—she could dig away enough of the disintegrating cement to remove the grate and to escape.

But it took only a minute to realize that even if she did manage to remove the glass and the grillwork, the opening wasn't large enough for her to crawl through, even if she could manage to pull herself up! She would just have to think of another way.

She had hardly put the furniture back into place when she heard the back door slam upstairs, and Miss Dimple sank into her chair with the beginnings of a quilt in her lap. She had been able to tell right away the man harbored bitter resentment and certainly wasn't the brightest bulb in the chandelier. And although he tried to disguise it, his voice sounded vaguely familiar. She had heard it before—but where? And what did he mean when he said, "It isn't money we're after"? Dimple Kilpatrick thought that frightened her most of all.

102

Cornelia Emerson was tall, even taller than she was, Charlie noticed. She wore her dark hair in a pompadour, a round gold watch on a chain around her neck, and responded with a nod when the principal introduced them, saying in a clipped accent that she hadn't taught in a while and hoped they wouldn't be disappointed in her.

Everyone assured her that she would be just fine, although of course no one mentioned how grateful they were to be rid of Alma Owens. The woman wore a dark green suit with a gold lapel pin in the shape of the letter C, and in spite of the new teacher's admission of misgivings, Charlie decided right away it could have stood for *Confidence*.

"If you have any questions, just give any of us a holler," Geneva said with a smile. "We're kind of like family here, and everyone's always glad to help."

"And that goes for me as well," Froggie added, before bustling away to investigate a ruckus on the playground.

Annie held out a hand. "I didn't have a chance to welcome you to Phoebe's last night, but I think you'll find it about as close to home as you can get without actually being there. Some of us enjoy a game of bridge now and then after supper, and if you're interested, we're always looking for a fourth."

"I see." Cornelia's expression didn't change, but Charlie got the distinct impression she considered playing cards a waste of time. "I understand your Miss Kilpatrick was quite skilled in that area."

"She *is*, yes," Annie said, accenting the present tense. "I don't know anybody who enjoys trumping an opponent's ace more than Miss Dimple."

Cornelia fingered her watch and frowned. "I don't suppose you've learned any more concerning her whereabouts?"

"Not yet, but we're hoping . . . we're hoping *something* will turn up soon." Charlie swallowed a lump in her throat. She didn't think she would ever get used to seeing another teacher in Miss Dimple's classroom.

"But isn't it true that she left a note?"

"Right." Annie nodded. "But you'll have to ask Miss Phoebe about that."

The first bell rang just then and Cornelia followed Geneva to supervise the lower grades as they lined up by the front steps.

"So, what do you think?" Annie asked as she and Charlie took their customary stations by the back door.

"I don't think we'll be hearing any more games of musical chairs or fruit basket turnover," Charlie said. "I couldn't help noticing how interested she was in what happened to Miss Dimple, but I guess I'd be curious, too, if I were in her place."

Annie, who had come outside without a wrap, hugged herself for warmth. "Peculiar accent. I can't place it."

"Scandinavian, maybe?" Charlie clapped her hands. "Get in line, now, Marshall! The bell's about to ring."

"But, Miss Charlie, Willie says a spy's been sleepin' in the tool-shed! He's been eatin' in there and everything."

Charlie looked at Annie and groaned. That child saw spies in his sleep. "That toolshed always stays locked, Marshall. No one's been sleeping in there. I'm afraid Willie has an overactive imagination."

"No, ma'am, it's true," Ruthie Philips said, shoving Marshall aside. "There's cans of Vienna sausage and baked beans in there, and a pile of old empty ones, too. Willie found burlap sacks all piled up like somebody's been sleeping on them. Mr. Faulkenberry said they've done gone and broken the lock."

❧

"Probably Delby O'Donnell," Geneva said when they discussed it during their midday meal. "Some of you might not remember, but Fro— uh, Mr. Faulkenberry had to run him off a couple of times last year."

"That's right." Velma Anderson inhaled the aroma of her chicken pie and dug in with as much delicacy as she could muster. "Had too much to drink and his wife wouldn't let him in the house."

"Disgusting!" Lily Moss made a face to match. "Do you think he might have been the person who broke into Miss Dimple's desk?"

"Not unless there was booze in there!" Geneva said, laughing in spite of Elwin's disapproving glare.

The new teacher, Charlie noticed, didn't have a lot to say during the meal, but concentrated on her food. The morning had been quiet and uneventful. The first-grade line had never been straighter as they walked to and from the building, and she had glanced in the doorway to see them sitting docilely in their assigned places, reciting their sums in unison.

"Any news from Miss Dimple's brother, Henry?" Annie asked Phoebe over Odessa's apple cobbler.

Their hostess shook her head. "He did say he was going to look into things, and I keep thinking I'll hear something any day, but I've seen neither hide nor hair of him."

Charlie downed her last swallow of coffee. "I find that most peculiar," she said, and several others agreed. But Elwin Vickery, she noticed, excused himself and left the table.

CR

"Do you think Delby O'Donnell really might have been the one who broke into Miss Dimple's desk?" Annie asked as she and Charlie walked to the library later that afternoon.

"I doubt it," Charlie answered. "Geneva said Bobby Tinsley dusted for prints but the desk had been wiped clean except for the ones left by Alma and a couple of the children. Delby wouldn't have worried about that. He probably left fingerprints all over the toolshed along with his stash of canned goods. Besides, that happened in the daytime, and it sounds like Delby only takes advantage of the sleeping accommodations there at night."

She found herself peering into store windows as they passed the drugstore and straining to see if she could catch a glimpse of Hugh at the counter or inside the family dry goods store, hoping she might see him just one more time before he left.

"If you want an excuse to go inside, I need a couple of pairs of rayons," Annie said, urging her across the street. "What I wouldn't give for some decent nylons! I only have one pair left and even those have a run in them."

But Charlie kept on walking. "This is Emmaline's day and I'm not going to spoil it for her," she insisted.

"Huh! You know you want to see him! You're afraid of the old bat, aren't you?"

"I'm afraid of Hitler, too, and I'm not going to drop in on him, either," Charlie told her. "Come on, now, let's hurry before the library closes."

Virginia Balliew looked up as they returned their books to the stack beside her desk. "You're just the two I want to see," she said, taking her pocketbook from a drawer. "I have something to show you."

Silently she laid the tiny twist of purple yarn on the desk in front of them. "I found this caught on a crape myrtle bush between Phoebe Chadwick's and the Elrods'," she said, her voice almost a whisper.

Charlie looked closer. "What? It looks like—"

Annie frowned. "Do you think it might have come from Miss Dimple's purse?"

"It could have, according to Willie Elrod," Virginia said, and told them the story the child's mother had related to her. "And if there's any truth in his tale, that's exactly the thing Dimple would do . . . if she had time to think." The librarian's voice broke and her eyes filled with tears. "Every day I think maybe, just maybe, we'll have some kind of explanation, but to tell you the truth, I'm very much afraid we'll never see our old friend again."

"Don't say that, please!" Charlie, who felt like crying, too, put an arm around her. "Willie's full of all kinds of wild tales about spies and creatures from Mars. He told me the same story just the other day. I wouldn't put too much faith in what he says."

Virginia fingered the shred of yarn and returned it to her purse. "Then where is she?"

"Did you show that to the police?" Annie asked. "It's not much, but at least it's something to go on."

Virginia sighed as she began to sort the returned books. "Bobby promised he'd come by and look at it but the man hasn't darkened my door yet!"

"Then we'll just have to see that he does," Charlie said, frowning, although she really didn't think Bobby Tinsley would know what to do with a clue if it slapped him in the face. "Have you ever met Miss Dimple's brother?" she asked Virginia.

"Henry? Yes, he's treated us to dinner in Atlanta on several occasions. The two of them have always been close. She practically raised him, you know, although"—Virginia lowered her voice—"I don't believe Dimple cares very much for his wife."

And that was when Charlie decided she would try to find out why Henry Kilpatrick hadn't shown up to look for his sister. If Annie could manage to get his phone number from Phoebe Chadwick, she would telephone him tonight.

But her mother and Aunt Lou were holding a record-breaking phone conversation when she got home later that day, and every time Charlie approached to interrupt, Jo Carr covered the mouthpiece with her hand and gave her daughter a "go away" look. Charlie finally gave up and escaped to the kitchen where she opened a can of Spam for supper.

A persistent knocking on the front door startled them later as she and her mother finished putting away the supper dishes and Jo immediately switched off the overhead light. "Could that be Jesse Dean? Hurry, Charlie, and get the curtains! I didn't know we were having a blackout tonight! Did you hear the siren?"

But it wasn't Jesse Dean standing on the darkened porch. It was Hugh Brumlow, and Charlie forgot all about telephoning Miss Dimple's errant brother.

Chapter Twelve

Bessie Jenkins smiled at herself in the mirror. That new hair color really was becoming—not nearly as brash as the cheaper kind, and hadn't Ollie said it made her look even younger? "Even younger." Those were his very words, and tonight he would be bringing a slice of country ham and some of that good stone-ground corn meal from his employer's larder. Old Paschall Kiker couldn't afford to pay him much, but he was generous in other ways, and now that Ollie had that job at the school, he had even hinted at taking her out to supper. Bessie fluffed the bow at her throat. It helped to hide her sagging chin, and the striped print of her cotton blouse brought out the green in her eyes. She had stayed up well past her usual bedtime the night before to finish sewing it and was pleased with the way it turned out.

In the kitchen, Bessie paused to admire the single pink sasanqua blossom floating in a cut glass bowl and centered it on the table. Her camellia bush had bloomed late that year and this would probably be the last of them.

Hearing a slight noise outside, she hurried to turn on the outside light for Ollie. He usually brought his bicycle up on the porch when *he came as it was almost impossible to buy anything made of metal now and somebody had even stolen a neighbor child's roller skates just the other day. She glanced at the clock. It was already dark at a little after six, but Ollie wasn't due for another fifteen minutes. Bessie narrowed her eyes as she peered through the living room window before turning on the light. What was Ollie doing out there? Why didn't he come on in? She had her hand on the doorknob to call to him when she realized it wasn't Ollie, but Jesse Dean Greeson who stood right there in the middle of her front yard obviously studying her house.*

"They're up to something," Charlie said the next morning.

"They who?" Annie asked, soothing a sobbing second grader, who had skidded in the gravel. The two had playground duty and several of the children in the lower grades were engaging in the popular pastime of "boys catching girls."

"Mama and Aunt Lou. I can't keep an eye on them all the time and, of course, they take advantage of it."

Annie sent the injured child to the office for Mercurochrome and a bandage. "How? What've they done now?"

"Well, for one thing, they're gone," Charlie explained.

Annie gasped, thinking, no doubt, of the missing Miss Dimple. "What do you mean, gone?"

"Mama wasn't there when I got up this morning, so naturally I called Aunt Lou. No answer. They're together, all right. I know they've been plotting something."

"Hey! No shoving!" Annie called out suddenly. "Where do you think they might be?"

"Oh, I know where they are," Charlie said. "They're out trailing the milkman."

"Did you see which way he turned?" Lou asked. "What's wrong with you? For heaven's sake, Josephine, sit up, will you? You can't see anything all bent over like that."

Her sister, who had crouched beneath the dashboard, pulled herself erect. "Well, I don't want him seeing me, either. I'm almost sure he turned left onto Wintergreen Street but it's hard to tell in the dark. Wait . . . isn't that him? That's Amos, all right, stopping at Edwina Foster's . . . and he'll probably be there a while, too. With all those children, there's no telling how many gallons they'll need."

"Must cost them a fortune. I hear he's going up on his prices next month and we're paying eighteen cents a quart already. Outrageous!" Lou muttered as she maneuvered the car silently forward.

"And last week ours was nothing but that nasty old 'blue john,'" Jo added. "No cream in it at all that I could tell. And if Amos lets his cows get into the wild onions like he did last summer, I'll have to buy from somebody else." She frowned. "Uh-oh! I think he's seen us."

"So what?" Lou snorted. "We have just as much right to be here as he does."

Jo shivered and wrapped her coat closer about her. The car had no heater. Lou's husband, Ed, had bought the Studebaker before the war and rarely used it now that gasoline had become rationed. She thought of that now as they crept at a respectable distance behind the other vehicle. "Maybe we ought to turn back, Lou. Ed won't like it if we use up his gas."

"Don't guess we'd like it, either," Lou reminded her, "since we'd have to walk all the way home. But don't worry. I'm sure there's plenty."

"What do you mean, 'sure'? Don't you know?"

Lou tapped the gas gauge with the tip of her finger. Well, this thingamabob's a little persnickety, but I know Ed put gas in the tank last week . . . or maybe it was the week before."

The sun was beginning to come up as they drove out of town,

and, following a cloud of dust behind Amos Schuler's once-black pickup, turned onto a two lane dirt road edged with tall overhanging cedars. "I wonder who lives down here," Jo said.

Her sister didn't know but thought it possible he might be leading them to where he had hidden Miss Dimple, and wouldn't it be exciting if they found her? Jo Carr didn't believe for a minute the morose milkman was guilty of abducting Dimple Kilpatrick, but her sister's outlandish schemes took her mind off Fain and the war for a little time at least, so she let herself be carried along with the plan.

Winter pastures on either side were brown and bare of all but sparse patches of green and there wasn't a house or a living creature in sight. Jo thought with anticipation of the small ration of coffee that awaited her at home. At this point, she would even welcome a hot cup of the hated substitute, Postum. She scanned the road in front of them for a sign of the dust-streaked truck but the milkman seemed to have disappeared. Jo yawned. "I'm afraid we've lost him, Lou."

"Or he's lost us." Lou sighed as she looked for a place to turn around. "Oh well, tomorrow is another day."

Her sister laughed. "I think that's already been said, Scarlett." But her laughter faded, along with the noise of the car's engine as the vehicle shuddered to a protesting stop.

"I thought you said Ed put gas in the tank," Jo said, eyeing the desolate road behind and before them.

"He did. I'm just not sure when." Avoiding her sister's accusing eyes, Lou twirled a red knitted muffler around her head and tucked it into the neck of her coat. "Guess we're going to have to walk, at least until somebody comes along to give us a ride home."

Jo didn't speak but pulled on her gloves and reached for the door handle. Why did she let her sister rope her into these crazy escapades? Well, never again! She had one foot on the ground when Lou pulled her back inside. "Wait! We're in luck. There's a car coming this way now!"

It was not until the vehicle drew closer that they recognized Amos Schuler's truck.

"Did you notice how soon Cornelia showed up after Miss Dimple disappeared?" Charlie asked Annie as they walked to Phoebe's during the noontime break. "It's almost as if she'd been waiting in the wings."

Annie jammed both hands in her coat pockets as they waited to cross the street. "She's pleasant enough, but seems to want to keep to herself. You don't think she might've had something to do with Miss Dimple's disappearance, do you?"

Charlie shrugged. "At this point, I don't know what to think. I meant to try and speak with Miss Dimple's brother by telephone last night if we could get the number from Phoebe, but Hugh dropped by to tell me good-bye and I never got around to it."

"Ahh! And, by any chance, did he ask—"

"Annie Gardener, you're hopeless! He *asked* me to write to him, which I will. I'm sure Hugh knows I'm not ready for anything permanent, and neither is he." Charlie gave her friend's arm a tug. "And I still want to see if we can talk Miss Phoebe into giving us Henry Kilpatrick's phone number—*after* I call to see if my wandering mother has returned."

Accustomed to her aunt's inclination for spontaneous adventures, Charlie hadn't been seriously concerned about her mother's sudden absence; surely she would be back at home by noon. Standing in Phoebe Chadwick's hallway, she listened to the telephone ring six . . . seven . . . eight times, before asking to be connected to her aunt's number.

"You're not going to find her at home," Florence McCrary, the operator, told her. "Myrtle Abercrombie was trying to get in touch with her a couple of minutes ago—something about that Thanksgiving basket for her church circle, I think—and Harris Cooper just called to tell her he didn't have any cranberries in yet but he reckons they'll be in by tomorrow."

"Well, ring her anyway, would you, please, Florence? Sometimes it takes her a while to get to the phone." Charlie tried to keep the anxiety out of her voice, as the local telephone operator was a notorious gossip, but when no one answered after multiple rings that seemed to go on forever, she finally gave up.

Annie frowned as she hovered nearby. "What about your aunt's husband? Maybe he knows where they went."

But Ed Willingham had left his office on some kind of errand an hour or so before and hadn't returned, his receptionist told her, adding that he might've dropped by the drugstore for a sandwich.

Probably because her aunt Louise wasn't at home to give him dinner, Charlie thought as she hung up the phone. *Where in the world could they possibly be?*

"Now, Uncle Ed's gone, too," Charlie said, telling Annie of the conversation. "And I'm really getting worried."

"Why don't you go ahead and eat, then give your uncle another call?" Annie suggested. "He's sure to be back by then."

The other diners had gathered at the table and Charlie signaled them to start without her. She had lost her appetite. "Don't wait on me, please," she advised Annie. "There's one more person I want to try first. . . . Hello, Florence, would you ring Bessie Jenkins for me, please?"

"I'm sure she's all right," her neighbor said, but the hesitation in her voice didn't do much to calm Charlie's fears. "I slept later than usual this morning since we didn't have to work at the ordnance plant today, so I didn't see your mother leave. Still . . ."

"Still what? Miss Bessie, you know it's not like Mama to go off for this length of time. If you know anything—"

"It's probably nothing," Bessie began, "but I have noticed that young man who works for Harris Cooper—the Greeson boy, you know—"

"Jessie Dean? What about him?"

"Well, he was standing out in my yard last night—just standing there—and then I heard him walking about, around the house and all. It unnerved me, I can tell you! Said he was taking over your uncle Ed's route as air-raid warden and wanted to become familiar with the neighborhood, but he stayed out there a little too long to suit me. I just don't know about that one. Why isn't he serving his country like everybody else?"

"He did try, Miss Bessie," Charlie explained. "They wouldn't take him because of his eyes."

"Huh! So *he* says, but if he wanted to become familiar with the homes on his route, why didn't he do it in the daytime?" Miss Bessie made a hissing sound. "I'm telling you, Charlie, something isn't right about Jesse Dean Greeson."

Charlie hung up the receiver feeling worse than ever, but Odessa, who was replenishing the creamed potatoes, caught her eye. "You best get in here and eat your dinner before them biscuits get plumb cold." She lowered her voice as Charlie approached the table. "And I made some of them butterscotch squares you like for dessert."

Charlie thanked her and took her seat knowing it wouldn't do a bit of good to argue with Odessa Kirby. Besides, she would have to give Uncle Ed a chance to get back to his office before calling him again.

Odessa had just passed around the dessert tray when Phoebe rose with an irate look on her face to answer the telephone's shrill ringing. "Now, who can that be? Everybody in this town should know we're all sitting down to eat.

"Charlie?" Her hostess held the receiver at arm's length. "Your uncle Ed's on the phone." Lowering her voice, she whispered, "And he sounds a bit put out to me."

Charlie could feel everyone's eyes on her as she answered the phone but the French doors to the dining room stood wide open and there was nowhere to hide.

"Well, you'll never guess what your mother and your aunt Lou have been up to!" Her uncle's booming voice was so loud Charlie could imagine the chandelier shaking over the heads of the diners and she was sure they could hear every word. She had a good idea what the two had been up to, but were they all right?

"Amos Schuler called to tell me those two were way out on Tuckers' Pond Road this morning *picking up pecans!* At least that's what they told him."

"Why would they be doing that? Aunt Lou said she couldn't keep up with the pecan trees you have in your own yard."

"Exactly." Charlie could picture her uncle's red face. "Amos said he thought they might've run out of gas and even offered to give them a ride back to town, but they insisted they were out there looking for some woman he never heard of who said they could have all the pecans they wanted. Of course there wasn't a bit of truth in it!"

"Where are they now?" Charlie pictured her middle-aged relatives plodding through miles of mud in their sensible oxfords, and it was enough to make her shiver.

"Should be home by now. Had to borrow a car from Asa Weatherby at the Gulf Station. Thank God he let me have enough gas to get them back!" Charlie thought she detected a chuckle. "They'll have to use a shovel to get all that mud off their shoes!"

Well, so much for that! Charlie thought as she replaced the receiver. She could hardly wait to get home and ask her mother about her disastrous adventure. She was about to join the others in the dining room for dessert when Charlie saw the name and number scribbled on a notepad by the telephone and quickly copied it on a scrap of paper. She would try her best to reach Henry Kilpatrick tonight.

"I'll be embarrassed to look Amos Schuler in the face," she confessed to Annie as they walked back to school. "He must wonder why they wouldn't accept a ride with him."

Annie laughed. "I wouldn't want to ride with the old sourpuss, either."

"His face would curdle milk, I know, but that doesn't mean he had anything to do with Miss Dimple's disappearance," Charlie said.

Annie was silent for a minute. "But who else is out that early every morning?"

"The paperboy for one, but Ernie Adams is only twelve and he'd have to stuff Miss Dimple into his bicycle basket." Charlie paused to scoop up a drifting scrap of paper from a candy bar and thought of Miss Dimple's tidy habit of collecting litter. "Maybe her brother can give us an idea of who might have taken her—and why."

"What makes you think you'll actually reach him?" Annie asked.

"Because I mean to keep trying until I do."

CHAPTER THIRTEEN

Dear Private Mote,

I am in the third grade at Elderberry Grammar School. Miss Charlie—she's my teacher—says you went to school here, too. We got new swings and a slide for our playground last year but I'd rather play ball. Do you like ball, too? We had an air raid last week and had to crawl under our desks, but I don't think that would do much good if a bomb dropped through the roof. I'm not scared though because we know you are fighting to protect us. My tinfoil ball is almost as big as a grapefruit and I'm real careful not to waste paper but I sure do miss bubble gum!

Your friend,
Junior Henderson

Charlie smiled as she read through the letters her class had written for their language assignment that afternoon. Jack Mote had been a couple of years behind her in school and was currently undergoing training for the army at Fort McClellan in Alabama. His older brother Chester had been killed in April when his plane ran out of fuel and crashed during General Dolittle's bombing raid over Japan. When school was over that day Charlie planned to take the letters to the boys' mother, Marjorie, whose neat white bungalow was a few blocks from town. Her mother and Aunt Lou made it a point to visit the Motes often, sometimes taking a loaf of home-made bread or a few flowers from the garden, but Charlie could hardly bear to pass by the sad home with the gold star in the window. That would now be joined by a banner with the familiar blue star like the one they had in their window for Fain. There was scarcely a house in town without one.

&

"Charlie! Do come in and tell me all about school. It seems like yesterday that you and Jack were children there yourselves . . . and what do you hear from Delia? I hear you're going to be an aunt."

Marjorie Mote greeted her at the door as if she'd been watching from the window, and Charlie followed her into the room, momentarily relieved that so far they had avoided the subject of Chester's death. His photograph and Jack's faced one another on a table by the window.

"I thought you might like to see these before I send them on to Jack," she said, giving her the folder of letters. "Some of them are kind of funny and I expect he can probably use a laugh."

"That he can, and it was thoughtful of you to think of him. He's doing all right—or at least he wants me to think he is—and I know he loves mail from home."

Charlie sat in a large overstuffed chair by the fireplace and sipped homemade blackberry wine while nibbling on ginger cookies as they talked of her sister's pregnancy, Jack's news from Fort McClellan, the upcoming Thanksgiving holiday, and, of course, Miss Dimple's mysterious disappearance.

"I can't imagine that school without her," Marjorie Mote said. "Why, I almost expect the buildings to crumble into dust! Have you not heard any word at all?"

Charlie told her about Miss Dimple's brother and his perplexing absence from Elderberry. "And I don't know if it means anything or not, but Virginia Balliew found a small scrap of purple yarn on the crape myrtle next to the street not far from where Miss Dimple lived . . . lives." She fingered the crocheted doily on the arm of the chair and felt herself wanting to doze. The house was warm from the wood burning fireplace and smelled richly of wood smoke, spices, and sweet summer wine.

She had baked her customary fruitcake that morning, her hostess explained. "I had to make substitutions, of course, and used a lot of hickory nuts and honey, but I think it's important to carry on with traditions even though it's just the two of us this year." Marjorie Mote's lips smiled bravely but Charlie thought her eyes held more pain than a person ought to bear.

"And Fain," she asked as Charlie was leaving. "Any word from him?"

Charlie shook her head. "Not for a while," she told her, and when they said good-bye, Marjorie clung to her for a long, long time. It was not until she was on her way home that Charlie remembered they had not once mentioned Chester's death.

"I didn't even tell her how sorry I was about Chester," Charlie confessed to her mother when she got home.

Jo put aside the article she was writing about the Magnolia Garden Club's autumn reception and spoke softly to her daughter. "Don't you think she already knows that? Just your being there assured her that you care."

Charlie took two small pork chops from the Frigidaire and sliced potatoes and onions for frying. "I told Mrs. Mote I planned to try and reach Miss Dimple's brother tonight and she agreed it was a good idea."

"And why would you do that?" her mother wanted to know.

"I thought he might be able to give us some idea of why she was taken. After all, he *is* her brother and should know her better than anybody. I can't understand why he hasn't come here to help look for her."

"That could be because there are things he doesn't want us to know," Jo said, setting her writing tablet aside to put plates on the table.

Charlie frowned. Sometimes her mother said the strangest things. "Why not? What kinds of things?"

"Think about it, Charlie. He lives in Kennesaw—that's near Marietta and the Bell Bomber Plant. And Miss Dimple told me one time her brother was an engineer of some sort . . . not the train kind," she added with a wave of her hand. "We don't know what they might be working on there."

"Do you really think somebody might be holding her for ransom?" The shortening in the frying pan began to smoke and Charlie quickly added the vegetables before it started to flame. Was this really happening right here in Elderberry? And to quaint Miss Dimple of all people! It was like something out of a movie. Now she was even more determined to speak with Henry Kilpatrick.

Charlie shoved the potatoes and onions aside to sear the meager chops before adding salt and pepper, wishing she could bottle and sell the fragrance of the sautéing onions. Neither Charlie nor her mother had mentioned the morning's fiasco with the milkman *yet*, but Charlie didn't mean to let the opportunity pass. She waited until Jo stood at the stove warming up leftover butterbeans before asking her mother if they happened to find Miss Dimple hidden under the milk bottles in the back of Amos Schuler's pickup.

Jo concentrated on stirring the beans before answering. "All right, I'll admit I'd almost rather go through childbirth again than let Lou drag me along on one of her outrageous ventures, but the morning wasn't a complete waste of time."

"What do you mean?"

"Well, you know your aunt—she just out and out asked Amos Schuler if he ever saw Miss Dimple out walking while he was on his morning route."

Charlie flipped the pork chops to the other side. Knowing her aunt, she wasn't a bit surprised. "And what did he say?"

"He said something like, 'You mean that old lady with the umbrella everybody's been talking about? Sure I've seen her.' Said he just about ran over her once when she stepped behind his truck just as he was backing out of somebody's driveway."

Charlie shrugged. "Still, that doesn't prove anything."

"But that's not all," her mother continued. "*Then* Lou asked him if he'd seen her on the morning she disappeared, and I'll swear, Charlie, that man has the most unpleasant expression—looks like he just ate a rotten potato with a hair in it . . ."

Charlie made a face at the image that brought to mind. "And had he? Seen her, I mean?"

"Didn't say. Drove off and left us standing there in the middle of nowhere, but if looks could kill, your aunt Louise and I would be laid out as cold and stiff as yesterday's grits over there in Harvey Thompson's Funeral Parlor!"

"He didn't even offer you a ride back to town?"

Her mother spooned butterbeans into a bowl. "He did at first, but you could tell he didn't really want to. Anyway, that was before Lou asked him all that about Miss Dimple. By then we'd already decided we'd take our chances on somebody else coming along." She sighed. "But I sure don't know what I would've done if your uncle Ed hadn't shown up when he did. I thought I was going to wet my pants!"

Charlie waited until they had washed the supper dishes before placing her call to Henry Kilpatrick. She had no idea what his working hours were or when he ate his evening meal. She did know he was married because Virginia had hinted that Miss Dimple wasn't particularly fond of her brother's wife. If she wasn't able to speak with Henry, however, maybe his wife would tell her what she wanted to know.

But she soon learned that wasn't going to happen.

"My husband isn't available." When the woman spoke it sounded as if each word had been chopped off with an ax. "May I ask your reason for calling?"

Charlie took a deep breath. She could sympathize with Miss Dimple's opinion of her sister-in-law already. Be calm, be pleasant— or at least sound pleasant, she reminded herself as she explained who she was and where she lived. "I not only teach with Miss Dimple, but I was also once one of her students. We're all concerned about her absence and are hoping her brother might be able to give us some idea of why this has happened. Do you know if he plans to come here to Elderberry anytime soon?"

"He most certainly does not! This is a private matter, and I have no intention of discussing it with you or anyone else."

"Who is it, Hazel?" A man's voice interrupted and Charlie overheard a rather loud whispered explanation of her identity: "Some woman who says she teaches with Dimple in that town where she used to live."

Used to live? Did they know something she didn't know? Was Miss Dimple already dead? When Henry Kilpatrick came on the line, it was all she could do to keep from crying. "We all care deeply for your sister," she told him, "and frankly, we're worried that something terrible has happened," Charlie began. "I don't suppose you've heard—"

"I share your concern, believe me," Henry said, "but I give you my word that everything possible is being done to assure my sister's welfare."

At that Charlie breathed a little easier. "I—we thought it might help if you came here to . . . uh, kind of assist in the . . . uh, investigation." *Why was she stammering so? Just come out and say it, Charlie!* "I mean, you should know her better than any of us, and we hoped you might have some idea—"

"I'm sorry, but right now that would be impossible. However, I do appreciate your concern, and I thank you for calling."

And Charlie Carr stood in her chilly hallway on Katherine Street listening to the terminal click as he hung up the phone.

How could anyone be so callous? Wasn't the man worried at all? His *sister* has disappeared! Henry Kilpatrick should be right here in Elderberry, dragging the river if necessary! Charlie stood with her fist knotted around the receiver and reminded herself to breathe.

"Well, I'll be!" Florence McCrary muttered from her switchboard in the Elderberry Telephone Office. "Don't that just beat all?"

"Didn't anyone ever tell you to hold up your shoulders?" Miss Dimple said. "A proper posture is so important. It affects your entire physical well-being . . . gives your internal organs space to do what they're meant to do." She put aside the Agatha Christie book, *Murder in Three Acts*, one of several he had brought earlier and which she found she hadn't read. "I had an uncle once with stooped shoulders like yours. Uncle Leon. Such a sad thing—died fairly young, I'm afraid. Of course he didn't eat right. Perhaps you should try deep-breathing exercises."

Her jailer set her supper tray on the table with a rattle and muttered as he turned to leave. She seldom understood him when he spoke from behind the mask—another witch one today, and he was obviously making an effort to disguise his voice—but Dimple Kilpatrick knew enough to realize the man was cursing under his breath.

How far could she push him? For all she knew he probably wouldn't hesitate to kill her if it wasn't in his interests to keep her alive and minimally healthy. He had demanded she give him the gold brooch that had belonged to her mother along with the message for Henry—to prove, she supposed, that she was, indeed, their prisoner. She was fond of the brooch as it was the only possession of her mother's she had, but she hadn't hesitated to comply with his request. After all, she assumed it would end up in Henry's hands. The message to Henry had been brief and to the point, letting him know she was alive and well, and although her jailer had suggested it, she did not beg her brother to go along with any demands.

As soon as he slammed the door on his way out Dimple rose to see what he had brought for her supper: a baked potato, a small dish of canned tomatoes, a wedge of cheese, and a slice of baker's bread—the presliced kind that came wrapped in wax paper. She was pleased to see it was accompanied by a large mug of steaming tea. She sniffed. Not ginger mint, but it was hot and strong, and she sipped it gratefully. She didn't plan to give up on the ginger mint, just as she had continued to ask for mystery novels. This one, she noticed, had come from the local library. Would her friend Virginia take note? Not that she was the only mystery reader in town, but it was worth a try. She had even left a message—several, in fact—within the pages of the books, but she suspected her captor didn't mean to return them.

Miss Dimple broke off some of the cheese, added it to the still-warm potato, and spooned canned tomatoes on top. Surprisingly, she found it quite palatable.

Earlier that day she had leapt to her feet and run to the window when gravel crunched under the wheels of a vehicle close by. It sounded as if it might have been a heavy truck or perhaps a van, but it didn't come near enough for her to see it or call to anyone. Although she had on occasion crept to the top of the stairs to listen to what went on above her, Miss Dimple had never heard anyone talking. A telephone rang now and again in some distant room and she could hear someone walking about. She wasn't certain how many people were staying in the place where she was being held, but there was one thing about which she was sure. She now knew who her jailer was.

After her meal, Miss Dimple stacked the empty dishes on the tray and carried it to the top of the stairs as she had been asked to do. An overhead lightbulb suspended from the ceiling over the stairway burned day and night, and from the very first day, a plan had begun to form in Miss Dimple's mind, but she wasn't ready to put it into action just yet.

Miss Dimple sat in the rocking chair by the gas heater and began sewing on her patchwork quilt of patriotic colors in red, white, and blue, and it was coming along quite nicely, she thought. As she stitched, she thought of her brother. Poor Henry! What a dilemma he must be in, but she knew he would make the right choices. Her freedom, and possibly her country's depended on it.

CHAPTER FOURTEEN

*C*ornelia Emerson lingered in her room until the very last minute when she heard the cook—Odessa something or other—ring the bell for supper. Actually, it wasn't her room but belonged to Miss Dimple, or it had until recently, and everything about it was modest and unassuming: the small oak desk by the window, the white-painted bureau against the wall, even the neat single bed with its white tufted counterpane. The tiny closet, which had been emptied of the former occupant's clothing, was spacious enough to hold all she would need for a while at least. The room suited Cornelia just fine. That Chadwick woman who owned the place had informed her in no uncertain terms the arrangement was only temporary until Dimple Kilpatrick returned. Well, that was all right with her!

Wetting her fingers, she tucked a stray strand of dark hair into place and pinched her cheeks for color. The others should be seated by now and were probably waiting for her. Well, let them. She had promised— very much against her will—to submit to a game of bridge after supper. Cornelia sighed before going downstairs. It was all part of the job, wasn't it? But at least the food was good.

Charlie stood on the corner and watched them, what seemed an unending line of khaki-colored trucks filled with soldiers lining benches on either side. She smiled and waved as they passed, and most of them waved back. They looked so young—*were* young—many younger than she, and when they tossed addresses from the truck, she tried to write to as many as possible. She still heard from a couple of them, but recently, many of her letters had gone unanswered.

Last night she had written her brother again. It had been almost a month since his last letter and it had become literally painful to watch her mother wait for the mail. Charlie tried to find peace in the anesthesia of *not knowing*. If you didn't know, then he couldn't be somewhere fighting for his life or wounded, or lying dead on a distant battlefield. Fain would be safe until the boy on the black bicycle knocked at their door with a telegram from the War Department. *We regret to inform you . . .*

Charlie didn't know the name of the boy who delivered the telegrams or why he rode a bicycle of that color. Maybe it was his only choice when the war began, or maybe he painted it himself thinking his mode of transportation should be somber, befitting the occasion. Of course, it would make no difference if the bearer of such grim news pulled up to their porch on red, blue, or sparkling gold, and her breath caught in her throat whenever she saw him pass.

Ollie Thigpen's bicycle was steel gray with a basket and headlight on the front and a small motor on the back. While at school he kept it just inside the basement door near the room that housed the monster furnace Annie had nicknamed Ladon for the mythological dragon that guarded the tree of golden apples. Tall and gangling, when riding his bicycle Ollie resembled one of those dancing puppets with hinged legs, and he walked with great loping strides, but the old building now shone from his daily efforts. He arrived early to stoke the furnace, rode back to the farm to see to the needs of Paschall Kiker, and returned to the school in the early afternoon. Although the bicycle had a motor, because of the scarcity of gasoline, Ollie seldom used it. Sometimes, Charlie noticed, their principal would give him a ride, and when Ollie visited their neighbor, Bessie usually hauled him and his bicycle back to the farm in her ancient Chevrolet.

How the man sustained the energy for courtship with his rigorous schedule, Charlie couldn't imagine, and supposed it must be love. She wished it would hurry and happen to her. Tonight, she decided, she would write to Hugh, even though he had been gone only twenty-four hours.

"I can't believe Thanksgiving is just about a week away," Annie said at the noon meal that day.

Velma Anderson spoke up. "And do you realize it's been a week now since our Dimple disappeared?"

"A week and a day," Lily Moss added, shaking her head. "I'm afraid it's not looking good. Why, with each passing day—"

"We're all aware of how long it's been," Elwin Vickery said. And he set his knife across his plate with such a clatter Charlie halfway expected the china to crack. She told them about phoning Miss Dimple's brother.

"And he refuses to come here and even try to help?" Elwin glared at Charlie as if it had all been her fault. "What a cold, unfeeling person he must be to care that little about his own sister!"

But their hostess shook her head. "Now, Elwin, I don't think that's true. From all I've heard from Dimple, the two had—*have*— a very good relationship. As you know, Dimple isn't the kind to make a fuss over someone, but it's easy to see she adores him. He always remembers her with that lovely fruit at Christmas, you know, and at the end of every school year she joins him for several weeks at his summer place in the mountains."

Geneva Odom paused while buttering her biscuit. "*Summer place?* Do you think there's a possibility she might've gone there?"

"Without saying anything about it to us?" Phoebe frowned. "I can't imagine why, but I'm sure her brother has mentioned the possibility to the police."

"Well, from his callous response to your questions," Elwin said to Charlie, "I wonder if the man's been of any help at all."

"There might be more to this than he's able to tell us," Charlie said, repeating what her mother had told her about the possibility of Henry Kilpatrick's connection to the Bell Bomber Plant.

"Do you mean someone might be holding Dimple for *ransom?*" Lily asked, wide-eyed.

Odessa set a tray of cups on the sideboard with a rattle so loud everyone jumped. "Here's you all's coffee if you want it," she announced before fleeing back into the kitchen.

"What on earth's wrong with Odessa?" Lily asked, frowning.

Charlie and Annie started to rise at the same time. "She's *crying*," Annie said. "Something must've upset her. I'll go see what's wrong."

But Phoebe held up a hand. "No. Just leave her be. Odessa's emotions have been in turmoil since Dimple disappeared. There's a closeness there, you know." She lowered her voice. "Odessa couldn't read when she came here and Dimple worked faithfully with her for over a year. Taught her how to read."

Velma dabbed at her eyes and nodded. "And Odessa taught Bob Robert."

❧

"Did you notice anything kind of peculiar about the conversation today at dinner?" Charlie asked Annie as they walked to town after school that afternoon.

"About what?"

"Cornelia Emerson."

Annie hopped daintily over a puddle. "What about her?"

"Well, nothing really," Charlie answered, "except she never said a word."

"Come to think of it, she didn't, did she? Took the last biscuit, too, and I had my eye on that."

"I can't figure her out," Charlie admitted. "The other day when she first came she asked so many questions, I felt like I was being interviewed, but lately she mostly just sits and listens."

"And eats," Annie added grimly. "And what about Elwin? Think he might know more than he lets on?"

"I doubt it," Charlie said. "He seems to get genuinely upset whenever the subject of Miss Dimple comes up."

But Annie disagreed. "I'm not so sure about that. Remember that quote from *Hamlet*: 'The lady doth protest too much . . .' Except in this case it's a man."

Charlie just shook her head. She couldn't even imagine Elwin Vickery being mixed up in Miss Dimple's disappearance. She looked at her watch. They would have to hurry if they were to drop by the library to speak with Virginia before meeting Janet Delaney at the drugstore. Afterward the three planned to see Joel McCrea and Claudette Colbert in *The Palm Beach Story*.

The librarian had pulled several books from one of the mystery shelves for a patron whose back was turned but she paused to greet them when they entered, and from Virginia's wearied expression it was obvious to Charlie she'd had very little sleep. She didn't recognize the woman browsing through the volumes as Cornelia Emerson until the newcomer headed for the check-out desk with a stack of books in her arms. Charlie noticed *Hangman's Holiday* as the title on top as she passed and mentioned that she'd read and enjoyed it. "But I like just about everything by Dorothy L. Sayers," she added.

Cornelia nodded. "It helps to pass the time," she said, frowning as she looked about her. "But such a tiny library! I've never seen one so small."

Charlie, who had always loved "the cabin," as they called it, wasn't sure how to accept that comment, but she rose to the occasion and gave the woman the benefit of the doubt. "Cozy, isn't it? It was built by the Woman's Club about fifty years ago and they still use it for meetings. Once in a while when it's really cold somebody will build a fire in that big stone fireplace, and in summer people like to read on the porch in the shade of the wisteria vines."

"And it's not unusual for someone to stop for a while and play a few tunes on the piano over there," Virginia added as she checked out Cornelia's books.

Cornelia thanked her and left without further comment, and the three of them watched her from the window. "Thoughtful of her to offer me a ride back to Phoebe's," Annie said wryly.

"But you aren't planning to go there yet anyway," Charlie reminded her.

Annie shrugged. "She didn't know that, did she?"

Virginia turned to Charlie. "Tell me about Henry. Have you spoken with him yet?" And Charlie told her of her disappointing conversation with Miss Dimple's brother. "Don't waste your time looking for him in Elderberry," she said. "He practically hung up on me when I mentioned it."

Virginia was silent as she straightened books in the children's section. "I wonder if Elwin Vickery might be able to shed some light on that," she said.

"Why Elwin Vickery?" Annie asked.

"I'd almost forgotten this," Virginia told them, "but I believe Dimple mentioned once that Elwin had gone to college with her brother."

"You wouldn't have guessed that by the conversation at noon," Charlie said. "If Elwin's ever known Henry Kilpatrick, you could've fooled me."

"And from his comments during dinner, he certainly didn't seem to think much of Henry's refusal to come," Annie added.

"Mama thinks Henry might be working on something important at the Bell Bomber Plant," Charlie told them.

Virginia followed them to the door. "If that's the case," she said, "whoever took Dimple might *want* her brother to come to Elderberry. There's a possibility they mean to use her for bait."

Charlie's high school friend Janet Delaney had been so enthusiastic in her response when invited to meet them for a Coke and a movie, Charlie felt guilty for not asking her sooner. She wasn't surprised to find her scooping up the last of a chocolate soda while waiting for them in a back booth at the drugstore.

Janet smiled when she saw them. "Sorry, but I just couldn't wait—been craving this all day!"

Charlie, who remembered when her friend could hang by her knees from the apple tree in her backyard and turn cartwheels all the way down the front walk at school, couldn't help noticing there was scarcely an inch of space between Janet's growing stomach and the edge of the table. It startled her to think that her younger sister would soon be in the same situation.

Janet spoke with pride of her husband Ben, who was training as a gunner at the Army Air Field in Las Vegas and had recently been given his first chance to train in the gun turret of a B-17. "He's due to graduate in another two weeks," she told them, "and I'm expecting him home on leave before they have to—"

"So he'll be home soon after Thanksgiving," Charlie said, seeing Janet's lips tremble. "You must be excited!"

Janet drained the last of her soda before replying. "We're waiting

133

to have Thanksgiving until he gets here. His mother's ordered a turkey and Aunt Opal's making a coconut cake—if Mr. Cooper can get any coconuts. Jesse Dean's promised to hold one for us if they come in."

Janet leaned forward. "Say, what's all this about Miss Dimple up and vanishing? Have you heard anything yet?"

"Not a word," Annie told her, "and we're getting more worried every day."

"I wish there were something we could do . . ." Janet folded her paper napkin and set it aside. "I've always thought a lot of Miss Dimple. Remember that little boy who started out with us in the first grade, Charlie? He was called by his initials: T. W., or something like that."

Charlie nodded. "C. W. Can't remember his last name, but I think his family moved away before the end of the year."

Janet smiled. "Miss Dimple probably wouldn't like me telling this, but I was on my way home for dinner one day and I remember C. W. sitting out there on the wall all by himself. His folks were poor as Job's turkey, you know, and he hadn't brought anything to eat. Anyway, I saw Miss Dimple take a quarter from her purse and kinda bury it in the dirt with her foot, and I thought it was a strange thing to do until she called that little boy's attention to it and asked him if it was his. He just looked at it and shook his head. . . ."

"I doubt if he'd ever seen a quarter before," Charlie said, remembering the shabby clothing and sad little face.

"Miss Dimple said, 'Well, I guess it's yours now. You found it, didn't you?'" Janet continued, "and she stood there and watched that child run to that little school store where you could buy a grilled cheese sandwich and a candy bar. Then she saw me standing there and frowned so it just about scared me to death. 'What you just saw is between you and me, Janet, and you must promise not to tell a soul,' she said. And I haven't until now."

"And that's just one more reason we have to find her—and soon!" Annie said, and everyone agreed. But nobody knew exactly how to go about it.

"I thought you might have something exciting to tell me today," Janet said to Charlie in an obvious attempt to lighten the mood. "Didn't Hugh just leave for the navy?"

Charlie stirred her Coke with a straw and rolled her eyes. "If anything happens between me and Hugh, I'll put you on the list to be informed," she said, and then felt ashamed for being curt. Janet was only asking a friendly question, but why did everyone think it was imperative that she become engaged?

She looked at her watch. "Hadn't we better hurry? It's almost time for the movie to start."

CHAPTER FIFTEEN

*G*eneva Odom hugged herself as she walked through the park on her way home from her sister's. Not because she was cold, but because she didn't want to relinquish the delightful feeling of a tiny baby in her arms. Her younger sister, Sandra, had given birth to her third child, a little boy, two weeks before, and with her husband away in the army, she had her hands full coping with the newborn, a five-year-old, and a toddler underfoot. Geneva had taken dinner and stayed to get the older two to bed, then lingered to rock tiny Donald to sleep. She and Sam had thought about adding to their family, but with their two girls in high school now, they had to consider the cost of their college years ahead. She smiled remembering the strains from a lullaby their mother used to sing, "Bye, baby bunting, daddy's gone a hunting to get a little rabbit skin to wrap his baby bunting in . . ." How lucky she was to have her sister's young family close by!

The lamps in the park cast yellow circles on the grass and Geneva heard the trickle of the fountain as she approached. Now and then a car circled the courthouse square a couple of blocks away, their headlights like candles in the dark night. It had been after eight o'clock when she left Sandra's and traffic was usually light at this time of night. Sam hadn't liked the idea of her walking home alone, but Geneva reminded him she had come that way many times before. Except for the shadows around the two large magnolia trees on the other side of the bridge, the path was well lit and she had never felt afraid here. Still, Sam had insisted on coming to meet her and Geneva knew it would be useless to argue.

The rattle of leaves in the magnolia to her right caught her attention as she crossed the bridge and Geneva thought she saw one of the limbs move as she passed. She walked faster as the crunch of footsteps behind her grew louder. Was Sam trying to frighten her? If so, he was doing a pretty good job of it and it wasn't funny! Geneva paused at the edge of the pathway. "That's enough, Samuel Odom! You're going to be sorry!" she called.

She didn't have time to cry out at the sharp pain in the back of her head before darkness overtook her.

"They said it was a limb," Charlie said the next morning at school. "You know how some of those magnolia branches hang over the pathway in the park, and they seem to think one could've broken off just as Geneva walked underneath."

"Geneva doesn't think so," Lily Moss said, drawing her lips into a tight line. "From what I heard, she thought somebody was behind her. Must've come out from under that big old magnolia. Geneva had no business walking in that park by herself that time of night, especially after what happened to poor Dimple. It's a good thing Sam came along when he did or who knows what might've happened."

"She's going to be all right, though, isn't she?" Annie asked. "I mean she was still stunned but already sitting up by the time Sam found her."

"But she'll have one heck of a headache," Charlie added. "Doc Morrison says she's going to have a knot as big as a hen egg, but she'll be okay."

The three teachers had early-morning playground duty and news of Geneva's injury of the night before was on everyone's lips.

"I hope she hurries back . . . for more reasons than one," Annie said with a groan as they noticed Alma Owens hurrying into the building.

"Oh, Lord! Hide the rhythm band instruments!" Charlie wailed.

"Well, I, for one, intend to find out just what Geneva heard last night," Lily informed them. "With what's been going on around here, I'm almost afraid to go anywhere in Elderberry anymore."

And although Charlie was dying to talk with Geneva as well, she didn't want to add fuel to Lily's apprehension. Instead, she brought up the subject of the Thanksgiving party the town was planning for the servicemen due to pass through the next day.

"Mr. Faulkenberry's letting us out early tomorrow so we can meet the train," Charlie told them. "I'm going over after school today to help decorate."

Already volunteers were busy cleaning and setting up tables in an empty store near the depot and many of the women had signed up to provide a Thanksgiving dinner for the young men, most of whom were probably homesick already. In the post office the week before, Charlie had noticed a large poster showing a family gathered around a dinner featuring a turkey that looked so real you could almost smell it. Lettering at the top read OURS TO FIGHT FOR, FREEDOM FROM WANT. If the servicemen passing through couldn't make it home, at least they could give them the next best thing, she thought.

"Odessa's already made cornbread for the dressing," Annie said, "and the whole house smells like onions. She won't let anybody near the kitchen—even Miss Phoebe."

Aunt Lou planned to take sweet potato soufflé and apple pie, and Charlie was going to make peanut butter cookies using brown sugar and corn syrup.

Her mother and aunt were already smoothing crisp white sheets over the long tables when Charlie arrived that afternoon, and she took her turn draping the walls with flags and buntings. "Wouldn't it be festive if we could gather a lot of red, white, and blue balloons and hang them from the ceiling?" Aunt Lou said, but most of the rubber was being used in the war effort and Charlie couldn't remember the last time she had seen a balloon.

Emmaline Brumlow busied herself decorating some of the tables with mounds of fruit and nuts, and Bessie Jenkins, in a bright blue flowered turban that matched her crisply starched housedress, arranged ears of dried corn, pumpkins, and winter squash on others. When Bessie wasn't looking, Charlie saw Emmaline sneak along behind her and adjust what she'd done.

Working up her courage, she approached Emmaline and said she supposed Hugh had reached his destination in Virginia by now. The woman frowned as she silently studied the table, then picked up an acorn squash and put it back in the same place. "I wouldn't know," she said finally. "He hasn't seen fit to telephone his mother. I don't suppose *you've* heard anything?"

From the look she received, Charlie was frankly relieved that she hadn't. "I really didn't expect to," she told her. "I doubt if he has access to a telephone."

Annie, who had been listening, spoke with a grin. "You know how the song goes about not having private rooms or telephones," she reminded her, referring to Irving Berlin's popular hit, "This Is the Army, Mr. Jones." Emmaline, apparently not amused, went back to sorting vegetables.

Elwin, accompanied by Velma Anderson, came in just then with arms full of brightly colored chrysanthemums Bob Robert had harvested from Phoebe's backyard garden and Charlie welcomed the opportunity to help them round up vases.

"Have you had a chance to ask him?" Charlie whispered to Annie as they filled the vessels with water.

"Ask who?" Annie jumped back as she sloshed water on her skirt.

"*Elwin!* Remember? You promised to find out if he knew Henry Kilpatrick in college. Virginia said that Miss Dimple said—"

"I know! I know! I just haven't had a chance. At dinner everybody was talking about what happened to Geneva and I haven't been able to catch him alone."

"I guess there's no time like the present. I'll ask him now." Charlie set the vase aside and crossed the room to where Elwin was helping arrange a row of chairs to surround a space to dance.

Elwin nodded when he saw her. "Good, we can use your help. You can look through that stack of records somebody brought and pull out the best ones for dancing."

Charlie found the records next to the old Victrola that had been shoved into the corner and began sorting through them, glad to have something to do with her hands. *How was she going to word this without sounding accusatory?*

"You probably know Miss Dimple better than a lot of us," she began, setting some of the records aside. "Did you ever have a chance to meet her brother?"

Elwin turned away to push a chair into line. "Why do you ask?"

"I just can't understand why he hasn't been more help in trying to find out what happened. I thought maybe if *you* talked with him—"

When he faced her Elwin Vickery's answer was as rigid as his stance. "I went to the university with Henry Kilpatrick years ago, but I hardly knew him well. At any rate, I doubt if anything I might say would have the slightest influence."

Charlie found herself staring at his back. "Well, so much for that," she said to Annie, who had been eavesdropping under the pretense of helping sort the records.

Annie shivered. "Why do I feel like I've been doused with a bucket of well water?" she asked. "Somehow I get the notion Henry Kilpatrick isn't Elwin's favorite subject."

Charlie shrugged. At the moment she didn't have time to worry about it as Ray Richards and his wife, Ellie, arrived with boxes of dishes and flatware from their restaurant and wanted to know where to put them.

When they left the building a few hours later, what had earlier been a grimy abandoned store was converted into a festive and welcoming holiday room where their young guests could enjoy themselves and forget for a little while the destination that awaited them.

Annie paused to glance back as they left. "It really looks beautiful, doesn't it? And I think we'll have plenty of food. This is going to be fun, Charlie! I found some new Glenn Miller records in that stack so let's hope we have some good dancers!"

Charlie was looking forward to it, too. Helping to entertain the troops would take her mind off the approaching holiday without Fain and Delia—for a little while, at least. She would see Hugh when he completed his medical training sometime after Christmas, and Delia had hinted that she would probably come home when and if her husband was shipped out, but they weren't even sure where her brother was. Charlie knew only that this year Fain wouldn't be able to eat his fill of Aunt Lou's cornbread dressing and sweet potato pie, or if he'd have any kind of Thanksgiving dinner at all.

But she wasn't going to think about that.

"Aunt Lou has ordered her Thanksgiving turkey from Mr. Cooper," she told Annie, "so we'll all be in for a treat, and she usually makes about five kinds of desserts, but with rationing, I guess we'll be lucky to have one or two." Last year their family had joined her aunt and uncle for Thanksgiving dinner that had included escalloped oysters along with the customary bird, but she knew better than to expect that this year.

"I hope she doesn't mind the extra guests," Annie said as they turned down Katherine Street for home. "You've seen how Joel can put the food away and I wouldn't be surprised if Will couldn't hold his own as well."

"Aunt Lou should've had at least five children. She can't wait! I know she plans to make a jam cake and Mama's donating sugar for a lemon meringue pie. Does your Will have a favorite dessert?"

"Oh, you are a sneaky one!" Annie laughed. "If he's like the rest of us he'll be glad to get any dessert—and he's *not my* Will!"

In her letter to Hugh that night, Charlie told him about helping his mother decorate the store for the troops they expected the next day, adding that she wished he could climb on a magic carpet and drop in among them at least long enough for a dance or two. There weren't many opportunities to dance in Elderberry, Georgia, and the first, last, and only time she'd danced with Hugh had been at a fraternity party during his last year in college. She didn't mention, of course, that Emmaline Brumlow was in a royal snit because he hadn't telephoned.

After supper Charlie made peanut butter cookies for the next day's party while her mother washed the dishes and put them away. "Have you noticed that Bessie has started wearing everything blue?" Jo asked as she hung up the dish towel. "She's made scarves for several of the ladies at work, all from that same flowered pattern. Frankly, I've never cared much for blue, but I don't guess it matters what color you wind around your head when you're making ammunition."

"Why blue?" Charlie asked as she slid the last of the cookies into the oven.

"Can't you guess? It's Ollie's favorite color." Her mother smiled. "It wouldn't surprise me one bit if those two didn't have an important announcement to make before long."

"It's about time. They've been going together for as long as I can remember," Charlie said. "But what about old Mr. Kiker? Would Ollie bring Bessie to live with them out on that farm?"

"I don't know. Now that he has a job over at the school, maybe they'll find somebody else to help out there." Jo sighed. "Poor old Paschall. His wife's been gone twenty years if it's a day. Shame he never married again."

Jo was quiet as Charlie washed the mixing bowls in the dishpan and scalded them with boiling water. "Ben Morrison got down-right short with me today, and for the life of me I can't figure out why," she said, sinking into a kitchen chair.

Charlie frowned. "Ben Morrison? *Doc* Morrison? When did you see him?"

"I have as much right to get my blood pressure checked as the next person," her mother said with what could only be called an air of indignation.

"I never said you couldn't, but I didn't know you were having a problem. Why didn't you tell me?" Charlie became suddenly concerned. "Have you been feeling dizzy lately, light-headed?"

Her mother waved her away. "Of course not, but I had the morning free since I didn't have to go into Milledgeville today, and I wanted to ask him some questions."

Uh-oh, Charlie thought. "What kind of questions?"

"About Wilson Malone." Jo drew herself up and folded her arms in front of her. "We've never had any kind of rational explanation about what happened to him, and then the very next day Dimple Kilpatrick just up and vanishes from the face of the earth. Can you tell me that's not strange?"

"Of course it's strange." Charlie admitted that she felt the same way. But what did that have to do with Doc Morrison, she wanted to know.

Her mother took the broom from the pantry and began to sweep the floor with brisk, angry strokes. "All I know is that when I asked him what killed Wilson he as much as told me to mind my own business."

That night Charlie Carr dreamed her sister Delia had enlisted in the navy and put her newborn on the train for home. When Charlie went to the depot to greet the baby, a tiny infant wearing a blue flowered turban stepped off holding a huge turkey drumstick in one hand and an American flag in the other.

CHAPTER SIXTEEN

*N*ine days. She had been here nine days. Dimple Kilpatrick had read four mystery novels, a copy of The Farmer's Bulletin (circa 1924), in which she learned about the early mechanics of home canning; stitched together quilting squares until she dreamed in red, white, and blue; started a journal on the yellowed paper she'd found lining a dresser drawer; and learned to be an adequate liar. In fact, Miss Dimple thought, her performance of the day before would have been worthy of a standing ovation had she been onstage.

Mr. Smith had come downstairs with her usual midday meal of canned soup, stale soda crackers, and a banana that had seen better days. Lying fully clothed on top of the bedclothes, Miss Dimple lifted her head weakly from the pillow and asked him to take it away.

"What's the matter with you?" he said, setting the tray on the table. "There's nothing wrong with this food. You have to eat, you know."

"No, I most certainly do not. The very smell of it makes me ill. Please take it out of my sight." She uttered the last sentence in a rasping voice that grew weaker with each word and let her head fall back on the pillow. Earlier, Miss Dimple had made a thick lather with the Ivory

Soap in her bathroom and let it dry on her face, then wiped it away leaving a powdery dusting. She coughed daintily and closed her eyes.

"Well, look, what is it you do eat? You're not sick, are you?"

She turned her face away as she heard his footsteps approaching, creeping cautiously as if he were afraid she might be contagious. "You have to eat," he said again. "You'll be sick if you don't . . . you could starve."

Miss Dimple fluttered her eyelids and allowed a low moan to escape her pale, dry lips. She had no intention of starving. She had saved an apple from an earlier meal, dry cereal from her breakfast the day before, and a slice of buttered bread from last night's supper, and stored them in a fruit jar beneath the underwear in her dresser drawer.

"I wouldn't be surprised if I were contagious," she croaked. "Weakness . . . loss of appetite . . . you'll know when it happens to you."

She heard his impatient intake of breath as he turned away, heard him pace to the stairs; she counted his steps as he moved to the outside wall where the small high windows let in cobweb-filtered light, then back to the table where he'd left the tray. "Then tell me what you want and I'll try to get it," he said through his teeth, and Dimple Kilpatrick knew by her captor's tone of voice that if he didn't need her alive, he would gladly lock her away in this dank room with no hope of ever being found.

Sitting on the side of her bed, she took paper and pen from her handbag to make a list of some of the ingredients she used in her muffins, hoping that the person who held her hostage wasn't aware that Dimple Kilpatrick was identified by her Victory Muffins almost as closely as Wimpy in the Popeye comic strip was famed for his love of hamburgers.

She gave him the list when she finished and watched him while he read it.

"Soy flour!" he exclaimed. "Where in the world do I find that?" He mumbled as he read: "Whole grain cereal, light molasses, raisins, whole wheat flour, honey, dried figs . . . dried figs? Are you being serious?"

Miss Dimple nodded solemnly. "I most certainly am. You'll not find a better aid for digestion, and I can tell by the way you walk you're not eating the right kind of foods. It's in the slope of your shoulders. I had a cousin who walked like you do. Planned to be a doctor . . ." She shook her head. "Such a shame!"

"I don't care about your blasted cousin—" he began.

"Of course if Mr. Cooper doesn't have the figs, I've sometimes substituted dried apples. And a dash of cinnamon if you have it," she said, ignoring him. "Oh, and don't forget the tray!" she added as he turned to leave.

When he'd brought her breakfast of lumpy oatmeal that morning she'd made a point of thanking him for remembering her tea. It wasn't ginger mint but it was hot and it was good. She wondered where he'd gotten it. Now, Miss Dimple sat in her chair near the gas heater counting the colored rings in the braided rug at her feet: blue, red, green, yellow, purple, and then blue again. Is this what she had come to? She closed her eyes and recited aloud the whole of "Thanatopsis," by William Cullen Bryant, a poem about death she'd had to learn in school. Miss Dimple shuddered. Death? What on earth was she thinking? There must be some way to call attention to her plight, and taking a careful inventory of the room, she was struck with an idea. It might not work, but one had to try.

"You're back!" Charlie met Geneva with a hug in the hallway. "I didn't think you'd be here until Monday."

Geneva rubbed her head. "Well, the lump's going down, so now I just have half a headache."

Charlie gently touched the tender knot. "Wow! That must've been some limb that fell."

"Fell, nothing!" Geneva muttered. "Whatever hit me had some elbow grease behind it."

After their janitor's death and Miss Dimple's disappearance,

Charlie thought she was prepared for just about anything, but she gasped in spite of herself. "Did you have a chance to see who it might've been?"

Geneva unlocked the door of her room and unloaded a stack of papers onto her desk. "I thought I saw somebody moving under that big magnolia—the one to the right of the bridge—but it was too late to turn and run." She shrugged. "I just walked a little faster and hoped it was the wind or Sam playing a trick—and then I heard footsteps behind me."

Charlie frowned. "But why? Did they take anything? Say anything?"

"Nary a mumblin' word. Must've been the strong, silent type." Geneva managed a slight grin. "Well, strong at least, and I didn't have my purse with me, so if he was after money, he was out of luck."

"I suppose you've told Bobby Tinsley about this."

"Uh-huh." Geneva nodded. "But I could tell he didn't believe me. There was a place right over the pathway where a limb had broken earlier, and maybe that *was* what hit me, only somebody used it to knock me into next week! I know the police have their hands full dealing with what happened to Miss Dimple, but Bobby as much as told me I'd have to get in line."

❦

"I just can't imagine *why*, and I haven't even gotten around to wondering *who*," Annie said when Charlie told her about her conversation with Geneva.

It was morning recess and Charlie stood at the top of the back steps watching Lee Anne Stephens jump rope at "hot pepper" forty-six times before she missed. "I think whoever hit her did it to keep her from seeing something," she said.

"Or someone," Annie added. "Do you think it could've been somebody she knew?"

"Anybody's my guess," Charlie said. "What about Elwin? He lives in the same house as you. Any idea where he was at about that time Wednesday night?"

Annie laughed. "Miss Phoebe doesn't require us to sign in," she reminded her, "but several of us did start a game of Monopoly after supper. I remember Velma asking Elwin if he wanted to play but he said he had a letter to mail and wanted to get it to the post office so it would go out the next morning."

"Do you remember what time he left?"

"It was already dark but he didn't take his car. Said he didn't want to waste the gas and needed the exercise," Annie said.

Charlie thought for a minute. "I wish we knew more about him. There's something kind of secretive about Elwin. He never talks about where he came from or where he lived before now . . . there must be some way we could find out . . ."

"Oh, no, you don't! I know what you're thinking, Charlie Carr, so don't even look my way!"

"Did I say anything?" Charlie pretended innocence. "But it would only take a minute to slip into his room while he's out. We might find *something* we could go on."

"*We*? You mean *me*, don't you? And just what do you expect to find? I wish you'd leave poor Aunt Mildred alone! If Elwin Vickery is an enemy spy, he sure has a darn good cover . . . and what am I supposed to do if he walks in?"

"That's where I come in," Charlie said. "I'll stand guard in the hall and—

"Marshall Dodd, don't you even think about throwing that rock! Put it down this minute!

"Naturally we'd have to wait until everybody's busy doing something else," she continued.

Annie shook her head. "What about Jesse Dean? Didn't you tell me your neighbor said he'd been prowling around her house after dark? And surely you haven't given up on Amos Schuler."

"Jesse Dean has an excuse. He's taken Uncle Ed's route as an air-raid warden and was just checking out the territory."

"So he says." Annie rolled her eyes.

"And I think Mama and Aunt Lou have put the fear of God into Amos—for a while at least." Charlie laughed, remembering. "After they trailed him all the way to the end of nowhere, if he really is up to something, you'd think he'd be afraid to try anything right away."

The bell rang just then and the children scurried to be first in line.

"Well, whatever we do will have to wait until tomorrow," Annie said, clapping her hands for order. "Stop that shoving, Pricilla Jean!

"I intend to spend what little free time we have today getting ready for our Thanksgiving party for the troops, but for now, 'I go, and it is done—the bell invites me,'" she added with a flair.

$\mathcal{R}$

"Well, hi there, sugar! Are you rationed?" The young soldier looked as if he had barely started to shave and stood almost a foot shorter than Charlie. "I'm not today," she said, and smiling, took his arm and led him to the punch table. His name was Paul and he was from a little town in Nebraska. Charlie danced with him to Dinah Shore's "Blues in the Night" and part of Glenn Miller's "At Last" before a tall red-haired soldier from Tennessee cut in. Alvin, she quickly learned, played basketball in high school, had an aunt who once met Eleanor Roosevelt, and apparently never tired of dancing. After the fourth number, Charlie begged for a break and passed him along to Annie. "Here's somebody who likes to dance as much as you do," she said as the two whirled onto the floor to "The Jersey Bounce." After two cups of punch and an exchange of addresses with a serious young GI from Oklahoma, Charlie searched for the two on the dance floor but Alvin was dancing cheek to cheek with Loretta Scoggins, who clerked at the drugstore and Annie was deep in conversation with a dark-haired lieutenant who couldn't seem to take his eyes from her face.

"Well, hi-de-ho! What's buzzin', cousin?" Charlie allowed herself to be led onto the floor by Skipper, an amiable sort from Kentucky who had dropped out of his junior year in college to enlist in the army. In the following hour, she danced with a "Biscuit," a "Skeeter," and a "June Bug." She discussed movies with "Topeka Tom," and with "Doc," the pre-med student with earnest face and ready smile, talked of all the places they'd never been but would someday like to visit. Like personal trophies, their names had been earned and were as much a part of them as the color of their eyes, the way their ears stuck out or their hair grew. Labels of love, the nicknames had been given to them by the friends and family who knew them best and wanted them safely home.

During a quiet moment Charlie shared family photographs with a young father who had left a wife and two small children in a small Ohio town, and listened as he told her of his toddler son's first words and his daughter's first-grade accomplishments. "My wife's parents live just a few blocks away," he added, in an obvious attempt to be positive, "so I know they'll be in good hands. I just wish I could be there for Christmas." The soldier turned away, his voice thick with emotion, and Charlie was at a loss to comfort him.

"I hope by next Christmas you'll all be home," she said softly.

He put the pictures back in his wallet and nodded. "They know I had to go," he said, and smiled. "Something sure smells good. I could eat a bear!"

Charlie laughed. "I hate to disappoint you but we're having turkey."

She looked for Annie and saw her still with the dark-haired officer dancing to Frank Sinatra's "Night and Day." Annie's partner was so tall the top of her head barely came to his shoulder but she didn't seem to mind. When Emmaline barked that it was time to find a seat for dinner, the two didn't even seem to notice when the music stopped.

Annie introduced him as they moved through the serving line. He was a Georgia boy named Frazier Duncan and had earned his engineering degree from Georgia Tech. Charlie found herself sitting between Doc and Skeeter during the meal, and wasn't surprised when Frazier found a place beside Annie.

When the dinner was over, somebody put on Bing Crosby's new record of "White Christmas" and those who knew the words joined in. After exchanging thanks, good-byes and a lot of addresses, the men filed out to board the train for Columbus and Fort Benning.

"What are you smiling about?" Annie asked as they helped return serving dishes to their rightful owners and folded tables to put the room back in order.

"I'll have you know I'm the cat's meow," Charlie informed her. "At least that's what I was told."

"Well don't flip your wig," Annie told her. "According to Alvin from Tennessee, not only am I a killer-diller but I'm cooking with gas."

"Is that good?" Charlie stood on a chair to take down a banner.

"I'd like to think so," Annie said, laughing, but her smile faded as she picked up a poster promoting the sale of war bonds that had fallen to the floor. On it a young soldier with a bandaged head asked, DOING ALL YOU CAN, BROTHER?

❧

When they finally finished cleaning up, Charlie went through the slips of paper she had tucked into her purse. "I must have five addresses here. Hope I can keep up with them." She glanced at Annie. "And how many did you collect?"

Annie grinned. "Just one."

"I think I can guess who that would be. You two really seemed to hit it off. What's Will going to say?"

Annie shrugged. "Will and I aren't exactly serious, you know. Besides, Frazier was our guest. I was just being a good hostess."

"You certainly were!" Charlie laughed. "I don't think the two of you even noticed anybody else in the room."

"Oh, don't be silly! I doubt if I'll ever hear from him," Annie said, flushing.

It was dark as they walked home together and Charlie turned up her collar against the chill in the air. She was tired, but it had been a successful party and everyone seemed to have a good time. As she and Annie parted at Miss Phoebe's it occurred to her that they had spent an entire evening without once mentioning Miss Dimple's disappearance.

CHAPTER SEVENTEEN

Jesse Dean brushed his hair as soon as the siren sounded. Although he would be wearing a helmet, he felt he should be as properly groomed as the servicemen he saw passing through. He wished air-raid wardens were required to wear uniforms, but at least the helmet and arm band gave him some distinction. He looked in the mirror once more to be sure his "smile could pass the test" as the advertisements for Ipana Toothpaste warned. Surely the colored striped toothpaste was the best deterrent to the dreaded "pink" that seemed to terrify the curly haired lady in the magazine ads. He hurriedly screwed the top back on the plastic tube, remembering when not too long ago toothpaste—and many other things—had come in metal containers. You couldn't buy anything made of metal now, or rubber. Tires were made of synthetic material prone to punctures and blow-outs, and even pencil erasers made ugly black marks on the paper.

Stepping back from the mirror, Jesse Dean adjusted his bow tie. It was green with brown stripes, which was as close to military colors as he could find. He didn't have to wear a tie at all, but he thought it made him look more responsible and self-assured. There was no doubt that people seemed to take him seriously when he knocked on their doors to warn them about a showing of light. Jesse Dean was strict about that. He took his job seriously.

Fingering the metal whistle around his neck, Jesse Dean began his rounds, and was pleased to see the streets dark and empty. The party for the troops in the old appliance store had been over for almost an hour so everyone should've had a chance to get home. Quickly—or as quickly as possible for Jesse Dean—he walked the streets of the town. Downtown was as silent as Cemetery Hill and most houses loomed in utter blackness. At the Sullivans' house across from Phoebe Chadwick's, a glimmer of light peeped through an upstairs window. The new baby was probably suffering from colic, he thought as he rang the front doorbell, and sure enough, young Mrs. Sullivan answered the door with a crying baby in her arms, looking as if she hadn't slept in a week.

"I'm sorry to bother you," he began, "but there's a light—"

"Oh! Of course. I'll take care of it. Thank you for letting me know," she said, not giving him time to finish. And seconds later the light was extinguished. Jesse Dean smiled as he walked away. She knew he was doing his part. He walked a little straighter.

He had made a circle now and was at the end of his rounds near the park when he saw the car. It was partially hidden by an overgrown hedge in the alley beside the library at one end of the park and it hadn't been there before . . . or had it? There seemed to be someone inside, maybe more than one, but he didn't want to turn on his flashlight unless it was absolutely necessary. Still, the car was parked very near to the place where Geneva Odom had been struck down only two nights before. Jesse Dean crossed the street to get a closer look. The car didn't look familiar but it was hard to tell. In the darkness they all looked pretty much alike. People weren't supposed to park here but they weren't showing any lights. Probably a sparking couple, Jesse Dean thought. Well, it was none of his business. Let Bobby Tinsley worry about it. He started to move on but curiosity got the better of him. What if it was the person who attacked that teacher? He could at least give them the number of the license plate.

Creeping closer, Jesse Dean reached for the flashlight that hung from his belt and felt for the switch with his finger, but before he could turn on the light, the car's engine came to life, and with a grinding of gears, the driver took off into the night.

Jesse Dean stood watching the car as it was swallowed in the surrounding darkness. The feeble flashlight beam was of little use now. Whoever was driving was in one great hurry to get away, he thought. They were driving with no headlights.

❧

"I can't come here anymore," the visitor said. "It's too risky. After that little scene in the park the other night they'll be keeping a close watch over there."

"It wasn't my idea to hit that woman over the head," Mr. Smith answered. "It's a wonder she wasn't hurt worse than she was."

The visitor laughed. "What did you expect me to do? Another few steps and she would've seen you."

"I didn't agree to this—to kill people."

"A little late for that, isn't it? And now we're going to have to speed things along."

"We? Isn't that supposed to be your job? I've got the woman just like we planned. It's up to you to deal with her brother."

"I gave him the proof he demanded—that note in her handwriting and the pin she claimed belonged to her mother. Now he's playing us for time and time is running out! If that doesn't convince him, we can see how he responds if we send him a whole finger!"

Mr. Smith tried not to show his revulsion. He hadn't been feeling so well lately—throat definitely felt scratchy. He was probably coming down with something, but it was too late to back out now, and besides, he was afraid of what might happen to him if he did. "I don't think I'll be able to stay here much longer," he said. "You know the situation."

His visitor shrugged. "Then take care of it. The colonel's getting impatient and I told them we'd have those plans by December. I suggest you take a look at your calendar."

"Didn't you tell me Hugh said Elwin Vickery owned a house somewhere in the country?" Annie asked over breakfast the next morning. Odessa didn't cook for Miss Phoebe on Saturdays so the roomers usually helped themselves to cereal and toast in the kitchen. Today, Charlie had invited her friend over for waffles, which was the only decent thing her mother could make.

Jo Carr poured batter into the sizzling iron and closed the lid. "I believe he bought the old Brumlow property out on the Covington Highway. Hugh's uncle Martin owned it for the longest time. Raised cotton out there. I don't know what in the world that fellow would want with it as far out as it is."

Charlie glanced at Annie who pretended innocence and made a point of sipping from her cup, but her sharp-eyed mother knew a furtive look when she saw one. "Why?" she asked, frowning. "Why are you two interested in that old empty house?"

It took only a few seconds for the light to dawn and she thumped the honey jar on the table with a bang that made the dishes jump. "You think Miss Dimple's being held out there, don't you?"

Charlie groaned aloud. "Mama, everything we mention doesn't necessarily have something to do with what happened to Miss Dimple. I'll swear, you're getting as carried away over this as Aunt Lou . . . and hadn't you better check those waffles before they burn?"

"Speaking of Lou," her mother said, "she'd never forgive me if we went without her. I'd better let her know we're going . . . and snatch that waffle out, will you, honey?"

Frowning, Charlie did as she was told. "Going where?" Of course she knew.

"Why, to find Miss Dimple, naturally. I'd never forgive myself if that poor soul was being held prisoner out in that God-forsaken place and we didn't do something to help her." And she shut the kitchen door firmly behind her as she hurried to phone her sister.

Charlie forked the crisp waffle onto Annie's plate and passed her the margarine. "Now, why did you have to go and mention that?" she asked crossly.

"Just think about it, Charlie. It only makes sense to check there *first*. I refuse to invade that poor man's privacy by snooping in his room unless we have a darn good reason." Annie scooted her chair closer to the table and reached for the honey. "There's no telling what we might find in there."

"That's exactly why I wanted to check out his room at Phoebe's," Charlie insisted. "We might discover something that would lead us to where she is."

"If Elwin really does have anything to do with it, she must be at that house he owns," Annie said. "And we should be okay if we hurry. He said he planned to work on something at his office this morning."

"He *said* . . . hmm, maybe we oughta let Bobby handle it." Charlie ladled more spoonfuls of batter into the hot iron. "I mean, if she really is being held there, it could be dangerous."

"We wouldn't have to go in," Annie said. "We could just sort of ride by and try to get a closer look, see if it looks like anyone's there. . . . Is there enough of that batter for us to have more?"

⬧

Aunt Lou, who had insisted on driving, slowed as they passed a produce stand by the side of the road. Although the air was brisk, the mid-morning sun shone brightly in a blue November sky. "Remind me to stop here on our way back," she said. "I'd like to get a couple of small pumpkins and maybe a few ears of dried corn for the Thanksgiving table."

"Since I won't be able to bring anything to help out with dinner, why not let that be my contribution?" Annie suggested. "It's generous of you to include the three of us, and I know it will be a special treat for my brother and Will."

"This will be our pleasure," Lou protested. "If I could, I would invite the whole United States Army."

"What about the navy and marines?" Charlie asked.

Her aunt laughed. "Them, too."

They passed a farmer on a combine harvesting fodder for the winter, and farther down the road a man in a big straw hat plowed under bare brown stalks of what had been a cotton field, now picked clean. Charlie drank in the peaceful landscape, knowing it was deceptive. The two farmers were doing what they had to do so that life could go on as usual. Did they have sons in the war? Did they dread the hateful telegram as she did? If only things could be as they were before! Earlier she had received her first letter from Hugh. Fairly brief, it was composed mostly of a description of his first jolting days, the food, and the barracks. His bunkmate was called "Slim." That figured, Charlie thought with a grin. *Our picnic together was a perfect send-off,* Hugh wrote, *and sharing it with you made it even more special.* He had signed his name *with love,* and Charlie filed his letter away in an empty candy box until she had a chance to read it again.

"I think that place is just a mile or so past this country store up ahead," her mother pointed out. "It's on the right if I remember correctly. Help me watch, now. Don't let us go past it."

"That must be it where that car is turning out," Lou said a few minutes later. "Right past that big pine tree . . . looks like the mailbox is about to fall down." She coughed as the passing car kicked up red dust on the dry unpaved road.

"Wait a minute! That looks like Cornelia's car!" Annie turned to look out the window. "It *is!* What's she doing out here?"

Lou slowed and glanced at her over her shoulder. "Cornelia? Who's she?"

"Cornelia Emerson," Charlie explained. "She's teaching Miss Dimple's class, and it did look like her, Annie, but are you sure that's her car?"

"Had to be. There was a dent in her back left fender where Velma backed into it in Phoebe's driveway the other day. But what in the world would she be doing out here?"

"Maybe the same thing we are," Jo answered. "Unless, of course, she's lost."

"'There are more things in heaven and earth, Horatio, than are dreamt of . . .'" Annie muttered under her breath.

Charlie recognized the lines from *Hamlet* and smiled. Her friend was fond of quoting Shakespeare from time to time. "What's that supposed to mean?" she whispered.

"Tell you later," Annie said.

Weeds grew knee-high on either side of the battered mailbox and brushed the underside of the car as they turned into the rutted drive.

"Sure doesn't look like anybody's been living here for a while," Jo said, wincing as a scraggly bush scraped the door on the passenger side. "Louise Willingham, don't you dare get us stuck out here at the end of nowhere!"

"It was your idea to come," her sister reminded her. "Look, there's the house—or what's left of it. Porch has just about fallen in. I can't see anybody using this place for much of anything."

"I can't, either," Charlie said. "Let's go." She was beginning to feel uneasy and there was only one way out.

Her aunt ignored her. "I just want to see what's around back," she said, bumping over ruts in the weed-grown yard.

The same thing that's around front, Charlie thought. But she was wrong. Someone had obviously begun work on rebuilding the back porch. Steps that still smelled of fresh pine led up to a partially refloored porch and what appeared to be new shutters hung at the four rear windows. Remnants of lumber filled a wooden box beside the door.

"I'm going to see if anyone's home," Annie said, and slipped out of the car before Charlie could stop her. She watched as Annie knocked several times at the sturdy oak door, then peered in one of the windows and motioned for Charlie to join her.

"Keep the motor running," Charlie told her aunt, and tried not to think of the waste of precious fuel.

They looked into a kitchen bare of everything except a rust-stained sink, an ancient woodstove, a small table, and two mismatched chairs. "There's no place like home," Charlie said. "Can we go now?"

But Annie had moved to the windows on the other side of the door. "Shoot! The shades are down." She tapped on the glass. "Can't see a thing."

"How inconsiderate of them," Charlie said as she started back down the steps.

"It seems that Elwin or somebody is renovating this old place," Lou called from the car. "Maybe he plans to live here."

"Or rent it to someone else," Jo added. "Did you see any signs of Miss Dimple?"

Annie shook her head. "No, but it looks like somebody's been using that kitchen."

"Really? I didn't see anything. How could you tell?" Charlie asked.

"Didn't you notice those dirty dishes piled in the sink? Most un-Elwin-like, though. I knocked on a window to see if I'd get a response, but of course she might not be able to call out," Annie said.

The idea of the serene and steadfast teacher she had admired since childhood being treated in such a way made Charlie want to kick in the windows and charge inside. She turned and studied the house. "Do you think she could be down here?" she asked, noticing small basement windows below the back porch. Not waiting for an answer, she snatched up a stray scrap of lumber and beat a pathway through the weeds to see inside.

"See anything?" Annie asked behind her.

"Not much. Looks empty." Charlie shoved aside a clutching weed before realizing it had thorns. "Ouch! Watch out for the blackberry bramble." Squatting, she looked inside. "Wait, there're several boxes—packing crates, I think—and something that looks like an umbrella stand. That's about it."

"Of course Elwin would have an umbrella stand," Annie said grinning, "but I don't see any signs of anybody being held down here."

"Well, I'm hollering anyway," Charlie said, and did. "What do you think Cornelia has to do with this?" she asked as they brushed themselves off. "It looks to me like Elwin started remodeling this house, and for some reason, stopped. I suppose he could be planning to sell the place to her." She lowered her voice. "And what did you mean back there with that quote about Horatio?"

"It's about Cornelia," Annie whispered. "I haven't had a chance to tell you what happened last night. She said she was going to bed early . . . made kind of a big issue of it I thought. We were all tired from the Thanksgiving party but several of us stayed up to listen to *Lum and Abner* on the radio, you know how funny they are—"

"I know, I know. Go on!"

"I didn't go up until after the news, and the door of her room was closed so I assumed she'd gone to sleep. It must've been about two o'clock when I got up to go to the bathroom—all that coffee, you know—and from the bathroom window I saw Cornelia coming across the back lawn."

"At that hour? I wonder where she was going," Charlie said.

"I don't know, but I'm sure there was 'a method in her madness,' and she wasn't *going*, she was *coming*! She must have cut across underneath that weeping willow in the Elrods' yard so she wouldn't be seen, and she didn't take her car, so she must have gone out to meet somebody. I ran and got back in bed when I heard her come upstairs." Annie made a face. "Something tells me it wouldn't be a good thing if Cornelia Emerson found out I saw her."

CHAPTER EIGHTEEN

The sound of voices woke her. She wasn't accustomed to hearing people talking in this place. Miss Dimple sat up in bed and listened. There were two of them; one she recognized as her jailer but they were speaking so low she couldn't identify the other. She had turned down the heater for the night and the room was damp and cold. Heated or not, it made little difference. She was living in a basement. It smelled like a basement, felt like a basement, and if she wandered too far from the heated area, the dankness seemed to permeate her very core.

Miss Dimple wrapped a quilt about her and felt for her shoes in the dark. She had seen cockroaches on several occasions and had almost stepped on one before she learned to look first. The nasty, disgusting beetles scurried away when she turned on the light but tonight she didn't want anyone to know she was awake. She felt her way across the room and stood silently at the bottom of the steps listening to snatches of muted conversation. It didn't sound friendly.

Miss Dimple took a step up, and then another. From the cadence of what was being said, she guessed they were arguing—probably about her. If only she could hear what they were saying! Should she dare *venture farther? Dimple Kilpatrick put one tentative foot on the next step and the board beneath her groaned and creaked with such a racket that she jumped in spite of herself. Surely they must've heard it. She froze where she stood, clutching the handrail and hardly daring to breathe until the sound of the voices diminished and footsteps moved away.*

Creeping quietly down the stairs, Miss Dimple waited until she heard a door close and the sound of a car driving away. She knew she had to do something soon. Tomorrow she would put her plan into action.

❦

"What time?" Charlie asked Annie after church the next morning.

"I really don't feel comfortable about this, Charlie. Are you sure this is necessary?"

"You saw that house yesterday and said yourself it would be the perfect place to hide somebody away. And what about those dirty dishes you saw?"

"But who knows how long they've been there." Annie shrugged. "From the looks of them, probably since the house was built! We didn't actually see anything that would lead us to believe anybody's *staying* there." She grabbed at her pert green hat with a feather in it to keep it from blowing away.

The service had lasted a little longer than usual since it was the Sunday before Thanksgiving, and after the sermon the choir had led the congregation in a number of patriotic songs. People lingered in clusters on the lawn talking mostly of war. *Have you heard from Sonny lately . . . my goodness, all the way to California . . . we expect them to ship out soon . . . so handsome in his uniform . . . their grandson lost an arm . . . did you hear . . . Gabriel Heater says the Russians counterattacked at Stalingrad . . . we won't have a Christmas like last year . . .*

Charlie spoke to Hugh's sister Arden, as she and her mother made their way through the throng. She wanted to tell her she'd

164

heard from Hugh, but didn't want to mention it in front of Emmaline in case she hadn't received a letter, too. Arden smiled and spoke but her eyes were red and Charlie could tell she'd been crying, as were many. Their last song that morning had been the stirring and beautiful "Navy Hymn," one of Charlie's favorites, but the line about "those in peril on the sea" made her think of the men who had lost their lives during the Battle of Midway and those who would probably share the same fate in the months to come.

"We have to do it sometime today," she said, leading Annie aside. "When do you think would be the best time?"

"Tonight, I guess. He usually goes to vespers at the Episcopal Church after supper, and most of the others will be listening to the radio. Fred Allen's on tonight and they never miss Edgar Bergen and Charlie McCarthy. Why don't you plan to come over about seven—and don't forget your magnifying glass, Nancy Drew!"

"What are you two laughing about?" Virginia Balliew waved to them as she approached and Charlie was glad she didn't persevere with her question. "I wanted to let you know that Bobby finally collected that scrap of yarn I found but I doubt if anything will come of it."

"What makes you think that?" Charlie asked, although she wasn't surprised.

"I got the definite idea he wanted me to back off," Virginia said. "Said it would be best if I just let the police handle things."

Annie shook her head. "Well, it's a good thing they're not *handling* the war or we'd all be speaking German!"

Charlie had fried a chicken and made creamed potatoes earlier that day and the whole house greeted them with a mouthwatering aroma when she and her mother returned from church. Both women quickly tossed hats and gloves on the hall table on their way to the kitchen, and Jo spooned potatoes into a casserole dish, spread melted margarine over the top, and put them in the oven to brown while Charlie took a Waldorf salad from the Frigidaire and set the table with her mother's fragile rose-patterned china. They had invited Bessie Jenkins to join them but she had declined as Ollie was treating her to dinner out. Bessie would drive, of course.

"Guess what Lily Moss told me at church today?" Jo said, taking threadbare linen napkins from a drawer.

Charlie looked up. "No tellin'."

"I know you and Annie made a big joke out of Lou and me following Amos Schuler the other day," her mother said, "but there might be more to that than you think."

Charlie didn't answer. She was still trying to figure out what Lily Moss had to do with Amos Schuler.

"Seems somebody told Lily what happened to us," she said with a glaring look at her daughter. "It wasn't you, was it? I'll swear," Jo continued, "you just can't keep a secret in this town! Anyway, Lily told me Amos had it in for Miss Dimple for holding back his grandson last year. Lily said he even went to the school board and tried to get Dimple fired."

Charlie filled the coffeepot with water. "If she held him back, I'm sure she had a good reason. I didn't know Boyd even had a son."

"Married fairly young, I think. Too young! Didn't last long. The couple divorced a short time later, and then Boyd went off and got himself into all that trouble in Atlanta, but Amos dotes on that little boy. If I'm not mistaken the child and his mother live out there with the Schulers."

"What's his name? I'd probably know him," Charlie said. She was familiar with most of Miss Dimple's students.

But her mother shook her head. "From what Lily says, they took him out of Elderberry and enrolled him somewhere else—some private school in Henry County. At any rate, there doesn't seem to be any love lost between Dimple Kilpatrick and Amos Schuler."

Charlie remembered what the milkman had said about almost backing over the teacher and how he'd pretended not to know her name. What if he had killed her, accidentally or otherwise, on one of her early-morning walks? They would never find her body on the Schuler farm, partially covered in dense woods and undergrowth. Suddenly she seemed to have lost her appetite.

"Do you really think he would?" Annie asked when Charlie told her later what her mother had said. "Kill somebody, I mean."

"I hope not, but I'm glad Mama and Aunt Lou didn't get in the truck with him the other day. They might've disappeared, too."

Several of Miss Phoebe's roomers were eating a light supper of sandwiches and potato salad in the dining room when Charlie walked the few blocks over that night, but she found Annie in the kitchen washing the dishes she had used and stacking them in the drain. Everyone was responsible for their own cleanup on Sunday nights so Odessa could go to meeting. Elwin, she said, had already left for church.

"Come on up, and I'll see if I can find that book I was telling you about," Annie said in a voice loud enough for the diners to hear. Aside to Charlie she whispered, "We'll wait until everybody's gone into the living room to listen to the radio. *Charlie McCarthy* comes on in a few minutes and just about everybody listens to that."

From Annie's room at the top of the stairs they soon heard the announcer's familiar voice hawking Chase and Sanborn Coffee followed by the ventriloquist's clever conversation with Charlie McCarthy, and even listening to it from a distance, the two friends exchanged smiles. The dummy with top hat and monocle seemed like a real person to most. They were halfway downstairs when Cornelia Emerson passed them going the other way.

"You're going to miss *Charlie McCarthy*," Annie said as the woman approached.

The new teacher shrugged. "Too many papers to grade. Guess I should learn to budget my time more wisely."

They hesitated until they heard her door close behind her before continuing. Elwin's room was the first door to the right just behind the stairs, and the two crept cautiously through the hallway, avoiding the living room where Velma Anderson's distinctive whinnying laughter could be heard above everyone else's.

Charlie darted a look upstairs. "Do you think Cornelia suspects what we're doing?"

Annie shook her head. "Why should she? But I'd like to know what *she's* up to! I don't think she noticed us when she passed us yesterday or I believe she would've said something."

"She was in too much of a hurry," Charlie said. "Do you think we should mention it to her? I'm dying to find out what she was doing out there."

"I can't figure that one out," Annie said. "Maybe we ought to wait . . . give it a little time."

But Miss Dimple might not *have* much time, Charlie thought as she stood guard outside Elwin Vickery's room. The door wasn't locked, Annie explained, so that Odessa and Bob Robert's niece, Violet, could get in to clean a couple of times a week, and Charlie couldn't resist a quick look inside. She found the room as neat and immaculate as she expected it to be. The bed was made with a blanket of a colorful Indian design folded neatly at the foot. Books jammed the shelves under his window and black-and-white photographs of the Grand Canyon and the cacti and mesas of the desert area hung in an orderly row above his bed.

Waiting outside the room, Charlie heard Annie open and close a drawer, and then another. She stiffened as the treads creaked over her head as someone from the living room hurried upstairs. "I'd better get my glasses if I'm going to work on that embroidery," Velma said, and Charlie heard her footsteps returning soon after. All the guest rooms except Elwin's were on the second floor, but Phoebe's room was next to his at the end of the hall. What if Phoebe decided to go back to her room or to the kitchen? There was no way she would miss seeing her. She took a deep breath and pressed her back against the wall. *Maybe this wasn't such a good idea after all!*

When the air-raid siren went off a few seconds later, she was absolutely sure.

"Quick! Somebody get the hall light," Miss Phoebe called from the living room.

"Oh, dear! I'll draw the blackout curtain," Lily offered in a quivering voice. "We just had a drill a few nights ago. Do you think this might be the real thing?"

"Annie and Cornelia will take care of things upstairs," Phoebe said, ignoring her, "but I guess we'd better check and see if Elwin left a light on."

"I'll do it," Velma offered, and, hearing her footsteps approaching, Charlie quickly slipped inside the door and switched off the light. "Velma's coming! Hide somewhere—hurry!" she called under her breath, and almost collided with Annie as they headed for the closet.

They heard Velma call out that the room was okay and the door closed behind her. "That was close!" Annie whispered. "I hope she couldn't see the desk drawer I left open. I didn't have time to close it."

"Then let's close it now and get out of here while it's still dark." Charlie felt her way across the room to where she remembered seeing the desk and gave the open drawer a shove. It squeaked.

"Aw—applesauce!" Annie groaned beside her. "Here, let me help," and together they managed to shut the drawer without further protests. They were on their way to the door when they heard voices just outside in the hallway.

"Is that you, Elwin? I thought you were at vespers," Miss Phoebe called from what sounded like the kitchen. "We're in here if you can find your way to join us."

"I was halfway to church when the siren sounded, so I decided to come on back here," Elwin answered. "Just let me get rid of this coat and I'll be right there."

Where else would you hang a coat? Charlie wondered from her hiding place in the closet. She huddled behind what felt like a wool jacket that made her want to sneeze and wondered where Annie had fled. This had really, really, really been a rotten idea!

CHAPTER NINETEEN

*M*iss Dimple was ready when she heard the car approaching. The first time she had done this had been many years ago on a fine, sunny day in May. She had gathered her small students on one of the rare grassy areas on the school playground with a large bowl of soapsuds and lopsided wands fashioned from wire. The children laughed and tried to catch bubbles like tiny rainbows as they floated over the school grounds bursting in midair. She had explained to the class about the colors in the spectrum and refraction of light, and wasn't sure at the time if any of them would ever remember what she'd told them. But she hoped as they slogged now through mud and freezing cold, or pitched about on an angry sea in some fierce and hostile land, that they might recall the beauty of the day, the gossamer bubbles drifting to the trees, and the blessed peace of being in such a place.

She had been working on the window for several days, first carefully removing the broken corner of the glass so that it could be reinserted without looking noticeably different from the rest of the window. The rusted grille had been made of stronger material and Miss Dimple had to wait until she knew he had left before pounding one of the slender metal bars with an empty Coca-Cola bottle—one of several stored in a wooden case in an unused corner of the basement room—until the weathered metal finally bent and broke. She had never really cared for soft drinks before. The carbonation brought a most uncomfortable feeling of effervescence—as if one might explode—but she was beginning to change her mind about the drink's usefulness.

The idea had come to her as she was rinsing her underwear in the bathroom sink, and she remembered that a wire clothes hanger, with one end bent to the approximate circumference of a fifty-cent piece, would make an acceptable bubble wand. Now, with a drinking cup frothing with suds, she climbed onto the table by the window and stood on a chair to put it to the test. The vehicle had pulled into the driveway on the other side of the house. Because of the loud, chugging noise, she thought it was probably an older car or maybe a truck. Possibly a delivery van of some sort, or the rural carrier bringing a package. Miss Dimple had heard it on several occasions, and this time she was ready.

It took only a second to remove the small wedge of glass from the window, and setting it carefully aside, Miss Dimple dipped her improvised wand in the suds, stood on her tiptoes, and sent bubbles the size of walnuts into the cold morning air. Minutes passed before the car door slammed and the rattling engine started up again. Oh, please look this way! Just once . . . please, please look this way! She had tried yelling, hollering at the top of her voice, but she was too far away for anyone to hear her.

Miss Dimple sent another flight of the delicate orbs skyward. Did anyone see them? All she could do now was hope.

❧

Please, God, don't let the lights come back on! Smothered by layers of jackets that smelled strongly of mothballs, Charlie backed into the closet until there was nowhere left to go. The door opened and she heard him fumbling in the darkness for a hanger. Metal hangers were in short supply now and people who ran the laundry and dry cleaners offered a penny for every one that came in. Most people, including Elwin, she noticed, had started draping two or three garments together.

Wouldn't you know Elwin would have to hang up his coat properly, Charlie thought. Anybody else would've just thrown it on the bed, but apparently the man was satisfied with his efforts and at last closed the door firmly behind him. Still Charlie didn't move.

"Are you in there?" Annie asked a few minutes later in a voice so low Charlie could barely hear her. Only then did she shove aside the clothing and venture from her hiding place.

"I thought I was going to suffocate!" Charlie gasped, taking a deep breath. "And I was terrified that he would see you. Where in the world did you hide?"

"Under the bed, and there was a metal footlocker or something under there. I think I have a knot on my head," Annie complained as they made their way to the door. "And if you get any more big ideas, Charlie Carr, you can count me out!"

"All this trouble and we didn't learn a thing," Charlie grumbled under her breath. "It wasn't even worth the effort."

"That's what you think," Annie said as they stepped quietly into the dark hallway and shut the door behind them.

"What do you mean?"

"Annie, is that you?" Miss Phoebe called from the kitchen. "I found some molasses cookies Odessa had hidden away and we're in here having an air-raid party."

"Sounds like 'a dish fit for the gods.' We were getting lonely upstairs," Annie said, making her way across the hall.

"I'll tell you later," she whispered to Charlie.

"I do hope I haven't left my little bedside lamp on upstairs," Lily said when they joined the others. "You didn't notice any light coming from my room, did you?"

Annie assured her that they hadn't. "And Cornelia's still up there. I'm sure she'd notice it."

"Jesse Dean would've been pounding on the door by now if you had," Phoebe told her. "If Elderberry gets bombed at night it won't be because Jesse Dean didn't do his job."

"Oh, I wish you hadn't said that!" Lily shivered. "Now I probably won't sleep a wink all night."

"Well, I, for one, plan to go to bed early," Velma said. "Those children are going to be wild for the next three days with Thanksgiving coming up this week."

"I'm glad you mentioned that," Annie said. "I still haven't bought my contribution to the basket for Paschall Kiker. Does anybody have an idea what he might need?"

"I asked Ollie," Charlie said, "but he wasn't much help. I think he's doing most of the cooking now, and I don't see how in the world he finds the time. I just brought a bag of oranges and some sweet potatoes. Anybody can bake a potato."

"Poor Paschall," Phoebe quipped. "God help him!"

It had been Geneva's idea for the faculty to contribute to a Thanksgiving basket for the ailing farmer since Ollie mentioned that he didn't get about much anymore and spent a good bit of time in bed.

"Ollie said a woman who lives down the road comes in to see about him a few times a week and will fix him something to eat if Ollie can't get there in the middle of the day, but he usually manages to get back to check on him," Lily told them. "The man's conscientious, I'll have to hand it to him. That school hardly looks the same since Christmas left, bless his heart. Bessie Jenkins better grab him while she can."

"Well, Annie, I suppose you and Alice Brady will be rehearsing the children for some kind of Christmas program as soon as Thanksgiving's behind us," Phoebe said, shoving the cookie platter across the table to Elwin. "You all might as well eat these up now. Odessa's going to find out we've been into them as soon as she comes in tomorrow."

"I think Alice has something in mind, and of course I'm always glad to help, but I don't expect a big production," Annie said. "There won't be much time to rehearse before we get out for Christmas; I hate to eat the last cookie . . ."

Charlie laughed. "No, you don't!"

She knew her friend would be miserable all week if she wasn't allowed to help with the school's Christmas show, and with Annie's magic touch, it was sure to be entertaining.

"I hope you saved your icicles from last year's tree," she said to Phoebe. "Mama said they told her at the five-and-ten they wouldn't be getting any because of the war."

"You won't be seeing anything else with metal in it, either," Velma said. "My nephew has his heart set on a bicycle but I'm afraid he's going to have to wait a while for that."

And he wouldn't be by himself, Charlie thought. She had tried to soft pedal the inevitable when her third graders discussed their wish lists. Most of the children in her class believed in Santa Claus and the few who didn't had been threatened with dire consequences if they ruined another child's sugarplum dreams. Even though Santa and his elves made the toys at the North Pole, she'd explained, they had to order some of their materials from distant places. Everyone has to sacrifice for the war effort, Charlie told them—even Santa. After all, she assured them, he's on our side.

"This air-raid drill seems to be going on longer than usual, don't you think?" Lily's voice rose to a crescendo. "I do hope we're not in any kind of trouble."

As if by signal, the siren sounded alerting everyone the drill was over and Charlie had to bite her tongue to keep from congratulating Lily Moss on being allowed to live another day. All this talk of Christmas made her sad. She wondered if Fain had received the package they had sent weeks before, and where he was sleeping tonight.

The Christmas when Fain had been twelve and she, nine, her

brother had received a new red bike for Christmas and Charlie, a blue one. The two of them had tired of riding in town and at Charlie's suggestion, turned onto a dirt road leading into the country. They were gone so long their parents had driven out looking for them and they were not allowed to ride their new bikes or to eat any of their stocking candy for the rest of the week.

Charlie had told her mother it was all her brother's fault when it had really been hers. Fain had gone along with her when she refused to turn back because he didn't want her riding alone.

If only she could take it back!

When Charlie got home that night she wrote a six-page letter to Fain and told him she was sorry. She also wrote to Hugh and to a couple of the men who gave her their addresses at the town's Thanksgiving party for the troops, and had every intention of writing more but when the lines began to blur from lack of sleep, she had to call it a night.

It didn't occur to her until she finally crawled into bed that Annie never told her what she'd found in Elwin Vickery's room.

Bessie Jenkins did a turn around the Carrs' sitting room and posed in front of the fireplace. "Well, what do you think?" she asked.

"I think it's lovely," Jo said, putting aside her notes on Katie Ann Gallman's sixteenth birthday party. "Gabardine, isn't it?" She felt the material between her fingers. "And such a becoming color blue. Where in the world did you find it?"

Their neighbor smiled. "Promise you won't tell? I cut it down from an old suit of Ella's. It's been hanging in the closet for ages so I'm hoping she's forgotten about it."

"I wouldn't worry about it," Jo assured her. Bessie's younger sister had been married and gone now for at least fifteen years. "You're getting to be a regular clothes horse. Is this for some special occasion?"

"I'm having Ollie over for Thanksgiving dinner, and I wanted to look especially nice." Bessie smoothed the collar of her jacket.

Charlie, who had been in the kitchen grinding cranberries for a Thanksgiving salad, overheard her as she entered the room. "What about Paschall Kiker?" she asked. "Ollie said he wasn't doing well, so some of the teachers are getting a basket together."

"Oh, he'll have his dinner in the middle of the day, and I think Ollie's asked Aileen Spragg to come and stay with him for a while. She lives just down the road." Bessie laced her fingers together and flushed. "I'm thinking—well, I've been seeing Ollie for a good long time now and I have a feeling something's about to change. I want everything to be just right when he comes Thursday, and I wondered if you'd mind if I borrowed your silver candlesticks. They'd look perfect on my table with my grandmother's crocheted cloth, and I promise to take good care of them."

"Well, of course you can!" Laying her notepad aside, Jo Carr got up from her chair and wrapped her arms about her neighbor. "I'll even polish them for you, but I'm sure the shine of the candles won't be able to compete with the light in your eyes."

"I didn't know we were Irish," Charlie said after their neighbor left.

"Maybe a little. Your great-grandmother O'Neal on my mother's side . . ." She frowned. "What makes you mention that?"

"Because you're full of blarney! All that bit about the light in Bessie's eyes. Where'd that come from?"

"I do write for the society page," Jo reminded her. "I'll have you know I've used every adjective in the book, and probably most of the adverbs, but I do want things to go well for our Bessie. She's always been a good friend and a good neighbor, and we all could use a little flattery from time to time."

"But Ollie!" Charlie made a face. "I mean, I like him okay and he does a great job at school, but I can't see the attraction."

"The attraction is that Bessie's almost fifty and has never had many beaus. She feels comfortable with Ollie, and apparently he, with her. I imagine she's lonely, Charlie."

Charlie caught the note of sadness in her mother's voice and stooped to give her a kiss. Once in a while she forgot there were times her mother was lonely, too. She was relieved when Jo began to smile. "I remember when Ollie's father, Reece, used to work for the post office," she said, "and we were on his route. It took him forever to cover it and you never knew whose mail you were going to get. People on our street had to run back and forth to exchange letters. It got to be kind of a joke." She laughed. "Of course there was this one neighbor—Esther Tuttle—dead and gone now . . . you wouldn't remember her, but I hated for her to get our mail."

"Why was that?" Charlie asked.

"Because you knew she always read it first."

CHAPTER TWENTY

*I*t would be two weeks tomorrow! Where in the hell was she? Henry Kilpatrick fumbled for his carpet slippers in the dark and reached for his robe on the back of the chair. There was no use trying to sleep.

His wife raised her head halfway from the pillow. "What is it, Henry? It's pitch black dark . . . you're not getting up already?"

"I just want a drink of water. Go on back to sleep, Hazel." She had no idea why he hadn't been able to sleep more than a few hours since Dimple disappeared—no idea at all. Hardly anyone did. He had told his wife and her sister, Imogene, who lived with them, that Dimple had suffered a nervous breakdown and was being treated in a private sanitarium. Naturally, he explained, she didn't want the cause of her illness made known. Not that Hazel actually gave a hoot. No love lost there.

The stalwart Dimple Kilpatrick giving in to a nervous breakdown! The idea almost made him laugh. Henry made his way into his study, poured himself a brandy, and stood at the window looking out at the empty street. Those bastards better not have hurt her! If he had his way, he'd tear out of here this very minute and knock down doors to find her, but his hands were tied. As one of a select group of engineers working to improve the design of an advanced bomber, the B-29 Super-fortress, he knew he was to blame for his sister's abduction and it nearly tore him in two. Other than a few officials in the Office of Strategic Services, no one knew he had been approached to turn over the plans for the plane in exchange for his sister's safe return.

Designed to reach Japan from Pacific Island bases, the four-engine B-29 would be capable of carrying up to nine tons of bombs internally and it was only a matter of months before they hoped to put it into action. Those investigating suspected the puzzling death of the school's janitor might have something to do with his sister's abduction and had taken the town's police chief, as well as the local doctor, into their confidence on a limited basis, explaining only that Henry Kilpatrick was involved in a matter of national security. Henry Kilpatrick was a man accustomed to finding solutions, but now he was fit to be tied. He would do anything to protect the sister who had raised him—almost anything. For there was no question that he would never betray his country.

Glass in hand, Henry watched the morning steal in slowly and cursed under his breath. He wasn't surprised it had been Dimple they chose to abduct instead of Hazel, who seldom left the house except in the company of her sister Imogene. How many times had he warned Dimple about walking alone in the predawn darkness while sensible people still slept? You never knew who was about at that hour or what they were up to—and now look what had happened. Damn stubborn woman!

Henry sat in his armchair sipping his brandy and reached for his pipe. He might as well smoke for a while. He couldn't do anything else. He smiled. Hazel hated it when he smoked.

Charlie cornered Annie in the faculty restroom the Tuesday before Thanksgiving. "You have five minutes," she said, looking at her watch, "to tell me what you found out about Elwin Sunday night."

The day before, Annie had spent most of her spare time, including her lunch hour, helping Alice Brady and some of her expression students plan an impromptu program for assembly before classes were dismissed on Wednesday, and Charlie hadn't been able to find an appropriate time to approach her.

Annie peeked under the toilet cubicle to see if they were alone and ran a comb through her unruly dark curls. It seemed to Charlie her friend had been taking a lot more time with her grooming lately. "'Oh, how poor are they that have not patience!'" Annie struck a dramatic pose. "I couldn't very well call you from that telephone in Miss Phoebe's front hall, and yesterday I hardly had a minute to breathe," she told her.

"Well, you seem to be breathing now, so cut the drama," Charlie demanded. "And hurry. The bell's about to ring." Leaning against the wall, she waited while Annie added a dab of lipstick in that new color, Fighting Red, and smiled at herself in the mirror. She smiled more often than usual, Charlie thought, probably because Will was coming for Thanksgiving. Annie had told her she'd received a letter from him just the other day and that Will was looking forward to spending time with her.

"I don't think we need to worry about Elwin being involved." Annie spoke so softly Charlie had to strain to hear her. "I believe he's keeping a secret, all right, but it isn't about Miss Dimple."

"Then what—"

"Excuse me, but is anyone in the toilet?" Cornelia Emerson marched in just then, slamming the bathroom door back on its hinges. "The children will be lining up any minute and I won't have another chance to go until recess."

"No, go ahead." Charlie stepped back, exchanging glances with Annie. The woman acted like she was the only person who was inconvenienced in that way. "We were just leaving.

"You were saying?" she whispered to Annie as the two stepped into the hallway.

"I think Elwin has a lover," Annie began.

"Really?" Charlie grinned. "Why would he keep that a secret? Do you know who she is?"

Annie tried to suppress a giggle, but she could see it was useless.

"*What?*" Charlie wanted to shake her. "What's so funny?"

"Look, I feel awful about this. We had no business prying into things that don't concern us. . . ." Laughing, she gripped Charlie's shoulders with both hands. "But I think we can stop worrying about Elwin being straitlaced and prudish!"

"What *are* you talking about? Does he have a girlfriend or not?"

Annie nodded vigorously. "I'll say he does!"

Charlie glanced behind her to see if anyone was around, but the hallway was clear. "So why would he want to keep it a secret?"

Annie shrugged. "Beats me, unless maybe she's married to somebody else . . . or he is. I mean, what do we actually know about him?"

"What makes you think that?"

They heard the toilet flush in the room behind them and knew Cornelia would soon be emerging. Annie took Charlie's arm and more or less propelled her down the hall to the back steps just as the bell began to ring. "There were framed photographs in his desk drawer, all of the same woman, somebody named Leila Mae, and they were signed . . . well, I won't go into how they were signed, but I can tell you for sure she's not his sister! And I found a couple of snapshots of her, too, and if her dress were cut any lower it would be down to her waist."

"No kidding? Who'd have thought it!" Charlie whispered. "What's she look like?"

Annie shrugged. "Frankly, I thought she was kind of plain, but she must have something. From what I read in her letters, they're planning to be together. Kinda hot stuff, if you know what I mean."

"Do you think that might be why he bought that farmhouse? Maybe this Leila Mae plans to join him there. Or, it could be she's there already," she added, remembering the dishes in the sink.

"If they really are having an illicit relationship, that would be an ideal place to meet, I guess. You know, sort of away from everything," Annie said as the children gathered in energetic clusters at the foot of the steps.

Maybe so, Charlie thought, but what was Cornelia Emerson doing out there?

The day before Thanksgiving the children were so excited they were like a roomful of jumping beans. After a brief assembly program during which Willie Elrod got to play the part of a friendly Indian and the school chorus sang, "Come Ye Thankful People, Come" and "Over the River and Through the Woods," it was a major effort to keep their minds on work. Several of the children in Charlie's class said that they wouldn't be traveling to celebrate Thanksgiving with their grandparents this year as they didn't have enough gas to get there and most of the space on trains and buses were reserved for those serving in the military. Willie, who proudly wore his Indian makeup the rest of the day, announced that his grandmother Cochran, who lived in Atlanta, was coming to spend the holiday with them because his two uncles were both away in the army.

"If they're this excited about Thanksgiving, I hate to think what they'll be like before Christmas. Why don't we combine our classes and create two teams for a spelling bee?" Annie suggested after lunch, and Charlie agreed. As soon as the children returned from their noon break, they lined them up facing one another in Annie's room, and since it wouldn't be fair to pit third graders against those a year ahead, they mixed up the classes into different teams.

"Why not call one team Indians and the other Pilgrims?" Charlie suggested, but Junior Henderson wanted his side to be the Americans and the other the Japanese.

"I'm not going to be on any old Jap team!" Willie protested. "I wanna be on the Indian side. If I was an Indian I'd sneak out at night and catch spies. Indians were so quiet you wouldn't even know they were there until it was *too late!*" And he jumped a little girl from behind and made her scream with fright.

"That's enough of that, William Elrod," Charlie said sternly. "If you're going to behave like that you won't be an Indian, a Pilgrim, or even a Japanese. Now, apologize to Shirley this minute."

"I'm sorry, Shirley. I didn't mean to scare you, honest. You can even have my moon rocket kit I got from Cheerios. I was kinda tired of it anyway."

And after a moment's hesitation, Shirley accepted gracefully. "Well, okay, I guess. Who you gonna spy on, Willie? Can I come, too?"

"Naw, you'd probably scream or something and scare them away, but I know how to be quiet, and I know where to find them, too, because I've seen the ev-i-dence."

The child was so good-natured, Charlie couldn't find it in her to punish him, and so it was determined that each student would draw a number from a hat. Those who drew a one would be Indians and the ones who drew a two would be on the Pilgrim team. Unfortunately Willie drew a two but in a matter of seconds he had talked Ruthie Phillips into swapping with him.

"I want to see you after class," Charlie told Willie when the spelling bee was over with only one fourth-grade Indian left standing.

"But, Miss Charlie, I promise I won't scare anybody no more, and Shirley's gonna come by my house to get that rocket kit soon as school's out."

"It's not about that and I won't keep you long. Shirley can wait for you on the playground," she assured him.

When the dismissal bell rang a short while later Charlie waited until the room emptied before taking a seat on the desktop across from Willie's and addressing him face-to-face. "I want you to promise me you won't even think of sneaking out alone at night, Willie. We all want to help with the war effort and we know how brave you are, but everybody would feel terrible if anything happened to you. If you want to help win the war, try not to be wasteful, and keep on buying savings stamps and collecting tinfoil. How big is that tinfoil ball of yours now?"

He beamed. "Bigger that a baseball, and heavy, too. I peel the foil off every piece of chewing gum I can find but Mama says she heard they're gonna start wrapping it in just plain paper."

"Well, it sounds to me like you're doing your part. Now I want you to forget all about this spying business." Charlie rose to dismiss him.

"But, Miss Charlie . . ." Willie's eyes grew wide. "I really do think somebody's been hanging around that old toolshed back behind the school. Why won't anybody believe me?"

"I think Mr. O'Donnell sleeps in there from time to time when he forgets the key to his house," Charlie explained in an effort to spare the man's reputation—or what was left of it.

"Aw, Miss Charlie, everybody knows Delby O'Donnell's wife locks him out when he comes home drunk, but this ain't Delby O'Donnell. There's cigarette butts all over the ground out there—and it's always Lucky Strikes. I've examined them."

Charlie smiled. "And I'm sure you have the makings of a fine detective some day, but how do you know they weren't Mr. O'Donnell's?"

"'Cause Delby O'Donnell smokes cigars. Ain't never seen him smoke nothin' else."

Charlie sighed. After assuring Willie the cigarettes were probably smoked by teenaged boys who could burn down the school with their carelessness and had no business out there, she wished him a happy Thanksgiving and sent him on his way. She really was going to have to do something about that child's English!

The basket for Paschall Kiker waited in the front hall underneath the stairs and Charlie was glad to see it was heaped with jars of home-canned fruits and vegetables as well as a couple of contributions of pickles and jams. True to her word, Charlie had donated oranges and sweet potatoes and Annie, who was from South Carolina, brought olives and a bag of rice. No table, she claimed, Thanksgiving or otherwise, was complete without rice and gravy.

"I hope you know how to make gravy," Charlie teased Ollie when he showed up a few minutes later to clean the hallway with the familiar cedar-smelling compound.

"No'me, but I reckon Mrs. Spragg does. She's coming over to help out with dinner. We've ordered a nice hen from Cooper's and it sure looks like we won't go hungry, at least not anytime soon."

Charlie knew Mrs. Spragg was coming over because Bessie had told her earlier, but of course she didn't let on. She wondered if Ollie had any idea that Bessie Jenkins expected more from him than a polite "thank you, ma'am" for his upcoming holiday dinner.

Annie was already locking her classroom door behind her when Charlie started back to her room to put assignments on the board for the next school day.

"You're in a hurry to leave," Charlie said. "What's the rush?"

Annie smiled and Charlie could swear her friend blushed. "Gotta run. I'm getting my hair cut this afternoon . . . well, just trimmed, you know, so it won't look so shaggy."

"You want to look your best for Will, I know—even though the two of you really aren't serious or anything like that!" Charlie grinned as Annie shrugged into her coat, shedding papers all over the floor.

"'Et tu, Brute?'" She made a face. "I'm not . . . he's not!" With Charlie's help, Annie scrambled to collect the papers. "I just want to look nice for Thanksgiving, that's all."

Charlie shook her head as she watched her hurry out the door. She had never seen her friend so excited, and she didn't think it had anything to do with the turkey and cornbread dressing her aunt would be serving—or even the rice and gravy.

Tomorrow would be Thanksgiving. Dimple Kilpatrick sat on the edge of her bed and thought about the children in her class. Most of them should be ready to move up into the more advanced primer by now but she worried about the few who lagged behind, the ones who didn't get enough sleep, or sometimes not even enough to eat, and whose parents were either too tired or too shiftless to care if they studied at home. Were they getting the extra help they needed at school? Certainly not if that silly Alma Owens had taken her place!

The book with the story about Tomochichi was still in her bag as it had been the morning she was taken and she drew it out and browsed through the pages. She always looked forward to reading that story to her children and telling them about how the Indians taught the settlers to bury a fish to fertilize the seeds when they planted corn. And her classes loved the improvised game, *This is what I'd take if I were going to the new world.* The first person listed something that started with an A, the next person added an item beginning with B, and so on, to see how far they could get down the alphabet. The ones near the end had a harder time of it, of course, because they had to remember all the subjects mentioned earlier, and the entire collection was always ridiculous and created much laughter.

Miss Dimple clutched the little book to her chest and said a few words to her Lord. *I'd be most grateful if you could see your way to get me out of this deplorable place, and if it's all the same to you, I'd appreciate it if you wouldn't leave Alma Owens in charge of my children.*

Odessa would be a real bear about now as she bustled about the kitchen, she thought, and Phoebe Chadwick's house would smell of cornbread dressing with plenty of onions, and of spice cake and sweet potato pie. It was one of the few times Miss Dimple forgot about what was good for her and enjoyed the rich bounty laid before her.

And Henry. Was her brother in danger, too? She sensed he was working on something important at the Bell Bomber Plant in Marietta but had no idea what it was. She only knew he would never give in to the demands of the despicable people who were responsible for locking her away in this dungeon of a basement. It was obvious they were up to something too horrible to contemplate.

What *would* they do with her if they didn't get what they wanted? And they *wouldn't*. Mr. Smith was nervous, even more so than usual, and Dimple Kilpatrick knew time was running out. She doubted if he'd have the nerve to kill her on his own, but he was afraid of someone as well. She looked out the window; it was too dark to see, and it was eerily quiet upstairs. He was usually walking about overhead before now. Also, he hadn't brought her anything to eat since noon and she was getting hungry. At least she'd saved a few soda crackers from lunch.

She woke hours later to the sound of footsteps upstairs. A door closed, and then another. Would he come for her now? Miss Dimple felt for the broken chair leg she'd concealed beneath her mattress and braced herself for what might happen—for the basement door to open and dreaded footsteps to descend the stairs. But the house grew silent once again, and finally she drifted off to sleep.

CHAPTER TWENTY-ONE

*H*arris Cooper tossed his dirty apron onto a pile with all the others and tucked the jar of olives he'd been saving in a bag with the pecans his wife had asked him to bring home. "I'm gonna let you close up, Jesse Dean. Lord, it's been a long day! I'm ready to go home and soak my feet in some Epsom salts." He pulled down the shade on the front door and looked about to see if he'd missed anything. "Now if anybody comes, just pretend you don't hear them. If they don't have it by now, they don't need it!" He paused. "I left some of those tangerines you like and a small fryer in the refrigerator for you, so don't stay too late—and you have a good Thanksgiving, you hear?"

Jesse Dean thanked his employer and wished him the same. Harris Cooper was a kind man and had always treated him fairly, which wasn't the case with everyone. He checked the cash register to be sure all the money had been deposited in the safe in the back of the store and discovered six dollars and thirty-seven cents that had come in during the last half hour. Well, it would just have to stay there until Friday. On the shelf beneath the counter he found what he was looking for, the lists of items he'd delivered that day. It wouldn't do to leave something off and have a customer fussing at him for ruining her Thanksgiving dinner.

Jesse Dean frowned as he read, and then he frowned some more. He hadn't paid much attention when he and Mr. Cooper had filled the orders earlier. They had been in too much of a hurry, he reckoned, to get everything delivered before they closed for the day. Because turkeys were expensive and sometimes hard to find, there had been numerous requests for baking hens, and so many customers wanted cranberries they had run out of those by noon, but here was an order for ginger mint tea and he didn't know but one person who bought that on a regular basis. The store had grown dark in the fading sunlight and Jesse Dean turned on another light so he could see a little better as he examined the list again: molasses—a lot of people cooked with molasses, especially now that sugar was rationed . . . nothing unusual about that; dried apples—his granny had made a darn good cake with hickory nuts and dried apples . . . called it "poor man's fruit cake," and they were good for pies, too. He scanned the rest of the items, then folded the list and tucked it in his pocket. He probably wouldn't have thought too much about it if it hadn't been for the last two items: whole wheat flour and raisins, things Miss Dimple Kilpatrick bought on a regular basis.

Of course she wasn't the only one who used whole wheat flour, he reminded himself. Mrs. Patterson rarely bought anything else for her weekly bread baking, and Estelle Huffstetler liked it in muffins, but those ingredients along with the ginger mint tea was a little too much of a coincidence.

Jesse Dean weighed a couple of sweet potatoes and took a can of green beans from the shelf to have with his Thanksgiving dinner, made a note of what he'd taken, and left the money in the cash register. Then, putting his purchases in a bag with the chicken and tangerines, he carefully locked the door behind him and started home, but he couldn't get the unusual grocery list out of his mind. Wasn't that the *same house where he'd seen those bubbles the other day? Maybe he should say something to the police.*

But Jesse Dean Greeson had been the butt of too many jokes to make a fool of himself without first finding out for sure.

◎

Charlie hurried home after school that afternoon to put fresh linen on the twin beds in Fain's room for Annie's brother Joel and his friend Will, who were due in sometime later in the evening. The two air cadets had just finished a couple of months in preflight school at Maxwell Field in Montgomery, Alabama, and were looking forward to a rare three-day pass. According to Joel, they planned to catch a flight to Souther Field in Americus, Georgia, where they were scheduled to begin the next stage of their training, and would hitchhike the rest of the way. Usually, anyone in uniform didn't have to wait long for a ride; it was considered unpatriotic to pass anyone in the service on the side of the road without offering to give them a lift.

Her aunt Lou had begged off from her duties at the ordnance plant that day in order to start cooking her Thanksgiving dinner, but Jo and Bessie had gone in as usual and Charlie knew her mother would be tired when she got home. She smoothed the blue corded coverlets on the beds and folded patchwork quilts at the bottom. A fire was laid on the hearth, waiting for someone to light it so the room would be warm when they were ready for bed. Bessie, on learning they would have guests, had brought over a vase of bronze chrysanthemums that Charlie placed on her brother's desk. The flowers seemed to brighten the room that had seemed bleak since Fain left. The gesture was one of the many thoughtful things their neighbor did and Charlie hoped she wouldn't be disappointed the next day in her hopes for that thick-headed Ollie Thigpen.

It would be good to have someone in Fain's room again, to hear

191

laughter and male conversation. Her brother always had friends about and Charlie missed them all. Every one of them was now serving in some capacity. She wished Hugh could be here with them, but she'd probably have to stand in line after Emmaline. He'd written that he and his new friends would join others in the mess hall on Thanksgiving for turkey with all the trimmings but there would be no passes for the occasion.

A friend of her mother's at the newspaper had generously shared with them a portion of smoked ham. It wasn't enough to divide among five people, as Annie would be joining them for supper as well, so Charlie planned to combine it in a recipe she'd found in her grandmother's cookbook that called for noodles, eggs, milk, and cheese. She hadn't been able to find noodles but wouldn't macaroni do as well?

Downstairs she glanced at the kitchen clock to find it was half after four. Hurrying about the kitchen, she chopped the ham into pieces, simmered the macaroni, and grated the cheese. She had combined the ingredients and the pan was ready to go into the oven when the doorbell rang.

"Heard anything from the boys yet?" Annie, looking pert and neat with her new haircut, stood in the doorway with an overnight bag in one hand and a plate of cookies in the other. Charlie had invited her to share her room that night so she would have more time with Will and her brother. "I sweet-talked Odessa out of the cookies when I told her Joel and Will were training to be pilots," Annie said, holding out the plate. "Thought you could use some dessert."

"You thought right." Charlie accepted the cookies gratefully and ushered her friend through the cold house and into a warm kitchen. "Haven't heard a word yet. What time do you think they'll get here?"

Annie shrugged. "Depends on how long it takes them to catch a ride." She looked about. "What can I do?"

"Have you ever made yeast bread?"

Annie frowned. "No, have you?"

"Nope, but I'm gonna give it a try. I found this recipe in the paper the other day for holiday coffee bread and it doesn't call for much butter or sugar, but it says it takes an hour to rise."

Annie looked at the clock. "Then I guess you'd better get started . . . but are you *sure* you want to fool with yeast?"

"You're just afraid that when your Will gets a whiff of that bread, he'll only have eyes for *me*!" Charlie laughed as she gathered the ingredients. She was joking of course.

But that was before she met him.

❧

Annie had spread a blue checked cloth on the kitchen table and was standing on a chair to reach the cups that went with Jo Carr's everyday daisy-splashed dishes when the doorbell chimed again.

"Can somebody get that? My hands are filthy!" Jo called from the sitting room where she was starting a coal fire in the grate, so Charlie left her bread to rise and quickly rinsed her hands at the sink before going to the door.

Joel immediately tossed his hat on a convenient chair and enfolded Charlie in a huge bear hug. He smelled of tobacco and Old Spice, and although he still demonstrated his college-boy exuberance, his face had a firmer, more chiseled look. His friend stood by while Charlie returned Joel's embrace with a kiss on the cheek and called to Annie in the kitchen.

Will stepped inside, set his luggage on the floor, and stood with his hat in his hand while Joel introduced them. Their hats, she noticed, were trimmed in blue braid against an olive drab background like their uniforms and neither wore an insignia designating rank as they had none as cadets. She also noticed that Will Sinclair looked at her as if he wanted to laugh. His mouth turned up in a flicker of a smile as he took her hand in greeting, and the

193

smile didn't seem to want to go away. His eyes—were they gray or green, or in between—were having a hilarious time as well, she thought, and obviously at her expense.

Laughing, Joel reached out and touched her on the nose. "You've flour on your face . . . and in your hair, too."

"And pretty much everywhere else!" Will didn't try to hold in his laughter any longer, and when Annie joined them, all three of them were howling over Will's concern that she hadn't left enough flour for the bread.

There was nothing outstanding about his face. His straight nose ended in the tiniest bit of a snub, he had a firm jaw line, and he wore his light brown hair in a crew cut like all the other men in the military. But his eyes had a gentleness about them, a mixture of humor and intelligence that made Charlie feel she'd known him forever. And his mouth . . . she wondered what it would be like to be kissed by Will Sinclair. Charlie had to force herself to look away.

What in the world is the matter with you, Charlie Carr, lusting after your best friend's beau? Will is here to spend time with Annie, not you, so you just back off and leave them alone!

Charlie chastised herself as she followed the group into the sitting room where her mother passed around dainty glasses of last summer's blackberry wine. Annie sat on one end of the sofa and Will perched on the arm with his hand resting lightly on her shoulder. Will was telling some tale about getting a ride on a truck with a farmer transporting a load of chickens and Annie glanced up at him and grasped his hand as she laughed. Annie was small and dainty with dimples and curly hair and when she laughed it made everyone else want to join in. Charlie reminded herself that Annie Gardner was the best friend she'd ever had.

"Guess I'd better go check my bread," Charlie said, excusing herself. She turned down Annie's offer to help and hurried into the kitchen. Why did she suddenly want to cry?

And when she took one look at her bread, she had good reason. It hadn't risen one bit!

"I just wanted to make sure you really did have enough flour left for bread."

Charlie jumped when Joel spoke behind her, then held up the pan for him to see. "Look for yourself, but I'm afraid it won't be fit to eat. The darned thing didn't even rise. Guess I'll have to throw it away."

"Don't you dare! After what we've been eating it will be like manna from Heaven." Joel sniffed the unbaked dough. "Mmm . . . what's in here? Orange peel? Cinnamon?"

"Both."

"Then into the oven it goes! I'm not missing out on that." Joel frowned and took her face in his hands. "Is something wrong, Charlie? It's more than the bread, isn't it?"

Charlie nodded silently. "I guess it's just—well, I don't know . . . I felt kind of teary all of a sudden. I wish Fain could be here, but I try not to let Mama know how much I miss him."

"Your brother? Annie says you think he might be with Patton in North Africa."

"But we don't know for sure and it's been a long time since we've heard anything." Charlie missed her sister, too, but she wasn't going to stand here and talk about all her worries when Joel and others like him were risking their lives every day. "We're hoping to get a letter from him any day," she added, popping the pan of bread into the oven. "And since you insisted on my baking this bread, I'm going to watch you eat it, Joel Gardner, even if we have to cut it with a hatchet!"

After supper, during which everyone gnawed politely on a hard hunk of bread, Charlie set up a card table in the sitting room and Will popped corn over the fire while Joel taught everyone how to play draw poker. Since nobody had any money to spare, they substituted pecans recently harvested from Aunt Lou's trees. Charlie wasn't surprised when her mother ended up wiping everyone out.

Jo entertained everybody with her account of a recent birthday party she'd written for the *Eagle*. The honoree was turning eleven and her mother, in keeping with the chilly autumn weather, had served sugar cookies and hot spiced punch, only somewhere down the line, the linotype operator had hit a wrong key and the town was aghast to read of their innocent children being served hot *spiked* punch.

While at Maxwell, the men had received extensive physical training, and during the classification stage were tested and examined mentally and physically to become classified as a navigator, bombardier, and pilot before their preflight training even began.

"What kind of planes will you be flying at Souther?" Charlie asked, turning to Joel.

His eyes brightened at the subject. "Probably the Boeing Stearman PT-17 to start with," he said.

"She's a two-seater," Will said, joining in. "Gets up to about one hundred twenty-five miles an hour. Nimble in the air, but I hear she's pretty tricky to handle on the ground."

Both men had been classified as pilots, and Joel had also received a high rating as bombardier, while Will got an additional classification as navigator. It was easy to see they were eager to get on with the next stage of their training and to receive their wings so that they could join fighting squadrons in Europe or the Pacific Theater. Charlie looked at their young, enthusiastic faces and thought of Fain who, a few months ago, had seemed very much the same. At least Fain was fighting on the ground. If a plane was shot down, it would be a long way to fall, and even if they managed to parachute, the crew became sitting ducks for enemy gunners. She rose abruptly to poke the fire.

Will, who after a few more hands of poker had begun to accumulate a fair supply of pecans, cracked two of them together, ate the nut meats, and threw the shells into the fire.

"Hey, you're not supposed to eat your winnings!" Annie told him, laughing, and he replied by snatching two of hers. The two seemed to have a friendly, relaxed relationship, and it was obvious they enjoyed being together.

"Annie's been keeping us up-to-date on your missing Miss Dimple," Joel said, throwing his cards down in disgust. "Any word yet?"

"No, and it's been two weeks today," Charlie told him.

Will shook his head. "And there've been no demands or evidence of any kind?"

"Very little that we know about." Annie told him what Willie said he'd seen and how Virginia had found the scrap of yarn.

"That Willie!" Charlie laughed. "He's convinced that spies are meeting behind that old toolshed in back of the school. Says he's found cigarette butts out there."

"Probably Delby O'Donnell's," Annie said. "I've heard he sleeps in there whenever his wife locks him out."

"That's what I told him, but Willie swears Delby only smokes cigars," Charlie explained, "and he claims these were all Lucky Strikes."

"Hey! I hear on the radio that Lucky Strikes have gone to war," Joel chimed in. "They're claiming the copper-based green dye on their old package can be better used to help manufacture tanks."

"I've noticed they've switched to red," Jo said, "but I think it's all a lot of talk. They were probably going to change the color anyway."

Charlie thought her mother looked tired, and suddenly she felt the same way. "I'm going to run up and light the fire in your bedroom so it will have time to take the chill off before you come up," she told the two men, motioning for Annie to stay when she offered to help. "I'm sure you three want a chance to visit, so stay up as long as you like. Just remember to bank the coals before you turn in, and I'll see you in the morning."

She was already in bed a little while later when she heard footsteps going up the stairs. *One set of footsteps.* Joel was probably giving his sister and Will some private time to themselves.

Once in a while during the evening Charlie had felt Will looking at her with an expression she couldn't quite fathom; probably her wistful imagination. She burrowed beneath the quilts and tried to think of Hugh. *Hugh. Hugh. Hugh.* But Hugh was only a good friend. Hadn't the two of them agreed to leave it that way? Charlie sighed. The only way she was going to get through this weekend was to put as much distance as possible between herself and Will Sinclair.

CHAPTER TWENTY-TWO

*She was hot . . . no, she was cold. Dimple Kilpatrick propped
on one elbow and shivered as she pulled the quilt to her
chin. Her throat felt as if she'd swallowed hot burning coals.
Across the room blue flames flickered in the gas heater and the gray
light of early morning seeped through dirt-streaked windows casting the
room in shadow. She reached for the glass of water on the table beside
her bed, almost spilling it when the man loomed up beside her.*

*"Here now, we can't have you gettin' sick." He doled two small
white pills into her trembling hand. "Take these aspirin and I'll bring
you some of that tea you like. Won't take a minute."*

*She glanced at the pills to be sure he wasn't dosing her with poison
and obediently swallowed them. They looked like aspirin and tasted
like aspirin, but if he had given her something that would kill her, she
felt she wouldn't have far to go.*

*As soon as he left the room she shoved the covers aside and pulled
on her robe and slippers. The quilt seemed to weigh a ton and her legs
wobbled so she had to hold on to a chair until she felt capable of walking to the bathroom. She must've picked up a germ somehow, she*

thought. Well, this wouldn't do. This wouldn't do at all! She needed every ounce of her strength if she wanted to get out of this place.

By the time her clown-faced captor returned, she had made her way to the rocking chair, and, wrapped in the shell of the quilt she'd pieced together, pulled the chair as close to the heater as possible. Her head felt as if someone had been playing kickball with it and every inch of her body ached.

Silently he handed her the mug of tea and put a pan of steaming water on top of the heater. "More hot water there as I reckon you're gonna need it," he told her. "I can't find a teapot, but there's a box of that tea and one of them little metal strainers over there on the table."

She noticed that he was keeping his distance, probably because he was afraid of germs, or it had occurred to him she would consider him a likely target for the pan of hot water—as she most certainly had. The tea was her favorite, ginger mint, and oh, it went down like a warm caress! Where had he found it? And was anyone paying attention or had they given up on her entirely?

Miss Dimple sipped every comforting drop and waited for the man to leave, but instead he pulled a straight chair up to the table and took out a pad and pencil. "If you'll tell me how to put them muffins together, I'll see what I can do," he directed.

"I think you'll find it much easier if I just write that down for you," she said, reaching for a sheet of her own note paper on her bedside table. She had given him a list earlier that had included ingredients for the muffins along with her request for ginger mint tea, but this time she made a point to print the lettering as large as possible. He hesitated for a moment as if thinking it over, then carefully laid his writing utensils aside. "I can't think of a more nutritious way to begin your day," she croaked as she began to print out the ingredients for the recipe in her own distinct style, so elegant it resembled illumination from ancient texts. "You'll be surprised at how much better you'll feel after using vitamin-enriched wheat flour, and soy if you can find it. I'm positively *certain you have a deficiency somewhere . . . take your fingernails for instance—not a healthy color at all."*

Later she heard him moving about upstairs in the kitchen, or at least she assumed it was the kitchen. Miss Dimple drank another cup of tea, ate a few spoonfuls of the oatmeal he'd brought her, and longed to go back to sleep, but she forced herself to get up and dress. By and by, if the aspirin did its work as it should, her fever would break and she must be ready for any event. She hadn't lied about noticing the man's fingernails, but the nails weren't discolored because of a vitamin deficiency. His nails were stained with soil, as if he'd been digging in the dirt. Had he been preparing a place for her?

Dimple Kilpatrick poured herself a third mug of tea and sat down to read a five-year-old issue of The Woman's Home Companion *for at least the third time. She looked at her watch. It was half after eight Thanksgiving morning, and for now she was thankful to be alive.*

◌

Aunt Louise took right away to Joel and Will, and Charlie's uncle Ed asked them so many questions, you might think he was writing a research paper on the subject, but the two men were happy to discuss the training behind them, and what would be expected in the challenging months ahead. They wouldn't receive their rank of second lieutenant, Will explained, until their training was complete.

They sat on scratchy horsehair chairs around her aunt's dining-room table and ate turkey and dressing with rice, gravy, and sweet potatoes, complete with most of the trimmings they were accustomed to with the exception of a few that were in short supply. Joel sat in Fain's usual place next to her uncle Ed, and Charlie was glad they wouldn't have to look at an empty chair. Annie sat next to him in Delia's accustomed place, with Will on her other side. The house was filled with the smells of turkey, spicy jam cake, and wood smoke from the big stone fireplace in the living room, and Charlie wondered where her brother was now and if he was thinking of home.

Anyone who didn't know her mother, probably wouldn't have noticed that Jo Carr was doing her best to "keep a stiff upper lip" as the British were fond of saying, but Charlie could tell from the look in her mother's eyes she was thinking of Fain and missing him. Jo dutifully kept up her end of the conversation as she and her sister told the men a little about their work at the ordnance plant in Milledgeville. They didn't speak about it often, and when they did it was only to a trustworthy few. Their jobs there weren't complicated, Jo explained, but munitions were essential to winning the war, and they were constantly being reminded that "Enemy agents are always near. If you don't talk, they won't hear!"

"I wonder if there *are* any spies around here," Annie said. "I can't imagine what they'd learn in Elderberry."

"I wish you'd convince Willie Elrod of that," Charlie reminded her. "But if there are any here, you can count on Willie to find them." She laughed when she said it, but she still had a feeling Miss Dimple's disappearance had something to do with her brother's work at the Bell Bomber Plant in Marietta.

After an early-afternoon dinner, Aunt Lou served rich boiled custard flavored with sherry and nutmeg with slices of her homemade jam cake. "But only a small one this year," she explained, "and from all I hear, I'm afraid next year's will be even smaller."

After the table was cleared, they all sat in front of the fire, too full and too comfortable in its warmth to do much of anything until Joel suggested Will entertain them at the piano.

Will sighed and stretched. "Would you mind bringing the piano over here to me? I don't think I can walk that far." But with a little encouragement and a lot of exaggerated groaning, he gave the piano stool a couple of spins and sat down to play, only on condition that the others join him in singing.

They warmed up with "She'll Be Comin' 'Round the Mountain," moved on to "Casey Jones," and were well into the third verse of "Home on the Range," when the telephone rang.

Jo's eyes lit up in expectation as she turned to Lou. "Oh, do you think it might be . . ."

It couldn't be Fain, of course, but Delia and Ned had access to a telephone at the base where they lived, and all eyes followed her aunt as she hurried to answer.

"It's for you," she said to Charlie, upon returning to the room. "Somebody important, I suspect." And then she winked and fluttered her eyelashes.

Charlie could feel the blood rushing to her face as she hurried from the room. Why couldn't she have normal relatives like everybody else?

"Can't talk but a minute," Hugh said. "Just wanted to wish you a happy Thanksgiving and let you know I'm thinking of you."

Charlie was so surprised to hear from him she was momentarily speechless. "And I've been thinking of you," she told him. "How did you know where to find me?"

He laughed. "Where else would you be on Thanksgiving? You've told me about your mother's cooking." He sounded surprisingly close, not at all like he was as far away as Virginia.

He told her that he was staying so busy with classes and drills, he fell asleep almost before his head hit the pillow every night. "I look forward to your letters," he said before ending the conversation. "Please keep them coming. And Charlie," he whispered, "don't forget me!"

"I won't, Hugh, I promise." Of course she wouldn't forget him! Charlie shook her head as she replaced the receiver. She'd detected a note of homesickness in his voice. It was Thanksgiving and Hugh was away from home. Just as he'd felt during the picnic at Turtle Rock, he was longing for familiar ground. Who could blame him?

Of course she'd continue to write . . . but things weren't exactly the same between them.

Annie grinned. "W-e-e-l-l," she said, making the word go on forever. "And how is Hugh?"

Charlie felt the hateful flush returning. "Busy," she told her. "He said to tell everybody hello." He hadn't.

"I need to get out and stretch my legs after all that good food," Joel said. "Why don't you two show us the town?"

"It won't take long to see Elderberry," Charlie told him. "The three of you go on and I'll stay and help Aunt Lou with the dishes."

Her aunt frowned. "Since when have you been so concerned about that? The dishes aren't going anywhere, so scat! Get on out of here and get some fresh air." She waved them along. "And take your uncle Ed with you!"

But Ed shook his head. "I'm allergic to fresh air," he announced, adding another log to the fire.

"Where should we go first?" Annie asked when they stepped outside. The days were getting much shorter now and sunlight was fading fast.

"I want to see where Miss Dimple got kidnapped," Will said, walking ahead with Annie. "Maybe we'll find another clue."

Charlie fell into step with Joel. "Believe me, we've looked," she told them. "This is where Willie says he saw Miss Dimple get into a car," she said, pointing out the spot after they walked the few blocks to the rooming house. From there they circled the school, and were passing Charlie's house on Katherine Street when Ollie Thigpen wheeled his bicycle out of her neighbor's driveway, waved in their direction, and pedaled off toward home. Charlie returned his greeting, hoping things had gone well that day for Miss Bessie. If the man had any sense at all, he would realize what a prize he had in Bessie Jenkins. She paused to look back at her neighbor's house where a light shone in the living room window, but none on the porch, and Miss Bessie usually turned that on when Ollie left and followed him out to say good-bye. Today she didn't see a sign of her, but there was still some daylight left, so a porch light wouldn't be necessary. *Why was Ollie leaving so early?* Charlie thought of her neighbor's nearly new suit, her elaborate preparations for dinner, and her dreams for the future, and had to suppress a strong urge to run and shove him off his bike.

Annie interrupted her thoughts. "What's Jesse Dean doing at your house?" she asked.

Charlie turned to see Jesse Dean Greeson in the truck he used for deliveries, slowly emerge from behind their house and turn into the street behind Ollie. "I can't imagine unless he was delivering something that came in late, but Mama usually leaves the grocery orders to me."

"I wouldn't think he'd be delivering on Thanksgiving anyway," Will said, frowning. "Maybe we'd better check and see if he left anything on your porch. Did you lock your doors when we left?"

Charlie smiled and shook her head. Nobody locked their doors in Elderberry.

"Maybe he was just turning around," Annie suggested when nothing was found on the porch.

"It does seem that all the suspicious activity lately has been taking place around the school and your rooming house," Joel said, turning to Annie. "Maybe you'd better change jobs and find another place to live."

"Not *all*." Charlie told him about Geneva Odom's painful experience in the park.

"Was she robbed?" Will asked. "Or attacked in—uh, any other way?"

"No, thank heavens!" Charlie said. "It's bad enough to get a blow like that on the head, but I guess it could've been worse."

"Then somebody must've been afraid she'd see or hear something . . . something there in the park. Let's go take a look before it gets too dark to see." Will took long strides as he spoke and the others hurried to catch up with him.

"Now what?" Annie shivered. Although it was not yet six o'clock, night had overcome them, and with it the penetrating cold of late November when the sun goes down.

They stood by the stone bridge in the deserted park and Charlie instinctively moved closer to Joel. He smiled and took her hand, and Will, linking his arm in Annie's, waded through the brittle leaves to the large magnolia where Geneva said she thought she'd seen someone. Parting the heavy limbs, he looked at the ground. "Wish we had a light. It's dark as a vampire's closet out here."

Annie backed away. "Did you have to mention vampires?" She and Charlie had seen Bela Lugosi in a horror movie the year before, and neither slept well for a week.

"It doesn't make any sense for him to come out and hit her when she was hurrying to get away," Charlie said. "Unless he thought Geneva had seen him."

"Or possibly someone else, or some*thing* else," Joel suggested. "Like a car."

"If they didn't want anybody to see it, it wouldn't have been parked in the street," Annie said. "But isn't there a little alley that runs behind the library?"

"It doesn't lead anywhere except to an area in the back where they unload books," Charlie told them. "Virginia Balliew, our librarian, parks there once in a while when she drives to work."

"I don't believe it was Virginia who was parked there the night your friend Geneva was attacked," Will said as they started back to Aunt Louise's.

⟡

They found the dishes washed but not dried, so upon their return, everybody pitched in to help while they listened to H. V. Kaltenborn on the radio with more news of the Russian counterattack at Stalingrad. It seemed the German general, Paulus, commander of the Sixth Army, was determined to fight on against the Red Army. Charlie had seen newsreels of the frigid Russian countryside and was glad, at least, that her brother wasn't there.

Aunt Lou insisted on serving leftover turkey for sandwiches before they left for home and everyone seemed surprised they had any appetite at all. But in spite of their objections, Charlie noticed, they managed to do all right for themselves.

Because it was dark when they left, Uncle Ed offered to drive them back to Jo's, but only Jo and Charlie accepted. Annie, who planned to spend the night in her room at Phoebe's, said she didn't mind the short walk, so Will went along to see her home. When Joel started to join them, Charlie pulled him aside. "I was hoping you might give me another chance at poker," she whispered, with a glance at his sister and Will.

"Oh." Joel shook his head and grinned. "Guess I wasn't thinking. Thanks for reminding me—and I'm sure Will will thank you, too."

And he would kiss Annie good night . . . and maybe he would kiss her again. After all, wasn't that the point of making sure the two of them had some time alone?

After her mother went to bed, Charlie and Joel drank Postum and played gin rummy at the kitchen table and had hardly finished the second hand when they heard Will return. Joel glanced at the clock and shrugged. "Must be too cold to cuddle!"

But Charlie knew Phoebe's parlor was warm, and probably empty as the other roomers had either left for the weekend or retired at their usual hour. What was the matter with Annie? Hadn't she even invited Will inside?

She would have to wait until tomorrow to find out. Before she went to bed that night Charlie stood at the living room window and looked out at the Jenkins house next door, hoping to see her neighbor moving about. But everything was dark.

CHAPTER TWENTY-THREE

*M*iss Dimple did not eat the muffins, nor did she partake
of any other nourishment that Thanksgiving except for
tea and a few spoonfuls of canned chicken noodle soup
in the middle of the day. Mr. Smith had seemed offended. "I made
them muffins just like you said, and you didn't do no more than nibble.
Seems like you'd at least try to do better than that."

Miss Dimple turned away. The very nerve of the man to complain
of ill treatment after robbing her of her freedom for these two weeks. "I
don't know how you'd expect me to eat them when you left out some of
the most essential ingredients," she said.

"Like what?" he pouted.

"Well, soy flour for one. Surely I wrote that down. And I'm sure
you didn't add the ginger or molasses."

This time she didn't have to pretend to be ill. The aspirin had helped,
but now the fever had come back with a vengeance and for the first
time Dimple Kilpatrick began to wonder if she would ever escape this
dismal place alive.

Now he sighed. "I haven't had a chance to pick up all them things
you listed, and stores aren't open today but I can try again tomorrow.

You gotta do better than this, you know." His shoulders sagged when he
walked, she noticed. In fact, his entire body drooped. It cheered her that
apparently things weren't going as well for him as expected and now he
was afraid she might die before he could make the trade for whatever
evil plan he had in mind. And Dimple Kilpatrick made the decision
right there and then that she didn't intend to die—not if she could help
it. "If you'll kindly bring me some hot salt water to gargle and a few
more of those aspirin, I'll try to get some sleep. Perhaps·I'll feel better
then."

Later she would not only need her strength but a whole lot more as
well. Miss Dimple missed reading her Bible, but doubted if there was
one in this foul place. Instead, she found comfort in a favorite Psalm
she'd committed to memory: "God is our refuge and strength, a very
present help in trouble . . ."

❀

"Did you and Will have some sort of disagreement last night?"
Charlie whispered to Annie when she phoned her the next morning. Her mother had left early for her work at the ordnance plant
and their two house guests were still asleep upstairs. "You *are* coming over this morning, aren't you?" The last thing she wanted right
now was to be left for any length of time with Will Sinclair when
Annie wasn't around.

"Of course I'm coming, and everything's okay with Will as far as
I know. Why?"

"Well, he certainly didn't stay long. I thought surely he'd hang
around for a while. Didn't you ask him in?"

Annie giggled. "I would have if I hadn't drunk all that tea last
night but I was about to die to go to the bathroom!"

Charlie never knew her friend to be so prim and proper she was
reluctant to admit that situation to her date, but she kept her opinion to herself. Maybe Will was unusually shy about things like
that, but he certainly didn't seem that way. Instead of pursuing the

subject, the two of them planned what they would do during the cadets' last full day in Elderberry.

Her mother seldom used the family car so Charlie had saved a fair amount of ration stamps to buy gas and over a late breakfast the four of them mapped out a tour of the area that would include several interesting and historic towns.

"There's a quaint little restaurant in Covington where we can stop for lunch," Charlie suggested, "unless it's closed for the holiday."

Which, of course it was.

The day had turned out bright and sunny with what Jo Carr liked to call a brittle coldness in the air, and Charlie was glad she'd thought to tuck gloves in the pocket of her warm corduroy jacket with the fleece lining. Joel was eager to get behind the wheel of a car again and Charlie happily gave him the opportunity. The old Studebaker, cantankerous at best, was forever stalling on inclines just to be exasperating, and she drove it only when necessary. In the backseat Annie chatted glibly to Will about the Thanksgiving program they'd had at school, her delight in a student whose goal was to read every book in the school library, and the sensitive issue of dealing with children over the sudden death of Christmas Malone.

"And did they find out what killed him?" Joel asked, overhearing.

"They'd like us to think it was a heart attack, but we never heard for sure," Annie said. She told them how the police had confiscated the wooden eagle with the broken wing. "Several of us have been wondering if somebody used it to hit Christmas over the head. Seems to me they're being very hush-hush about it."

"But why would anybody want to kill the fellow?" Will wanted to know.

Nobody had an answer.

During the morning they had paused briefly in the town of Eatonton, and stopped to stroll the quaint streets of Greensboro and Madison before continuing to Covington, so it was after one when they pulled up in front of Miss Eula's Dinner Table on the Covington Square and found it closed.

"I'm famished!" Joel complained. "Wonder if *anything's* open today?"

"There's a hamburger place between here and Griffin that's not too far away," Charlie offered. "Maybe we could get something there, and it's only a few miles from there to Indian Grave Mountain if you want to do any walking."

"Eat first, walk afterward," Will directed. "Meanwhile, why don't we sing something? It'll keep us from thinking about food and maybe we won't hear our stomachs growling." And with that he led off with "Oh My Darling, Clementine," and followed it with "Sweet Betsy from Pike."

Charlie was amazed not only at his true tenor voice, but also that he knew all the words. "How do you remember all that?" she asked.

"That's nothing. You should hear him on the guitar," Joel told her. "I tried to get him to bring it with him, but he didn't want to be bothered lugging it around. Everybody in Will's family plays a musical instrument. You'll have to get him to sing 'Scarborough Fair.'"

"Hey! Cut it out! That's enough of that." Will, obviously uncomfortable with the attention, pounded his friend on the back. "You make it sound like I'm the only person in the universe who can pick out a tune."

"Well, I don't like to brag," Joel said, laughing, "but I used to play a pretty mean triangle in the grammar school rhythm band."

They all laughed a lot during a lunch of burgers and fries in a tall wooden booth at Bart's Drive-in just outside the small town of Griffin. The place smelled of cigarette smoke, coffee, and grease, and they sat at tables carved with initials dark with age. There were only a few customers the day after Thanksgiving and the manager, whose name wasn't Bart, but Fred, insisted on treating them all to shakes after taking an interest in hearing about the cadets' flight training.

"The least you can do is to thank him by singing 'Scarborough Fair,'" Annie teased Will.

He grinned and put a nickel in the jukebox. "I'd rather dance with a pretty girl, but I'd die before I'd ask her."

Of course that was all Annie needed and the two of them took the floor with the Andrews Sisters' "Don't Sit Under the Apple Tree." Joel held out his hand for Charlie and both couples went through several nickels until Annie switched partners to dance with her brother to the "Pennsylvania Polka," leaving Charlie no choice but to dance with Will.

Will was a smooth dancer, leading her with only the slightest touch. The floor was of wide oak boards, worn and scuffed over the years, and the four of them had the whole space to themselves. Charlie started to go back to her seat when the record ended, but Will stubbornly refused to let go of her hand. "Just one more," he said with a grin and a tug, and Charlie sent up a silent plea for another fast one.

God must've been too busy on the battlefield to listen to her, she thought, as Will swept her onto the floor and into his arms with Glenn Miller's "At Last." His hand on her waist was firm and her head fit into his shoulder as if they were two parts of a puzzle. He smelled of some kind of shaving cream—Barbasol maybe, bracing and minty—and their lips were so close they could touch if she tilted her head the tiniest bit. They didn't speak, but now and then he glanced at her and smiled, and Charlie hoped he couldn't feel the racing of her heart.

"Maybe we'd better hit the road if we want to do any walking before it gets too dark," Joel suggested at the song's end, and

Charlie was relieved to escape to their booth where she'd left her wrap.

It had grown warmer by the time they drove the few miles to Indian Grave Mountain, and Annie, still with music in her head and dancing in her feet, ran ahead, leaving her jacket in the car. Inspired, the others followed. It was a picture-book day, Charlie thought, as a gentle breeze sailed downy clouds across a sky so blue it almost hurt her eyes, and although most of the trees were bare of leaves, the vivid green of pines and cedars freshened the pathway. Now and then a squirrel scampered across the trail, looking, no doubt, for last-minute supplies before winter set in. They walked Indian file on the narrow trail with Annie in the lead. Charlie hung back to walk with Joel but she couldn't avoid watching Will's every move in front of her. She liked the way he walked, the way he talked; in fact, she liked just about everything about him.

"Now," Annie said when, after about an hour of walking, they reached an inviting rock in the shade of the mountain and sat down to rest.

Joel looked up. "Now what?"

"Now's the time for Will to sing 'Scarborough Fair,'" Annie said, and folded her arms in expectation. So Will Sinclair stood with the tableau of the peaceful Georgia woods behind him and sang the old English riddle song about seeking his true love at Scarborough Fair, and Charlie Carr turned her face away so no one could see she was crying.

"I'm getting a little chilled," Charlie told them before hurrying back down the trail. "I guess we'd better leave if we want to get back before dark." The others agreed. She heard their footsteps behind her as she walked ahead, kicking pine cones out of the way, crunching leaves and twigs underfoot. It had been an almost perfect day—well, except for her heart aching, of course—and they couldn't have planned it better, but this wasn't the real world. The real world was somewhere in Europe, in Africa, and the South

Pacific, and it wouldn't be long before these two gentle, funny, courageous young men would be right in the middle of it. Her brother was already there.

Phoebe Chadwick had invited the four of them to share some of Odessa's soup and cornbread for supper, and as it had turned cold as soon as the sun disappeared from the sky, by the time they reached Elderberry the hot meal was as welcome as it was good. Elwin Vickery had left to spend the weekend with relatives, Phoebe explained, but Charlie, who tried to ignore Annie's knowing glance, thought he was probably spending the holiday with the alluring Leila Mae. Velma Anderson had driven her faithful Ford to be with her sister in Augusta, so, of the roomers, only Lily Moss and Cornelia Emerson remained to share the meal. After supper, the two men built a fire in the parlor where everyone gathered to listen to Edward R. Murrow, who, in ominous tones, reported semiencouraging news from Russia. Afterward, Lily finally acknowledged several meaningful looks from Phoebe and excused herself to follow their hostess from the room. Cornelia had retired earlier.

Joel and Will planned to catch a bus to Americus the next morning to return to the base on time and Charlie knew Annie wanted to spend time with her brother as well as with Will. Over protests from the others, as soon as the *Red Skelton* radio show was over, she excused herself to walk the few blocks home.

Joel followed her outside. "You really don't have to leave now, do you? If you're upset because I danced all over your feet today, I promise not to do it again."

Charlie laughed and kissed him on the cheek. "Silly! I thought I'd go home and keep Mama company for a while. She's not used to all of us being gone and it really made a difference having you and Will with us over Thanksgiving."

He insisted on walking with her to the corner and watched as she crossed the street, promising to be along soon.

Charlie had told the truth about wanting to be with her mother but she also didn't think she could bear watching Annie snuggle up to Will as they held hands on the sofa.

∞

True to his word, Joel returned about an hour later to join Charlie and Jo as they listened to a program of music on the radio. Charlie noticed her mother seemed restless, and when Jo paced to the window for the third time, she demanded to know what was the matter.

"I was just wondering about Bessie. You know how important this Thanksgiving was to her and she didn't even mention it today. She usually sits with Lou and me on the bus to Milledgeville, but today she sat several seats away and didn't have much to say."

"That doesn't sound good. I'm sure she would've told you if she had exciting news," Charlie said, explaining the situation to Joel. She told her mother about seeing Ollie Thigpen riding away on his bicycle when they were out walking the day before.

"No news is good news," Joel offered. "Or at least that's what my mother always says . . . so how about a few hands of poker?"

When Will returned a short while later, Jo excused herself to get ready for bed and Charlie went to the kitchen to make hot chocolate for the three of them, leaving her two guests arguing about which of them was the better poker player, the better dancer, and, of course, who would be the better pilot. She was still smiling over their horseplay when the kitchen door opened behind her and she turned to find Will standing in the doorway.

"Can I help?" With a hand on her shoulder, he peered into the simmering milk on the stove.

"Sure. Why don't you grab some mugs from the cabinet by the window?" *Damn! Could he notice the tremor in her voice?*

Charlie moved as far from him as possible to make a paste of the cocoa and sugar before adding it to the pan and he obediently gathered up three mugs and set them down in front of her, leaning so that his face was inches from hers. "You know, if I didn't know better, I'd think you were avoiding me, Charlie Carr."

She dribbled a little of the hot milk into the chocolate and tried to ignore him. "That's just plain silly and you know it."

Will lifted her chin with his finger. "Then why won't you look at me? Why all the excuses to run away?"

"You have a good imagination," Charlie told him as she stirred her concoction into the pan. "Besides, I was under the impression you came to visit Annie." *Why did he have to stand so close behind her? How much longer can I stand this?*

Before she knew it, Will reached around her to switch off the burner, took the spoon from her hand, and gently turned her to face him. "Look, I think a lot of Annie, and yes, we dated some when Joel and I were in school together, but there's nothing serious between us. There isn't going to be."

Charlie tried to turn away but his hands were firm. "Does Annie know how you feel?" she asked, staring into his collar.

He sighed. "We haven't discussed it, but I imagine she does. Annie doesn't care about me in that way, Charlie."

"But she writes to you, tells me all about your letters. I know she cares about you, Will!"

"Of course she does, and I expect she cares about all the others she corresponds with, just as I imagine you do."

Charlie turned back to the stove as he relaxed his grip. "But Annie's my friend. My best friend, and I—"

Again Will spun her toward him. "And wouldn't your best friend want you to be happy? Look at me, Charlie Carr, and tell me you don't feel something for me."

Charlie looked into his face—serious now, into his gray-green eyes that held her so that she couldn't turn away. "You do, don't you?" he insisted. "While we were dancing, tell me you didn't feel right in my arms."

And Charlie did the only thing she was capable of doing just then. She put her arms around his neck and kissed him. And that was all it took.

⚜

"You will write to me?" Will said at breakfast the next morning. "Promise?"

"Of course I will. I'll write to both of you." Charlie sat across the table from him because she couldn't bear to be any nearer, and forced herself to take her eyes from his face. *Joel knows . . . he must know . . . and Annie would soon know, too. She would have to find a time to tell her today—or tomorrow at least. What a faithless friend she'd turned out to be! How was she ever going to admit what she had done?*

Chapter Twenty-four

*C*harlie saw him coming from a block away. She had said her good-byes to the two cadets at the bus station and stood watching as the crowded bus pulled away and turned the corner at Harlan's Music Store. She had not confessed to Annie about Will and their mutual attraction to each other, and it had been difficult to send him away with a light kiss on the cheek as she had Joel. All the way to the rooming house her mind had been on Will Sinclair's lingering touch. She savored the pressure of his hand like a permanent imprint on her back and the imperceptible caress of his fingers against her face. If only she could keep them there—lock them away in her senses.

She had just dropped off Annie at Miss Phoebe's and was driving home, when Charlie spied the boy on the black bicycle.

The boy had pedaled down the backstreet from town as if he were ashamed to be seen on the main road, and Charlie faced him as she waited for the light to change at the corner. "Go down somebody else's street!" she said aloud, although she knew he couldn't hear her. "Don't you dare turn onto mine . . . please . . . please . . . please!"

But he did. The light turned green but Charlie stayed where she was and watched the boy on the black bicycle wheel onto Katherine Street. He'll go on past my house, she thought, as he had done before . . .

But he didn't. In slow motion he turned into her driveway, stepped off the bike, and laid it almost reverently by the steps—as if he were leaving a wreath, Charlie thought. She couldn't breathe, couldn't swallow, couldn't move. This wasn't happening, couldn't be happening.

A car pulled up behind her and waited patiently for Charlie to move on. Virginia Balliew pulled over to the curb, got out of her car, and slid into the passenger seat beside her. "You need to be there for your mother," she said gently. "Do you want me to drive?"

Charlie couldn't answer. She had turned to stone and stones don't speak. Finally, she shook her head and made the turn into her own street—the street that had sheltered them as children; the street where neighbors comforted them when they fell, watched them safely across the street, and called their parents if they were hurt or rude. Silently, Virginia put a hand on her shoulder. Charlie was glad it was there. Abruptly and with a grinding of gears, she bumped into her driveway and ran onto the porch, leaving Virginia to follow. She had to get to her mother first!

She was too late. White-faced, Josephine Carr stood in the doorway with the yellowed paper in her hands. The boy from the telegraph office hung his head, mumbled that he was sorry, and walked slowly down the steps. Charlie felt fleeting sympathy for him. What an awful job he had!

Charlie reached for the telegram. "Mama, let me."

"No," her mother said. "He's my son." She didn't look like Charlie's mother, but like a statue of a woman standing there in the doorway, halfway inside the house, and halfway out, and when she spoke, she sounded like how a statue might speak, Charlie thought. With shaking hands, Jo Carr opened the telegram, read it, and held it to her chest. Only then did she begin to cry.

"Let me see it, Mama! Let me!" Charlie had to pry the paper from her mother's fingers, and while Virginia put her arm around Jo and led her inside, Charlie sat on the porch bench by the front door and read the message from the Adjutant General:

Deeply regret to inform you that report received states your son, Fain D. Carr, missing in action in the Tunisian area November 10. Reports will be forwarded when received.

It was signed by Major General Ulio.

Through the screen door she could hear Virginia calling her aunt Louise on the telephone, and hurrying inside, Charlie held her mother in her arms and rocked her back and forth, crooning, "He's not dead, Mama! It doesn't say he's dead!" And all the while she felt her disloyal heart being twisted and wrung out inside her. Was she being punished for what she'd done?

ॐ

At two o'clock, Miss Bessie Jenkins gratefully turned over the ticket booth at the Jewel Theater to sixteen-year-old Patsy Brisco, who filled in on Saturday afternoons to earn money for Christmas. A notorious flirt, Patsy had a turned-up nose, luscious lashes, and enough freckles to make her adorable, and the boys lined up to see the movie even if they didn't give a hoot about watching Roy Rogers and Gabby Hayes in Man from Cheyenne. From past experience, Bessie knew that some of them would probably see the movie twice.

Bessie had eaten a hurried breakfast of cornflakes and toast hours ago but she wasn't especially hungry. The night before, she had only pecked at the chicken and dressing left over from Thanksgiving and she wasn't looking forward to facing it again. The afternoon was mild for the end of November and the coat she'd worn earlier was much too warm, but Bessie decided she'd rather suffer the discomfort than carry it. Although she sat during her hours in the ticket booth, her feet still ached from her work at the ordnance plant and the hours spent in the kitchen preparing Thanksgiving dinner.

And the whole thing had been a disappointment. Ollie had rushed through the meal, giving her some excuse about not wanting to leave Paschall Kiker alone too long. Bessie had reminded him in no uncertain terms that he left him every day while he worked over at the school, didn't he? And wasn't Aileen Spragg supposed to take him dinner?

Well, he got downright huffy about it. Said Mrs. Spragg was cooking for her son and his family and wouldn't be able to stay long. It was like trying to argue with a stump on fire so Bessie just gave up the effort to understand. After all her baking, that ungrateful Ollie had hardly eaten a thing, and she'd even borrowed Jo Carr's silver candlesticks to go on her grandmama's best tablecloth.

Bessie knew that behind her back people made fun of her relationship with Ollie Thigpen, and there had been times—such as this—when she wondered if he was worth her time, but then he'd come through and say or do something to make her feel special. Take Thanksgiving, for instance. Hadn't he said she was pretty as a picture in that blue suit? And he'd helped her with the dishes, too. He almost never did that. She'd been as mad as a wet hen at that man for rushing through dinner like he had, and he knew it, too. Bessie made sure of that. While they were finishing up in the kitchen she'd hardly said a word, and neither had he until he started to leave. And what was all this about her not going in to work at the munitions plant next week? He had a bad feeling about it, he said, and besides, he added, she looked tired. It was time she quit working so hard and took some time off. "Promise me!" he demanded, and she did, just to appease him of course. Then Ollie Thigpen had lifted her chin, kissed her gently on the lips, and told her things would be different soon. Now, what in the world had he meant by that?

For Christmas the year before, Ollie had given her a brooch with three tiny pearls in the center that had belonged to his mother. He wanted her to have it, he said, and she wore it often and proudly, but she didn't wear it today. Bessie usually felt at home with Ollie and looked forward to the evenings they spent together, but it was time to take their relationship to the next step if they were ever going to do it, she thought. She was tired of living alone, but several things had happened lately that made her feel uncomfortable. Take that odd conversation with Virginia Balliew, for instance. "How did you like *Murder in Three Acts?*" Virginia had asked her at church last Sunday. Had the woman gone crazy? Bessie had no idea what she was talking about and told her so.

"The book, *Murder in Three Acts.*" Virginia looked at her strangely. "It's a mystery. Ollie checked it out for you the other day. Said he thought you'd enjoy it."

"Well then, I guess he must have forgotten to give it to me," Bessie had told her. Ollie knew very well she never read mysteries. There was enough killing going on in the world without making up stories about it.

Marjorie Mote was deadheading the chrysanthemums by her front walk as Bessie passed her house, and of course she wanted to know how her Thanksgiving had been. Bessie didn't want to discuss her disheartening Thanksgiving, but how could one be abrupt with Marjorie after she'd lost her dear boy in the war? That hateful banner with the gold star was a constant reminder in the front window.

"I'm afraid it was 'eat and run' at my house," she said, pausing. "Ollie couldn't stay long because Aileen Spragg—"

"Oh, are the Spraggs back in town? I ran into Aileen at the ten cent store—I believe it was the day before Thanksgiving—and she said they were on their way to Macon to spend the holiday with some of their family."

How could that be? Surely Marjorie must be mistaken, but Bessie

222

wasn't going to argue the point. Her feet were about to give out on her and the thought of a good soaking in a pan of hot water was uppermost on her mind. As she hurried home she noticed Jesse Dean Greeson in his beat-up old Plymouth turning the corner behind her. He drove Harris Cooper's truck while making deliveries during the week, so what was he doing hanging around here on a Saturday? Bessie squelched a shiver and walked a little faster. She knew he couldn't help being different, but the man made her feel uneasy.

It wasn't until she was almost home that she saw all the cars parked in her neighbor's driveway. It wasn't unusual for Jo's sister, Lou, to be there, but unless she was mistaken one of the others belonged to the Methodist minister.

❧

"No! We never talked about that and I don't want to have anything to do with it!"

The speaker was clearly that of her jailer, "Mr. Smith," but Miss Dimple couldn't make out the other, only that it was a low rumble of a voice and the two were in the kitchen above her. The sound woke her from a restless sleep and the low blue flame of the gas heater cast a scanty light. Sitting up in bed, she shoved aside the heavy quilt and realized her gown was damp with perspiration, and for the first time in days, her throat didn't hurt. Her fever must have broken sometime during the night, and although her legs were a little wobbly, Dimple Kilpatrick felt some of her strength returning.

Switching on the lamp beside her bed, she groped for her glasses. There had been a time when she could see her watch plainly without them, but she could scarcely remember when. Why, it was morning already—almost six o'clock! In normal times, she would have been up by now and dressed for her walk about town. Miss Dimple missed her daily excursions, missed observing the shadows

223

lighten and lift as the town waked in its own time to greet the day. Lately, because of her illness, she even had to forgo her repetitious circuits of the room.

In the frigid bathroom she made hasty ablutions in the small lavatory and dressed once again in her own clothing she had washed days before. It felt good to be wearing her belongings instead of those other strange garments that made her feel as if she were incased in someone else's skin. Quietly, Miss Dimple made her way to the foot of the stairs and stood stock-still just as she had seen animals do when they sensed danger was near. After a lull in the discussion—or more likely, an argument—the two upstairs spoke again.

"I would never have given you the layout of that plant or told you anything else about it, if I'd known what they meant to do. I was told they'd be taking care of that on a Sunday when the place is empty," her jailer insisted once more. "There are those work night shifts during the week. Why, there might be people in there!"

Miss Dimple could scarcely hear all the reply but the threatening nuance chilled her through and through. As cold and calm as a blanket of snow the words drifted down to her: "A little late for an attack of conscience now, don't you think? And need I remind you that there's nothing you can do about it, my friend?"

She recognized the voice!

Was he going to kill her today? She knew there had been some kind of agreement about a December first deadline and time was running out. Today must be Monday—the Monday after Thanksgiving when everyone would be returning to school after the holiday. Miss Dimple thought fondly of her school, of her classroom, and the children who greeted her each day—even tattletale Joanie Lee Dixon, who bullied the other girls during recess. Would she ever see them again?

Somewhere upstairs a door closed firmly and she heard a car

starting up, then the scatter of gravel as it drove away, and Dimple Kilpatrick began to plan in earnest. Today would be the last day of the month. It had to be now or never.

❦

Charlie didn't think she would be able to bear the silent hugs, the sad smiles, the handshakes that squeezed and lingered. How could she face a roomful of boisterous third graders with any kind of enthusiasm when her brother might be dead or dying on some remote battlefield or captured by Hitler's horrible Nazi Army?

"You're not planning to go to the plant tomorrow?" Aunt Lou had asked her sister the day before. And Jo Carr lifted her chin, tucked away her lace-trimmed hankie, and said she most certainly was and had volunteered to fill in at the front desk a few hours after her day shift ended for a young mother who worked in their office. "Her little boy is sick," she explained, "and she doesn't want to leave him. Besides, I want—*need*—to keep busy. Bessie's working late tomorrow, too. They're trying to step up production at the plant and she said she'd rather do that than just sit around the house." Fain's being missing had only bolstered her incentive to do her part to win this war, Jo announced. And Charlie had no choice but to follow suit and go to school as usual. Now she was glad as it kept her from dwelling on all the "what-ifs" that might have happened to her brother.

They had telephoned Delia in Texas who, of course, cried at the news as they all had. Because of her sister's condition, Charlie hadn't wanted to tell her until they learned more, but her mother insisted that Delia had a right to know. As a child she had trailed after Fain adoringly no matter how much he teased her. The phone conversation was brief, and both Charlie and her mother promised to write often and to call as soon as they knew more, but there were too many questions unanswered and it was frustrating to have nowhere to turn. Was Fain still alive? Had he lost a limb? An eye? Or worse? Maybe he was a prisoner of war. Would they ever see him again?

Her class was so quiet and well behaved that day Charlie found herself wishing for at least a *small* ruckus, and as soon as the children filed in from their morning recess, she told them about Fain, how they had played together as children acting out the adventures of Tarzan and Jane in the apple tree behind their house, and how poor Delia complained because she always had to be Cheetah. It made the children relax and smile, and the day seemed to progress more normally once Charlie had shared memories of her brother.

Charlie had dreaded the midday meal at Miss Phoebe's, but found to her surprise that her fellow diners, other than offering their concerns, seemed committed to an upbeat conversation at the table.

Geneva Odom told a funny story about her first Thanksgiving dinner as a new bride when she had added so much rice to the pot it boiled over onto the stove and ended up on the floor. "Almost like that fairy tale about the porridge that flowed into the street!" she added, laughing.

Velma, who had spent the holiday with relatives, made everyone laugh with a description of what was supposed to be cornbread stuffing her niece had made and declared she was glad to be enjoying Odessa's good cooking once again.

"It was lovely to meet your brother and his friend," Lily told Annie over a dessert of bread pudding topped with tart quince jelly and meringue. She darted a look at Charlie and smiled. "It looked like the four of you were enjoying your time together." And Charlie, avoiding Annie's eyes, agreed that they had.

"What about you, Mr. Vickery?" Annie asked, nudging Charlie under the table. "Did you have a nice Thanksgiving?"

Elwin Vickery looked up from his coffee. "Very nice, thank you, however busy." It was obvious he didn't intend to enlarge upon that, but Cornelia Emerson, who had been quiet as usual during the meal, fixed him with her piercing gaze. "Oh? And how is that? Something interesting, I hope."

"I found it so," Elwin said, and setting down his cup, excused himself from the table.

"Well, that was strange," Annie said as she and Charlie walked back to school together. "Cornelia usually acts as if she couldn't care less about any of us. Wonder why she said that to Elwin. Did you see the look he gave her? If looks could kill . . ."

"It upset him, all right, and I noticed he didn't give her an answer," Charlie said. "But remember when we passed Cornelia coming from that house Elwin owns in the country? I imagine it has something to do with that."

Annie frowned. "Do you think she knows something about Elwin's love life? Maybe he thought she was teasing him."

"Somehow she doesn't appear to be the teasing type. I can't imagine her taking an interest in Elwin's personal life."

"I wouldn't want anybody prying into mine—such as it is," Annie said with a laugh.

The two had reached the edge of the school grounds and Charlie hesitated at the stone wall that marked the entrance. "Annie . . ."

The concern on her friend's face made it even harder to continue. "Are you all right?" Annie asked, her hand resting on Charlie's shoulder.

"It's not about me. Annie, I'm so sorry." Charlie turned away. How could she say this? "It's about you."

"About me? Oh, you mean my lack of romance? Heck, I'm no worse off than anybody else, and, Charlie! I've heard from him *already*—a letter came Saturday, and we have plans to meet in Atlanta when he gets leave before they ship out."

Charlie felt her legs turn to wood. "Does Will already know when they'll be shipped out? Don't they have a lot more training to—"

Annie laughed. "Will? I'm not talking about Will, silly. I meant Frazier—Frazier Duncan. Besides," she added, smiling. "I'm pretty sure Will's heart belongs to somebody else."

"Really?" Charlie felt her face was going to crack. "Who?"

"Why you, of course!" Annie threw her arms around her. "Do you think I'm blind?"

"But Frazier . . . isn't he that good-looking lieutenant you danced with so much at the party we gave for the troops? Annie, you only met him once. You hardly know him."

Annie hooked her arm in Charlie's as they walked across the playground. "And how long have you known Will? Sometimes, Charlie Carr, you just *know*, and when you do, you'd better grab the brass ring because you might never have that chance again."

Chapter Twenty-five

"Miss Charlie, I don't feel so good," Junior Henderson complained as the class lined up at the back steps after their return from dinner.

Charlie felt his forehead, and although the child was flushed, he didn't seem feverish. "Why don't you go wash your face with cool water and rest your head on your desk and see if that doesn't make you feel better?"

"I told him not to eat all that candy!" Willie said. "He won a nickel's worth of BB Bats from me playing marbles and Harry Taylor lost a whole bunch of jawbreakers to him, too."

"And he ate every one of the cookies Mama packed in my lunchbox," Marshall Dodd chimed in. "Serves him right if it makes him sick!"

Charlie reminded the boys that nobody made them gamble away their sweets at marbles, and they were walking down the hall to their classroom when Junior, whose face had turned the color of skim milk, threw up on the floor next to the water fountain.

Ruthie Phillips screamed and jumped back. "Eeeuuw! Don't you dare come close to me, Junior Henderson! I think I'm gonna be sick."

"I think you're going to be quiet and take your seat," Charlie told her sternly. She turned to Willie who was holding his nose and gagging. "Enough of that nonsense, Willie! Haven't you ever been sick before? Now, run down to the basement and ask Mr. Thigpen to please come and clean the floor for us—and hurry! The rest of you may sit quietly at your desks and read while I telephone Junior's mother to come for him."

Willie backed away, fanning the air in front of him but the class had already started filing into the classroom and nobody paid any attention to him. Maybe losing his candy to Junior hadn't been such a bad thing after all, he thought. If he stayed out long enough, he might even miss that boring science lesson, and he took his time on the way downstairs to Ollie Thigpen's headquarters in the furnace room. He'd found a dime one time on the landing and if he looked real good, maybe he'd find another.

But luck wasn't with him today and Willie decided he'd better do what his teacher asked and fetch the janitor. He sure didn't want Miss Charlie mad at him.

But Ollie Thigpen wasn't in his usual little room next to the furnace, although his jacket hung by the door. Willie called to him but it was plain to see the room was empty. He was probably cleaning somewhere in another building. Willie grinned. It might take a l-o-n-g time if he had to go and look for him, and he was turning to leave when he saw the small fold of paper showing just above the top of the janitor's jacket pocket. Less than an inch of it was exposed, but Willie Elrod didn't let anything get past him because he never knew who might be in cahoots with the enemy, and when he saw it, his hand shook so he couldn't put it back fast enough. It was a grocery list, kind of like the ones his mother wrote, only neater, and for yucky things like soy flour and stuff like that.

Not only was the list written in Miss Dimple's distinctive printing style, but Willie had seen that paper before. It came from a small note- pad bordered in some kind of purple flowers, and Willie had seen it more times than he'd like to remember when Miss Dimple had sent notes home to his mother.

He quickly stuffed the note back into the pocket and hurried up the stairs, taking them two at a time.

"Whoa, there! Where ya goin' in such a hurry?" Ollie Thigpen stood at the top, arms outstretched to stop him.

Willie ducked underneath and darted away as if Hitler himself were on his tail. "Junior's done gone and puked in the hall, and Miss Charlie needs you to come clean it up!" he shouted over his shoulder.

Thank goodness the days were getting shorter. She didn't think she would be able to wait for darkness much longer. He had brought a paper-wrapped bologna sandwich with her breakfast that morning and told her to save it for lunch but she had been too keyed up to have much of an appetite, and she had never cared for bologna. Who knew what part of the animal went into its making? But he usually brought her something for supper at a little after five and tonight she would be ready for him. Walking briskly, Dimple Kilpatrick prepared herself by making forty-eight circuits of the room: One circle for each state, and with every step she promised herself she would somehow manage to thwart the plans of the traitorous people holding her hostage. The longer she walked, the angrier and stronger Miss Dimple became until she felt like that comic-book hero the children read about, the one who changed his clothes in a phone booth.

She had seen the empty soft-drink bottles in a case behind the stairs, and now she dragged them out and placed them on their sides, two on each step, beginning at the top of the stairs. And although it took her several tries, she threw the local library's copy of Agatha Christie's *Murder at the Vicarage* until she hit the light-bulb in the ceiling of the stairwell and shattered it to bits. Surely Mrs. Christie would understand.

Just to make sure the room was good and dark, Miss Dimple stood on the table to cover the small windows with the quilt from her bed. And then she waited.

Darkness came early, but Mr. Smith was late. It was almost half after five when she heard his footsteps overhead, and Miss Dimple immediately turned off the lamp beside her bed, armed herself with the broken chair leg (in case the bottles didn't do the trick), and held her breath as the door opened at the top of the stairs.

"Why is it so dark down here? I can't see a thing!" She heard the repeated clicking of the light switch and a muttered curse before the blessed racket began. And when it did, it sounded more exciting than the fanfare of a thousand trumpets as Ollie Thigpen thudded, bumped, hollered, and rolled his way to the foot of the basement stairs and sprawled like a disjointed scarecrow at the bottom. Dimple Kilpatrick stood over him, holding the chair leg like a bat and had a strange desire to sing "The Hallelujah Chorus," but she didn't know all the words, and only the alto part at that. Handel would have to wait.

Was he dead? She had to be sure. Miss Dimple leaned closer, keeping her distance, of course, and saw his eyelids flicker as a groan escaped his lips. Good! She wanted him alive to get what he deserved. With one oxford clad foot, she shoved him aside and started up the stairs, taking care to keep a firm grip on the railing in case a bottle or two remained.

Ah! Sweet freedom! She stood in what looked like a farmhouse kitchen and assumed it belonged to Paschall Kiker as she knew that was where that poor excuse for a human being, Ollie Thigpen, worked. But where was old Mr. Kiker? Surely he couldn't be in on this. Miss Dimple looked in distaste at the dirty dishes in the sink and the plate of bacon from breakfast now covered in a gray greasy film. Maybe they were holding Paschall Kiker a prisoner as well, but she didn't have time to look for him now. Ollie Thigpen wasn't in this alone and that other one might be along at any minute. It saddened her to think who the other person might be, but it angered her as well. And she had always considered herself a good judge of character! An old-fashioned telephone hung on the kitchen wall and Miss Dimple hurried toward it. First she must call for help.

And that was when Elwin Vickery stepped in from the other room to block her way. "Ah, Miss Dimple, my friend! So that's where that racket came from! I was hoping we could avoid this, but I'm afraid we're going to have to ask you to accompany us to meet your brother."

"How dare you call me *friend*! And you're wasting your time with my brother. Just leave him out of this!" Still armed with the chair leg, Miss Dimple swung from the shoulder as the boys did on the playground. But she was no match for a gun.

❧

Why wouldn't anybody believe him? He had tried to tell Miss Charlie what he'd found in the janitor's pocket but she was too busy wiping Junior Henderson's face—the baby! Well, he guessed he'd just have to take care of this himself, and wouldn't they all be surprised? He would probably get to ride in a big parade with all kind of medals hanging off him.

Willie Elrod waited behind the big oak tree in the schoolyard until he saw the janitor roll out his bicycle and start for home. He'd brought his own bike back with him earlier when he'd gone home to tell his mother Miss Charlie wanted him to help her clean the blackboards that afternoon and he might be a little late. It was beginning to get dark as they rode into the country but Willie was afraid to turn on his bicycle headlight for fear of being seen. Ahead of him on the dusty road, Ollie Thigpen rode with purpose, his light making dim yellow circles in the fast-approaching night. Now and then a car passed, and Willie slowed and pulled over to the side of the road. He didn't have time to explain what he was doing there. Miss Dimple was in trouble and only he, Willie Elrod, could save her. Then wouldn't she be sorry she'd made him write all those sentences about not chewing gum back in the first grade?

But first he had to find out where Miss Dimple was being held, and then, when Ollie was out slopping the hogs or feeding the chickens, or whatever it was he did out there, he, Willie, would sneak in and set her free. Willie hid in a small grove of cedars not far from the house and waited for the janitor to come outside. It grew darker as he waited and still the man didn't appear. Willie's stomach growled. He was hungry and his mama was going to wallop him good! Ollie, he'd noticed, had parked his bike out back and gone in the back way, and a few minutes later he heard what sounded like that same door shut again. If he hurried, maybe he could find a door or window unlocked in the front of the house.

Willie's heart chugged double time as he crept across the lawn and took cover under some kind of scratchy bush. This wasn't nearly as much fun as he thought it would be. If he could find a foothold in the shrubbery, he might be able to climb in the window that was above him and a little to his right and had started moving in that direction when he saw that somebody else had gotten there first. The person who stood pressed against the wall looked like a shadow dressed in dark clothing with only the face exposed.

"Miss Emerson!" Willie yelped. "What are *you* doing here?"

"Be quiet!" she commanded, her hand clamping over his mouth. "You're going to give me away."

"A little late to worry about that," Elwin said from behind them. "I didn't know to expect a party. A shame we have no refreshments."

And the next thing Willie Elrod knew, he was being tied up in a kitchen chair along with that new teacher, Miss Emerson, and the missing Miss Dimple herself. He wondered if his mother would be sorry if he got killed. He knew his dog would.

CHAPTER TWENTY-SIX

*C*harlie froze when she heard the doorbell. The house had been bleak and cold when she arrived home from school a few minutes before and she had brought up a scuttle of coal and started to lay a fire so at least one room would be warm and a little more cheerful when her mother got off from the plant. And then she remembered that her mother would be working later that night as a favor for a coworker. And it couldn't be Bessie because their neighbor had volunteered to fill in as well.

Who could be ringing their bell? Had the boy on the black bicycle brought more news of Fain? Charlie stood and gripped the mantel, forcing herself to take deep breaths until her heart rate eased. If her brother had died she didn't think she'd be able to bear it . . . and she would have to face her mother. Damn this war!

But what if the news was good? What if Fain had been found alive and well and the army had made a mistake? The bell rang again and she risked a quick peek out the window to see if the bicycle was there. Instead she saw a strange van parked in their driveway. It was a blue van with white lettering on the side but she couldn't make out the words. Charlie hurried to see what they wanted. Anything was better than the black bike.

The container of flowers was so big she couldn't see the person's face behind it until he set the arrangement on the table by the front door where her mother kept a pot of ferns in warmer weather. The flowers were from a florist in Covington, the man explained. Charlie had to restrain herself from throwing her arms around his neck, and she couldn't seem to stop smiling.

"But we didn't order any flowers," she finally managed to tell him— especially these flowers, she thought, as they must have cost a fortune.

The man smiled. "Well, obviously somebody did." And he plucked the order form from his pocket and read the name and address. "I believe you'll find a card to explain it," he added, tipping his cap as he left.

Charlie took the vase into the sitting room and set it on the walnut chest that had belonged to her grandmother. The billowing arrangement of roses, gladiolas, and carnations in varying hues of pink was interspersed with tiny white chrysanthemums, baby's breath, and dainty ferns, and it brought blessed springtime into the room. Charlie sat in her mother's rocking chair next to the unlit fireplace to read the card addressed to her as well as to her mother.

"Our thoughts and love are with all of you," it read, and it was signed by Will and Joel.

After a good cry, Charlie propped the card on the table so her mother would see it immediately, and resumed her fire-building. The two cadets had brought chocolates to them as well as to her aunt Lou when they came for Thanksgiving, so the flowers must be in response to the news about Fain. Annie probably had telegraphed one of them— probably Joel—as soon as she learned what had happened.

Elderberry had put gentle arms around them in the only way they knew how. One of Odessa's chicken pies waited in the Frigidaire along with a congealed fruit salad from Virginia Balliew and potato salad

237

from Geneva Odom. Their neighbor Bessie had brought some of her homemade bread and butter pickles, and kind Marjorie Mote, who knew too well the heartbreak of losing a son, had called to say she would be bringing fried apple pies for their dessert.

She had just sat down to write thank-you letters to Joel and Will when Emma Elrod phoned to ask if she'd seen her Willie.

Charlie glanced at the clock. It was almost six. "Why, no, Mrs. Elrod. I haven't seen him since he left school at the regular time. Do you think he might've gone to the movies?" If Willie could come up with nine cents, the price of a ticket to the picture show, he'd been known to take advantage of it without first asking permission.

The woman's voice was choked with emotion. "I've already been there. They haven't seen him, and he's not with any of his friends. He came home earlier to get his bicycle and said you'd asked him to clean the blackboards, so I wasn't surprised when he was late."

Charlie drew in her breath. "Oh, Mrs. Elrod, I'm afraid that isn't true. I wouldn't have—"

"I know, I know! I ran into Annie Gardner at Miss Phoebe's and she said you'd left for home hours ago. I can't imagine where he'd be. Half the neighborhood's out looking for him, and his daddy and I are frantic."

Charlie didn't blame them. In fact, she was feeling the same way, but she tried to speak calmly. "I'm sure he's out playing somewhere and has just forgotten the time. I wouldn't be surprised if his stomach didn't remind him it's time for supper before too long."

"I hope you're right . . ." Emma Elrod didn't bother to hold back a sob. "I have to go now and help look for him. Can't just sit here and do nothing!"

"Has anybody looked over at the school?" Charlie asked. "I have a key to the building. Maybe he got locked inside."

Grabbing her jacket, she rushed out the door and dashed across the street and around the block to the school to find Annie already there, along with their principal and several other teachers.

"Any luck?" she asked Annie when they met in the front hall, but her friend shook her head.

"We've looked everywhere. It's so dark now and he's on his bike. I'm afraid . . ." Annie lowered her voice. "What if there's been an accident?"

Charlie turned to leave. "I'll get the car. Ride with me and you can look while I drive."

But where? Charlie wondered as they hurried back to the house. "There's no telling what Willie might have gotten up to with his wild imagination about spies. Why, just this afternoon he was trying to tell me some crazy story about poor old Ollie Thigpen."

"Then I guess that's where we'll start." Annie paused at the corner. "Do you think we have enough gas? Remember, we did all that riding around last Friday."

Charlie remembered. It wasn't so much the gas that concerned her, but she wasn't sure they had any rationing coupons left.

A car slowed as they crossed the street and Jesse Dean Greeson pulled over to the curb and rolled down his window. "Have they found the little Elrod boy yet?" he called to them.

"No, but we think we know where he might've gone," Charlie told him. "We're on the way to get the car right now. I'm just hoping it has enough gas to get us out to Paschall Kiker's farm."

" 'My kingdom for a horse!' " Annie muttered.

"Never mind that." Jesse Dean reached across and opened the passenger door. "Get in! We'll go together."

Charlie hesitated, but only for a few seconds and glanced at Annie, who nodded in agreement. If they wanted to find Willie, they really didn't have much choice.

"Maybe we should let Willie's mother know where we're going,"

Annie suggested as she stepped onto the running board and slid into the seat beside Charlie.

"But what if he's not there after all and we run into a dead end?" Charlie said. "I'd hate to get her hopes up for nothing."

"I tried to get in touch with Chief Tinsley but he's got some of his men out looking over at Etowah Pond," Jesse Dean said. Traffic was sparse and he quickly eased back onto the street and maintained a moderate rate until they came to the edge of town where he startled both of them by a sudden burst of speed.

Etowah Pond? Charlie felt a tightening in her chest. Surely Willie wouldn't have gone there this time of year! He knew how to swim, but he could've fallen in, panicked. "So you think he's at the Kiker place, too. Why?" she asked Jesse Dean.

"I have several reasons," he said, turning onto the two-lane dirt road, "but the main one is Ollie Thigpen." He turned to her. "What about you?"

Charlie told her what Willie had said about Ollie that afternoon. "Or he *tried to*," she said. "Some story about finding a grocery list in Miss Dimple's handwriting in Ollie's jacket pocket, but Willie's always seeing spies, and I was distracted by a sick child. Frankly, I didn't pay too much attention to him."

Jesse Dean nodded. "Grocery list. That makes sense to me. That's exactly what made me suspicious." He told them how Ollie had purchased Miss Dimple's favorite ginger mint tea, explaining that it was a gift for a friend. "Now she's not the only one who drinks that kind, and that in itself wouldn't have troubled me if it hadn't been for the other things," he added. "You know, like some of the peculiar ingredients she puts in those muffins she likes to make. He came in the store today and read them from a list."

"Did you see the list?" Charlie asked. "Willie said it was in Miss Dimple's handwriting."

Jesse Dean frowned and leaned forward, concentrating on the

rutted road ahead. "Never gave me the list, which I thought was kinda funny—and that's not all . . ."

"What do you mean?" Annie held on to the strap to keep from bouncing about. Their driver's eyesight was none too keen and she hoped they wouldn't end up in a ditch.

"Well, I make deliveries, you know. Been taking groceries out to old Mr. Kiker for a year or so now that he doesn't get around so much, but the last couple of times I was out there, I could've sworn I saw bubbles coming from somewhere."

"Bubbles?" Charlie smiled. Was he making that up? "What kind of bubbles?"

"Soap bubbles, I reckon. First time I thought I'd just imagined it, but then it happened again. It was the day before Thanksgiving and Ollie had phoned a couple of days before and said Mr. Kiker wanted a hen, but nobody answered the door when I got there so I left a note and told him he'd just have to come and pick it up—only he never did. That's when I saw the bubbles again."

"Did you find out where they were coming from?" Annie asked.

"Seemed like it was from somewhere in back, most likely from the basement, but they disappeared right quick, so it was hard to tell, and that day with all the orders and all, I didn't have time to check it out like I wanted to, but it puzzled me, and it still does."

"Maybe we shouldn't pull all the way into the driveway," Charlie suggested as they neared the Kiker farm. "If there is something going on, I wouldn't want them to know we're here."

The other two agreed that was a good idea. Jesse Dean turned off the road and parked near a weed-choked cornfield just down the road from the house. Charlie was glad she wore her low-heeled oxfords as the ground was uneven and dotted with puddles. A cold wind forced them to turn up the collars of their jackets and walk a little faster. As they drew closer they saw a dim light shining in one of the front windows, and without saying a word, the three of them began walking single file through the long grass that bordered the drive, taking care not to speak as they approached the house. Jesse Dean, who was the tallest, crept through the thick shrubbery to look in a window but returned, shaking his head. "I can't see anybody in there," he whispered, "but I know somebody's inside. Let's see if we can see anything around back."

"There's a car back here," Charlie said as they turned the corner of the house. It was hard to tell much about it in the dark, but she thought it looked vaguely familiar. Yellow squares of light lay across the back porch floor and Ollie Thigpen's bicycle was propped against the wall of the house.

It became immediately obvious to them that the three of them would make too much of a disturbance walking up the steps to the porch while trying to avoid being seen, so it was decided that Annie, being the smallest and most agile, should try to peek in the window while the others waited on the edges of darkness. Charlie armed herself from the woodpile with a length of firewood as long as her arm and motioned for Jesse Dean to do the same. Still, she hoped Annie would come up with a good story if she was detected: *Her car gave out on the road . . .* or, *Her Sunday school class sent her to visit ailing Mr. Kiker.* Knowing Annie, she had no doubt she'd think of something.

But Annie was back before she'd had time to worry and even in the darkness, her face looked as pale as a specter. "We've gotta get out of here!" she urged them, tugging at Charlie's sleeve. "They're in there—all of them—Willie, and Miss Dimple, and Cornelia Emerson, too. He has them tied to chairs."

"Who? Ollie?" Jesse Dean wanted to know.

"No, no, no! I didn't see Ollie, so there's no telling where he might be." Annie looked wildly about. "Come on! We have to get help *now!*"

Charlie stumbled along behind her. "Then who? If not Ollie, *who?*"

"Our good friend Elwin Vickery, that's who! Now *run!*"

The two women had turned the corner of the house when the back door opened and the porch light came on. "Who's out there?" a man's voice called. Elwin's. Annie slid into the shadows of a grove of pine saplings, pulling Charlie with her, and together they froze as one.

But it was too late for Jesse Dean, who was caught like a rabbit in the headlights. "It's only me—Jesse Dean. Just checkin' on Mr. Kiker," he said. "Thought I'd see if he needs something from the store so I can drop it by in the morning."

Charlie noticed something gleam briefly in his hand as he tossed it into the grass a few feet away.

"Who's with you?" Elwin called.

"Why, nobody. I was just on my way home, but if this isn't a good time, I can check back with him tomorrow." Jesse Dean sounded almost convincing.

The sound she heard next froze her inside as well as out. Charlie had heard it at the movies more times than she could count. It was the cocking of a pistol.

"I think not." Elwin's voice didn't sound like Elwin at all. "Why don't you come on up and join us? I'll get another chair."

Charlie pressed against the tree so hard she could feel the imprint of its bark in her back, and beside her Annie was doing the same. She heard Annie's sharp intake of breath as Elwin left the porch and came down into the yard to usher Jesse Dean inside. Would he see them? Would he see the ignition key Jesse Dean had tossed into the grass?

Jesse Dean distracted him by arguing as he was being shoved unceremoniously across the back lawn. "Well, I sure don't know what this is all about . . . you're funnin' me, aren't you? Come to think of it, though, it ain't too funny . . ."

Annie waited until she heard the door close behind them, and although the porch light remained on, darted across the lawn to comb the grass for what Jesse Dean had tossed away. Thank heavens it didn't take long to find the key. "I hope you can drive this thing," she told Charlie when, out of breath, they reached the cornfield where they had parked the car, "because I don't have the faintest notion how."

Not daring to turn on the headlights until they were safely out of sight, Charlie backed the car into the road, praying they wouldn't get stuck, and headed for town. She didn't remember it being this noisy on the way out. "If I didn't know how to drive it now, I'd sure learn in a hurry!" she said.

And 'a plague on both your houses!'" Annie yelled over her shoulder, meaning the curse, of course, for the wretched Elwin and Ollie. But only when they were a far-enough distance away.

Chapter Twenty-seven

Miss Dimple tugged at the bonds that held her hands behind her and tried to send a comforting look to poor little Willie Elrod who was bound to the chair across from her. Elwin Vickery of all people! His treachery was beyond comprehension. And what was this strange woman doing here? Maybe she had something to do with law enforcement because she seemed to have been armed with some sort of gun. Elwin had been holding it along with his own when he escorted the two inside.

What was this evil man planning to do with them? She wasn't keen on the idea of dying at all, but the child concerned her even more. Would this animal harm an innocent little boy? Not if Dimple Kilpatrick could help it!

At least she had put that disgraceful Ollie Thigpen out of commission, but you would have thought that by now at least someone in Elderberry might have caught on to one of her clues. She knew she wasn't the only mystery reader in town, but she had hoped Virginia might see the note she left in one of the books Mr. Smith had checked out for her from the library. The problem was that he'd probably never returned it, which was, to Dimple Kilpatrick, a sin in itself. And apparently no one had noticed her signal of bubbles, but Jesse Dean Greeson knew very well the ingredients in her Victory Muffins. She'd counted on better from him. Still, it wasn't too late.

Or was it?

Miss Dimple stiffened at the sight of Jesse Dean stumbling into the room, prodded from behind by the man who held them all. She had been snugly bound when that strange woman and Willie stumbled onto the scene and Elwin had forced the woman to bind Willie before he secured her to a chair, threatening to harm the child if she didn't cooperate. Now, scowling, he bound Jesse Dean. And while he was being tied along with the rest of them, Jesse Dean Greeson gave her the first sign of hope she'd had since she had been here. He looked up at her and winked.

The noise from the basement stairs alerted her before he stumbled into the doorway. Ollie Thigpen, bruised and bleeding, held the door frame for support and looked about him. "I don't know what you plan to do, and I don't want to know, but you can count me out," he said to Elwin. "I've done my part and I want my share." Leaning against the table he gave Dimple Kilpatrick a belligerent glance and turned away. "Just give me what's mine," he told Elwin, "and I'll go where nobody will ever find me."

Elwin's smile made Dimple want to cover her face. "Oh, come now! The colonel would be disappointed to hear you talk like that. He's been looking forward to meeting you."

Ollie turned away. "What about the plant? They're not planning to do anything tonight?"

"What's done is done, so don't concern yourself about it," Elwin told him. "What happens at that plant is not our problem anymore."

Ollie's voice trembled. "It's one thing to hold this old woman to get whatever it is you're after, but people I know work at that plant, some of them at night. Frankly, I don't care if they blow the place to blazes, but not while somebody's in it!"

"Well, isn't that just too bad? You should've thought of that before *you gave us all those helpful little details about the layout, don't you think?"*

Ollie closed his eyes. He really did look terrible, Miss Dimple thought, as if he might keel over at any second. "There are guards," he mumbled, wincing. "And they're armed."

"The colonel will take care of that," Elwin said. "Right now we have to meet a man about an airplane."

❧

What airplane? What man? Miss Dimple thought. *Not Henry! It couldn't be Henry!* She wasn't hearing this. And what was this about blowing up the plant? They must be referring to the ordnance plant where many of the Elderberry people worked. She thought immediately of Odessa's husband, Bob Robert, as he sometimes worked the night shift there. If only she could find a way to warn them!

Across from her Willie looked at her with imploring eyes and she wished she could give him an encouraging smile but that was impossible to do with a strip of cloth over her mouth. She could see he was trying not to cry. He was being very brave, Willie was, and she hoped she wouldn't let him down.

"We'll have to take her with us," Elwin said with a nod in her direction.

"But what about them?" Ollie asked, referring to the rest of the group.

"They won't be going anywhere, but I suppose we'd better take them down to the basement and tie them up again. It won't do to leave them sitting here in the kitchen," Elwin said.

Miss Dimple could see that didn't sit well at all with Ollie Thigpen. He'd had more than enough of those basement stairs, but he fished around in a kitchen drawer for a flashlight and kicked the broken glass and remaining bottles off the steps before untying the others to herd them down.

247

Ollie paused before releasing Willie. "What's gonna happen to them?" he asked Elwin under his breath.

"I don't know why you're so worried about *them*," Elwin said. "You didn't seem too concerned about that old man you worked for. Why don't you tell them what happened to Paschall Kiker?"

Ollie's hands trembled. "I had nothing to do with that! The old man died in his sleep—heart just wore out, I reckon, and on the day before Thanksgiving, too. Couldn't just leave him lying up there, could I? What was I to do?"

"Bury him, of course, which is exactly what you did do," Elwin Vickery said. "Now, hurry and get on with it! We have an appointment to keep." He made a point of addressing the other three as they stretched and rubbed their wrists. "And if you give us one bit of trouble down there, just remember your precious Miss Dimple here will be at my mercy, and I'm quickly running out of patience—and time."

They weren't going to let her live. Trussed like a holiday bird, Dimple Kilpatrick lay in the backseat of Elwin Vickery's shiny black Nash-Kelvinator and wondered where they were going. She knew her brother well enough to know he would not be exchanging plans of an airplane or anything else for her safety, so he must have something else in mind, but how did they intend to arrange it?

As if he knew what she was thinking, Ollie asked, "What if this guy doesn't show up?"

Elwin glanced at her over his shoulder. "He will if he wants his sister back alive."

"But . . ." Ollie began, and Miss Dimple could have finished the sentence for him because she was thinking the same thing: *How do we keep them from talking?* There was only one answer. And what was to become of the three back at the farmhouse? Earlier, Jesse Dean had led her to believe he knew something and it had given her hope, but Dimple Kilpatrick needed more than hope: she needed action. A plan formed in her mind.

Struggling, she managed to pull herself up far enough to see out the window, thankful for all those times she had forced herself to do early-morning sit-ups. Although it was black as a coal cellar outside, she recognized a dilapidated church on the other side of town, abandoned when the congregation built a new one farther out. Elwin Vickery seemed to know where he was going, and a few minutes later, when he turned into a rustic stone entrance, Miss Dimple realized his destination—one they would all reach eventually, but she was rather inclined to wait.

Elwin switched off his headlights as the car made its way over the narrow roads of Cemetery Hill.

Ollie peered into the darkness. "What about the colonel?"

"Believe me, he's not far away," Elwin told him.

"And Miss Dimple's brother? Isn't he supposed to meet us here?"

Elwin spoke brusquely as he pulled to a stop. "He'll be waiting by that large oak over there behind the Potts family mausoleum. Go and see if he's there and then bring him here to me," he instructed Ollie. "And be on the lookout for any chicanery."

The Potts "Apartments." Remembering the frivolous name the young people used for the ornate marble monstrosity, Miss Dimple knew exactly where they were, and as she watched Ollie scuttle away to do as he was told, Dimple Kilpatrick was confident that any blueprints her brother brought would not be authentic.

Rolling over onto her stomach she pulled herself up to a kneeling position, grateful that all her walking and healthy eating had allowed her the flexibility to do so. She didn't like what she saw. Elwin Vickery had taken a gun from underneath his seat and she didn't think it was meant for Ollie—at least not yet. The gun was intended for Henry . . . and possibly for her as well.

Twisting, she pressed her feet against the back of the seat behind her and rocked back and forth to gain momentum; then, with one great heave, she thrust herself over the back of the front seat, knocked the gun from Elwin's hand, and landed headfirst on the automobile's horn.

☙

"Dear God in heaven, Dimple!" her brother told her later. "That horn sounded loud enough to wake the dead."

Dimple Kilpatrick smiled as she touched the bump on her forehead. "Then we were certainly in the right place for it, don't you think?"

When she was able to gather her wits about her, she had seen two men dressed in dark clothing racing toward them from behind a nearby magnolia tree, and while Elwin fumbled for his gun, one of them wrenched open the door on the driver's side of the Nash and spread-eagled him against the car. Only then, as mist swirled and crept among the grave stones, did Henry Kilpatrick appear from out of the shadows and help his sister to safety.

The mysterious "colonel," who had obviously masterminded the plot, and who turned out to be the brother of Elwin's girlfriend, Leila Mae, was apprehended when he tried to escape by driving his car through a narrow gap in the cemetery wall.

In time to come, Miss Dimple would consider that night more exciting than any mystery she'd ever read, but at that point her major concern was for the three people back at Paschall Kiker's farmhouse.

The police had already been alerted about that, her brother assured her, explaining that someone—he didn't know who at the time—had escaped unnoticed in time to go for help and he had no doubt it was on its way. It was not until later she learned the identity of Jesse Dean's fellow rescuers and wasn't one bit surprised, but extremely proud, to hear they were teachers and colleagues.

"This wasn't all they had in mind for tonight," she told Henry and the grim-faced men who accompanied him. "Some of their accomplices meant to plant explosives in the munitions factory in Milledgeville, and several people are working a night shift there. We have to warn them!"

One of the men acknowledged her with an almost-smile. "That's already been taken care of," he told her, but refused to say more. On the ride back to town Henry confided that earlier someone had tipped off the police who immediately notified the Office of Strategic Services and they had been watching the place for days. Although no one ever read about it in the newspapers, Miss Dimple and the others involved knew that several armed persons found hiding in the wooded area near the ordnance plant were arrested that same night. Fortunately, they managed to convince Willie that the two bad men intended a mission somewhere far away, and the dedicated workers at the ordnance plant never knew of the danger that might have awaited them.

❧

"I hope you didn't think I'd abandoned you, but my hands were tied," Henry told his sister a few days later as they sipped hot toddies in Phoebe Chadwick's front parlor (strictly for medicinal purposes, Miss Dimple told herself. One can't be too careful after suffering a sore throat such as hers). She had to confess, she told him, that she was beginning to wonder.

As soon as he was contacted about her being held hostage, Henry told her, he got in touch with the proper authorities. "There wasn't a lot I could do on my own, and I knew they had the skills and the manpower to handle it. I think they suspected all along that you were being held somewhere in or near Elderberry, but we had to be careful not to leak any information to the public. It would've put you in even more danger and sabotage any plan to get you back safely."

His sister smiled. "But did you really have to let Hazel and her sister believe I'd been committed to a *psychiatric* institution? Really, Henry, I'd think you might come up with a better excuse than that!"

Henry Kilpatrick only shrugged. "Oh, I don't know. It seemed to work well enough, don't you think?"

Cornelia Emerson of the Office of Strategic Services, the newly formed United States intelligence agency, she learned, had been assigned to find out who was behind her disappearance and the subsequent threats to Henry. Miss Dimple wasn't told exactly what the enemy was after but she was almost certain it had to have something to do with a project her brother was working on in Marietta, and the Bell Bomber Plant there was among the few facilities in the country where planes were being produced. Henry had always loved fast cars, so she really wasn't surprised he would dedicate himself to helping to design something to do with acceleration. It wasn't until years later she found out that her brother was involved in helping to develop the blueprints for the B-29 Superfortress, an extended range bomber that would play an important part in history and a major role in winning the war.

But Elwin threw them off the scent with that farmhouse he bought in the country, and Cornelia had wasted her time keeping an eye on that. He had originally intended to hold Miss Dimple there as prisoner, but the house was unheated and the bathroom facilities, extremely primitive. He abandoned the undertaking when he learned of a vacancy at Phoebe Chadwick's where he could befriend Henry Kilpatrick's sister and possibly learn more about his project. Cornelia eventually discovered that several other people who were involved in the plot did meet there from time to time, but then, of course, she had no proof of their activities. According to Henry, the relationship between Elwin and Leila Mae began a year or so earlier when they lived in the same apartment building, and a romance had ensued. "Or at least it did on his part," he added. "I honestly think Leila Mae

Smallwood led Elwin along only to manipulate him into doing what she wanted."

"But who is this colonel I heard them mention?" Dimple asked. "It sounded as if he might be behind all this."

"Well, he's one of them," her brother told her. "Actually, he's Leila Mae's brother—real name's Peter Smallwood—and I'm sure there are others involved, but now that the colonel's in custody, I think it will lead to more arrests."

After hours of questioning and what Henry referred to as debriefing, Dimple Kilpatrick welcomed a day or so of rest and recuperation, but *only* a day or so, before announcing she was ready to return to her usual routine. Odessa insisted on cooking a second Thanksgiving dinner, only on a smaller scale, inviting everyone who had been involved with the heroic rescue at the Kiker farmhouse that November night. Because of her position with the government, Cornelia Emerson had to decline, but Willie's mother allowed him a brief visit during dessert. Henry put in a special appearance before returning to his mysterious project, and Jesse Dean was welcomed by both Charlie and Annie, and especially by Miss Dimple herself.

"That must've been Elwin who kidnapped you that morning," Phoebe said to Dimple over dinner. "Ollie Thigpen would've had a difficult time cramming you into his bicycle basket. I don't think the man even knows how to drive."

But Dimple shook her head. "That's what he wanted everyone to think, but that's where you're wrong. He was driving Mr. Kiker's car . . . kept it in the barn. I don't think he ever took it out in the daytime."

"I wonder if that was why Geneva was attacked in the park," Annie said. "The two men must have met there—Elwin and Ollie—and whoever hit her was probably afraid she would identify their car. It had to have been parked nearby."

"Probably Paschall Kiker's," Jesse Dean said. "Elwin would have walked. And they mentioned somebody called the colonel, who seemed to be the ringleader behind all this. It was pretty obvious that Ollie was afraid of him. Maybe the colonel—or whatever his name is—was planning to meet there that night, too. It would look suspicious if the three of them were seen together."

Odessa, helping Miss Dimple to one of her spicy peach pickles, groaned under her breath. *"Elwin Vickery! Huh! I shoulda put rat poison in his oatmeal!"*

Henry laughed. "Well, we won't have to worry about that one anymore . . . or Ollie, either."

Miss Dimple sighed. "Elwin Vickery is a cold, despicable criminal, but Ollie . . . well, Ollie is more to be pitied I believe. He blamed the government and everyone else for what he didn't have—and believe me, he really was slighted in the brains department! He wanted a better life and Elwin offered him a chance to have it."

"I wonder how those two got together," Annie said, shaking her head.

"From what I understand, Ollie Thigpen was helping with the potential renovation of that old place Elwin bought," Miss Dimple said. "Paschall Kiker couldn't pay him much, so he did odd jobs like that from time to time."

Henry nodded. "My guess is the two of them got to talking and Elwin found out that Ollie was bitter enough *and* desperate enough to do almost anything for money."

"I remember when Ollie's daddy carried the mail," Phoebe said. "Had a rural route for a while but he kept mixing up everybody's mail and some said he even threw a lot of it in the river. Naturally they had to let him go and the family eventually lost their land. I think Ollie held a grudge about that for years."

Charlie nodded. Their neighbor had told her as much. "Miss Bessie said Ollie was always disappointed that he didn't have a chance to go away to college because they didn't have the money."

"I don't suppose it occurred to him to work for it," Henry said. Miss Dimple only shook her head, but from the expression on her face you could tell she didn't think money would have been his major challenge.

Ollie had tried several times to abduct Miss Dimple before he finally succeeded. Once his efforts were thwarted when a former student joined her on her lonely walk in a deserted section of town. The second time she sensed danger and evaded him after he followed her to the park, and the third was when he climbed into her classroom window to wait for her to arrive. Elwin must have been waiting in the car to help lower her through the window. That was when Christmas Malone surprised him there and tried to summon help by ringing the school bell.

"Poor Mr. Malone!" Miss Dimple did the unthinkable and buttered a second yeast roll made of *white* flour. "He didn't have time to unlock the office and use the telephone there, so he took the stairs, in an effort to reach the bell rope in the storage room."

Charlie met Annie's eyes. *The wooden eagle.* "Ollie caught up with him and struck him with Ebenezer, didn't he?" she said. "From what we've learned, he had *two* head wounds—one was in the front from falling on the metal filing cabinet—but *two*? The other must've come from a blow from behind."

"That's what the medical examiner said," Henry told them. "The wooden eagle was heavy enough and they found a smear of blood where the wing broke off. In his hurry to get away, Ollie must've tossed the broken wing into the ditch.

"They couldn't let you know this, of course, but the local police were cooperating with the government on this case. They knew a lot more than they let on."

Phoebe Chadwick snorted. "You mean Bobby Tinsley's not as big an idiot as I thought? Well, that comes as a surprise!"

"What about Paschall Kiker?" Annie asked. "I heard Ollie buried him somewhere behind the barn."

Miss Dimple suppressed a shiver and started to speak but Jesse Dean interrupted. "I wouldn't be surprised if the old fellow didn't die of natural causes, like Ollie said. Ollie had ordered a small hen for Thanksgiving but never claimed it. If Mr. Kiker died that Wednesday like Ollie said, he'd have to do something with the body, and with Miss Dimple there in the basement, he couldn't just leave him lying upstairs."

"And to think, some of the faculty sent him a basket the very day he died," Annie reminded them. "Poor Mr. Kiker! Ollie said he loved olives so I made sure he had some."

"I think he'd been more or less confined to the upstairs for almost a year," Phoebe said. "I took him a basket of tomatoes from the Victory garden last summer and he looked frail even then."

"But I don't understand why Ollie stole Geneva's key to your classroom when he already had his own," Charlie said, addressing Miss Dimple. "It happened when we were all in the auditorium," she explained. "Somebody—Ollie, I guess—went through your desk looking for something, I suppose."

Miss Dimple nodded with understanding. "It *was* Ollie. He was looking for a bottle of pills I convinced him I needed. I didn't *have* to have them, of course, but Ollie didn't know that. I told him they were for my heart." Lovingly, she fingered the familiar pin at her throat. "I had hoped someone would discover him going through my desk."

Charlie frowned. "But why steal a key?"

"Probably to throw everybody off track," Jesse Dean suggested. "Why would he steal what he already had? Nobody would suspect him."

"I remember seeing him in the auditorium at the beginning of the program," Charlie said. "I guess he ducked out while everybody was all caught up in what was happening on stage. Nobody was paying attention to him."

"Remember those cigarette butts Willie was so sure about?" Annie said. "He was positive spies had been meeting behind the tool shed at school. Well, we found out yesterday they weren't spies after all. Delby O'Donnell has switched to smoking Luckies!"

Miss Dimple gave them her fiercest look. "Let's just keep that our little secret, shall we? Now aren't we about ready for dessert? It's almost time for Willie."

CHAPTER TWENTY-EIGHT

December 4, 1942

Dear Fain,

I don't know where to send this but I'm going to keep writing to you anyway and save them until I do. (I know you'll hardly be able to contain your excitement in getting all these letters from me!!) Mama is holding up better than I ever thought she would, and so am I because we know you're alive somewhere and that you have the faith and the stamina to endure so that you can come back home to us one day.

We have all read about the North African campaign and hear a lot about it on the radio. They call it Operation Torch and it sounds like it's going well over there with General Eisenhower and British Field Marshall Montgomery running things together. Geneva Odom, who teaches with me, said she saw films of the invasion on a newsreel at the picture show the other day but I haven't seen it. Mama and I plan to go next week to see Yankee Doodle Dandy with James Cagney. We both need to get out more and could use some music in our lives.

I wrote earlier about Miss Dimple disappearing. Remember Miss

Dimple from first grade? How could you forget? Well, she's been found, and believe it or not, Annie and I had something to do with it! She was being held captive in the basement of a farmhouse by these horrible people who wanted to ransom her in exchange for her brother's plans for some kind of special airplane.

Really, it was little Willie Elrod who led us to her—and is he ever going to be impossible to live with from now on! You'll never believe who actually did the dirty work and snatched Miss Dimple right off the street! It was Miss Bessie's good-for-nothing boyfriend, Ollie Thigpen, who took Mr. Malone's place as janitor. (More about that later.) Anyway, Willie became suspicious because he found a grocery list in Miss Dimple's handwriting in Ollie's jacket pocket and decided to follow him home. Unfortunately, Willie ended up being captured along with Cornelia Emerson who was filling in for Miss Dimple but is really an agent for the OSS.

Jesse Dean Greeson turned out to be the real hero, though. You know Jesse Dean—works at Mr. Cooper's store. Well, he'd been suspicious of Ollie for some time and teamed up with Annie and me to try and track down Willie, whose parents, by then, were getting frantic. Elwin Vickery, the nasty piece of work in cahoots with Ollie, must've heard us outside the house because he caught poor Jesse Dean, and you can't argue with a gun. Thank goodness Jesse Dean convinced him he was alone! First, though, he thought to drop the key to his car in the grass so Annie and I could go for help, so it all worked out in the long run, but of course we were scared to death!

Bobby Tinsley told us later it was a darn good thing we got word to them when we did because if those two had gotten away with it, they wouldn't have been inclined to leave anybody alive to tell their tale. I know Elwin wouldn't, but I'm not so sure about Ollie. Miss Dimple seems to think Elwin would have done away with him, too. And he's another one I had figured out all wrong. Annie and I did a little spying on Elwin that led us to believe the only thing he was hiding was a sizzling romance with some woman named Leila Mae. Turns out Elwin's girlfriend and her brother might have been behind the whole plot, and of course the OSS has all that information now, so I guess we'll never know. At any rate, everything's okay now. I don't know what will happen to any of that bunch, but I sure wouldn't want to be in their shoes.

Mama and I were feeling sort of sorry for our neighbor Miss Bessie as it seems she was an unwitting victim in all this. In fact, Mama even went so far as to bake her some banana bread, poor thing! (You know how that usually turns out.) When we got there, who did we find drinking tea in Bessie Jenkins's kitchen but Miss Dimple Kilpatrick and Jesse Dean Greeson! They had come to let our neighbor know that Ollie Thigpen, as rotten as he was, had considered her safety above his own. Of course, she pretended not to care and we pretended to believe her. She seems to be holding up well and is even planning to invite Wilson Malone's widow and daughters to spend the Christmas holidays with her. They don't have any family here and neither does she, and Bessie says she's just rattling around in that big old house.

And I'll just say this: it's a good thing Elwin Vickery and his accomplices didn't finish what they started out to do that night, or Miss Bessie, Mama, Aunt Lou, Bob Robert, and a lot of other folks would be out of a job—or worse! I think Miss Dimple's brother, Henry, filled her in on who tipped them off about that, but all she would tell me was it was "somebody right under my nose," and I think I have a pretty good idea that it was probably somebody right next door. Many of us are called upon to make all kinds of sacrifices for the war effort, some stranger than others.

Guess who's coming for Christmas? Our little sister, Delia! Well, she's not so little anymore as her baby's due in March. Ned's being shipped out next week so Delia will be living with us for a while and it will be wonderful for all of us to have a baby in the house. Just think, when you come home you'll have a brand-new little niece or nephew!

Oh, and by the way, I think I might be in love. Not with Hugh, although I do care a lot for him as a friend, but somebody new—probably too new to even go into it as I don't want to jinx anything, but I'll try to keep you informed.

I love you and pray for you every day, and every night, too, and promise to write often and keep you posted on the news, but you know how it is. Nothing much ever happens in Elderberry!

With much love from your sister,
Charlie

❦

Galoshes buttoned to the ankles, Miss Dimple Kilpatrick picked her way across a puddle, speared an offending bit of litter, and added it to her paper bag. Wind blew icy daggers of rain into her face and she paused briefly to adjust the purple woolen muffler around her neck.

Elderberry schools would soon be out for Christmas vacation and she planned to join Henry and Hazel for a few days in their rustic mountain retreat, but this morning she would walk.

The town still slept, with only the headlights from an occasional car reflecting bright yellow beams on the dark mirror of the streets. A worn, stuffed Santa Claus, surrounded by cheap plastic toys, smiled from the window of Murphy's Five and Ten, and a sign at the *Elderberry Eagle* encouraged readers to: SEND YOUR SERVICEMAN A SUBSCRIPTION! At the post office on the corner, a poster urged everyone to BUY WAR BONDS FOR CHRISTMAS!

What a peculiar season it was! Miss Dimple turned and made her way up Peach Orchard Hill, snatching another piece of litter along the way. If her class behaved themselves today, she would read to them from a favorite book, *Pinocchio*, while they glued colored paper chains for the class Christmas tree, a fragrant cedar that sat on a wobbly stand in the corner.

Contentedly, she patted her large handbag, which held two Victory Muffins and a container of her favorite hot beverage, and opening her umbrella, Miss Dimple tugged her lavender felt hat snugly about her ears and plunged forward.

It was a beautiful day!

MIGNON F. BALLARD

is "a must for readers who like
their mysteries on the cozy side."
—*Publishers Weekly*

**LOOK FOR the next
Miss Dimple novel...
December 2011
FROM MINOTAUR BOOKS**

"Ballard provides a nostalgic look at life in small-town
America during the war." —*KIRKUS REVIEWS*